THERE'LL BE SHELL TO PAY

Books by Molly MacRae

COME SHELL OR HIGH WATER

THERE'LL BE SHELL TO PAY

Published by Kensington Publishing Corp.

THERE'LL BE SHELL TO PAY

Molly MacRae

Kensington Publishing Corp.
kensingtonbooks.com

This book is a work of fiction. Names, characters, businesses, organizations, places, events, and incidents either are the product of the author's imagination or are used fictitiously. Any resemblance to actual persons, living or dead, events, or locales is entirely coincidental.

To the extent that the image or images on the cover of this book depict a person or persons, such person or persons are merely models, and are not intended to portray any character or characters featured in the book.

KENSINGTON BOOKS are published by

Kensington Publishing Corp.
900 Third Avenue
New York, NY 10022

Copyright © 2025 by Molly MacRae

All rights reserved. No part of this book may be reproduced in any form or by any means without the prior written consent of the Publisher, excepting brief quotes used in reviews.

All Kensington titles, imprints and distributed lines are available at special quantity discounts for bulk purchases for sales promotion, premiums, fund-raising, educational or institutional use. Special book excerpts or customized printings can also be created to fit specific needs. For details, write or phone the office of the Kensington Special Sales Manager: Kensington Publishing Corp., 900 Third Ave., New York, NY 10022. Attn. Special Sales Department. Phone: 1-800-221-2647.

KENSINGTON and the KENSINGTON COZIES teapot logo Reg. US Pat. & TM Off.

Library of Congress Control Number: 2025933139

ISBN: 978-1-4967-4430-2

First Kensington Hardcover Edition: July 2025

ISBN: 978-1-4967-4432-6 (ebook)

10 9 8 7 6 5 4 3 2 1

Printed in the United States of America

The authorized representative in the EU for product safety and compliance is eucomply OU, Parnu mnt 139b-14, Apt 123
Tallinn, Berlin 11317, hello@eucompliancepartner.com

For everyone who kindly sends me their favorite fig recipes, but especially for the Fig Ladies—Kathleen Thomas, Paula Diamond Román, and Roberta McLaughlin.

Acknowledgments

Over the years I've discovered that writing results in a grateful heart. To all the people mentioned here, I am well and truly thankful. For what they say (and sometimes don't say), for what they do, and for being in my life. The guys at home who cook, do laundry, and go shopping give me the time to tap away at the keyboard. What a team! Cynthia Manson, my agent, cheers for me every step of the way. This book—none of my mystery series—would be here without her. This Haunted Shell Shop series wouldn't be here, or in the good shape it's in, without Kensington Books, and especially my editor, John Scognamiglio, and publicist extraordinaire, Larissa Ackerman. It's a joy working with both of you. For two decades, Janice Harrington, Betsy Hearne, and I have been meeting on Sundays for the always refreshing, invigorating, and eagle-eyed critiquing of MABs. Thank you, and may we have the good health and good luck to meet for another two decades. Thanks also to the members of the Midwest Chapter of Mystery Writers of America who show up in our online group every single Saturday morning to write like mad for two forty-minute sprints. It's amazingly effective. Thank you to all the readers who've embraced the idea of a pirate ghost. Special thanks to Kathleen Thomas, Paula Diamond Román, and Roberta McLaughlin for letting me put you in this book and for waiting patiently to see how I messed with you. I've had a lot of fun hanging out with your alter egos (and messing with *them* quite a bit). And finally, thanks to anyone spurred to visit Ocracoke after reading this book. While you're there, stop by the real Books to Be Red, Howard's Pub, and Village Craftsmen—and be sure to take the Ocracoke Ghost and History Tour.

Chapter 1

On a Monday morning near the end of October, I sailed toward new adventures. Waves, curling and unfurling, carried my ship steadily closer to its destination—legendary Ocracoke Island, one-time pirate haven off the coast of North Carolina. Like diamonds, droplets of salt spray glittered in my fellow passengers' hair—also on the windshields of our cars because we were, in fact, aboard a ferryboat, the Croatan, plying its way from Hatteras to the landing at the north end of Ocracoke. Waves did curl, but out in the Atlantic, not on our sedate path in Pamlico Sound. Droplets and diamonds only glistened in my imagination, but new adventures did await.

As a storyteller—my late husband called me his fabulous fabulist—embellishments were my second language. It was no exaggeration, though, to say that I felt much better prepared for adventure on this trip than I had a month before when I'd arrived on Ocracoke at the tail end of a hurricane. That trip started with fears of sharks and foundering and ended with me waving goodbye to the ghost of a pirate. Again, not exaggerating. Quite a lot happened in between the fears and the farewell—getting zapped by an electrical short, being left for shark bait, and becoming the new owner of the Moon Shell, the island's storied shell shop, for instance.

A circus of gulls followed the ferry, begging for someone, anyone, to toss popcorn, French fries, a sandwich, stale bread, anything into the air for them to snatch. "Don't hold back!" they cried. "Throw something, you miserly meat bags!"

Try telling seagulls they shouldn't eat what humans toss for them. They won't listen. They have no time in their raucous, jeering schedules for nutritional advice. I hadn't taken my own nutritional advice, stopping in Buxton, on Hatteras Island, for lunch. Maybe the gulls smelled the softshell crab sandwich and onion rings on my breath. They might even have been interested in the few groceries I'd picked up in Hatteras Village before boarding the boat. Cupboard- and fridge-filling shopping could wait for the Ocracoke Variety Store.

Before heading from the passenger deck down to the vehicle deck and my car, I saw someone fishing near the dock. With miles of shore on either side of the island available for fishing, dropping a hook so near the oil-slicked dock waters seemed an unlikely choice. But, as a non-fisherman, what did I know?

This short, stout person looked shorter and stouter because of a heron-like hunch of the shoulders. The round, large-brimmed hat made the person look like a toadstool. It also hid the person's face, but I'd met someone of that general description a month ago—Doctor Irving Allred. Immediately and instinctively I shrank back from the railing. Allred, the island's elderly, and only, physician, had several hobbies, none of which I wanted to get involved in. Hoping he hadn't seen me, I returned to my car.

The deck vibrated as the ferry's great engines slowed us for mooring. With the vibrations, the excitement I'd kept in check for the day and a half it took to drive here began to stir. The boat came to its bumping stop against the dock's pylons. The excitement thumped against my rib cage and then burst out and took wing like a gull, begging me to race it to the village at the other end of the island. The gangplank lowered, clanged into place, and a crew member directed vehicles in a mannerly disembarkation. As soon as my tires touched land, I wanted to cheer. And I felt . . . a difference.

Jeff, my husband, used to say that wonderful places like Ocracoke only appear in reality as you approach them. He called it his *Brigadoon* hypothesis. (He'd seen the movie at an impressionable age and fell in love with tales of places, often under a spell or curse, that appeared and disappeared.) Was that what I felt? The frisson of a place too good to be true? Or was it the feeling of passing through a time warp to a place that harbors centuries-old stories and legends? I didn't believe either of those options, so maybe *I* was warped? No. I didn't believe that either.

I did believe that a month ago, when I'd landed on Ocracoke at the tail end of Hurricane Electra, I'd come close to drowning in assumptions. This time I hoped I wasn't drowning in rosy expectations for the success of this move, this new life.

The feeling grew stronger as I drove the spindly highway down the spine of the island and intensified to a prickling down my own spine. Not exactly unpleasant, but *not* something I'd expected. Did it have anything to do with the superstitious codswallop about traveling on a Monday that Doctor Allred loved to spout? What was it he'd said? *If you start a journey or vacation on a Monday, you drag bad luck along with you.* Today was Monday, but I wasn't here on vacation, and I'd set out on Sunday. Safe from Allred's warped codswallop.

Another possibility fizzed back and forth across my scalp as I entered the village. Did the feeling have anything to do with Emrys Lloyd? With the odd fact that he was a ghost and haunted the Moon Shell? Or the odder fact that I and almost no one else saw him or knew he existed?

Tourists thronged the sidewalks in town—thronged the street on bikes, in golf carts, in every kind of vehicle. I joined them, passing the harbor—called Silver Lake—on the left. Sailboats and the big ferry from Cedar Island crowded the docks. Eateries, souvenir shops, and rental kiosks for bikes, golf carts, and kayaks lined the shore.

I made the turn onto one-way Howard Street. A pair of crows sitting on the street's signpost cawed and flew off as I passed.

Chapter 2

Howard Street dripped with atmosphere the way Spanish moss dripped from live oaks here and there on Ocracoke. It was believed to be the oldest street in the village, the small village dating back to at least the early 1700s. Short and made only of sand, oyster shell, and gravel, Howard was really more of a slow-paced lane. Trees, houses, and lichen-crusted fences lined both sides. Many of the houses belonged to descendants of the original settlers. Small family cemeteries nestled in the deep green shade of the trees, the graves resting so quietly that tourists in vehicles or on foot didn't always notice them. Jeff and I used to visit Ocracoke with our sons when they were kids. Howard was our favorite street.

I slowed the car to a crawl as I came to the street's slight leftward bend and looked first at Glady and Burt Weaver's two-story house on the right. Either of the Weavers would be happy to correct me on the street's name and then be happy to argue with each other over which of them had clued me in first. Old Ocracokers, like the eighty-one- and seventy-nine-year-old sister and brother, knew Howard Street's official name—East Howard Street. Part of the street's charm was in discovering that no West, South, or North Howard ever existed to cause confusion with East Howard. That, of course, confused a few.

I smiled at all that and then looked at the smaller house opposite the Weaver's.

Glady and Burt had grown up in this second house, a neat one-and-a-half-story bungalow with a less generous, but still pleasing, front porch. Glady and Burt still owned the bungalow but fifty years earlier had moved across the street into the bigger house built and previously owned by an uncle. For the fifty years since they'd migrated, their birthplace had been home to the Moon Shell, the business started by Dottie Withrow (also called Mrs. Seashell) and carried on by her son, Allen. Now, by a weird quirk of luck, the business belonged to me, and the apartment in the half-story above the shop was my new home. My mind still wrestled a bit when I tried to wrap it around that quirk.

A couple of children jumped down the shop's four front steps, ran back up, and jumped down again. Even in the bright afternoon sun, the shop's lights shone through the front window and looked welcoming. Three golf carts sat in the small parking area in front of the shop. Golf carts—when I'd arrived in the village the month before, they'd surprised me. I didn't remember seeing a single one the last time Jeff and I visited. That only showed how long ago that visit had been and how little I paid attention to trends in vacation destination transportation. Golf carts made good sense, though. They were a quiet, efficient, friendly way for visitors and locals to get around. Along with the shell shop (and the rest of Allen's worldly goods and properties), I'd inherited his golf cart. Before I knew it, I'd be tootling around the village with the best of them, provided the police weren't still holding the golf cart as evidence. The quirk of luck hadn't come without baggage.

I followed a drive, more grass than gravel, around the side of the house to a more obviously gravel apron in back and parked. Unpacking the car could wait. Right now it was time to test expectation number one—that I would walk into the Moon

Shell's front door, and there would be Emrys, Bonny the shop cat, and Glady to greet me. Emrys with a doff of his tricorn hat, Bonny with a purr and a twine around my ankles, and Glady with open arms.

I trotted around to the front, called hello to the crows in the live oak that dappled the yard with shade, greeted the children, and bounded up the stairs with one of them. Taking a deep breath, I opened the door and walked in.

"Perfect timing, Maureen," Glady called, looking up from helping a customer. She went right back to peering over her glasses at the cash register, then at the customer, and back to the register: a busy businessperson's greeting. Couldn't fault her for that. If she'd sent a smile along with the greeting, though, I didn't catch it. It probably got distracted wending its way past the displays of seashells. Or got spooked by the stuffed seagull—new to me—beady-eyed and wings fully extended, hanging over the central display table. Where had *that* come from? It looked ready to snatch the ornaments off the driftwood Christmas tree standing in the middle of the display table.

"What can I do to help?" I asked.

Glady raised a hand. "Not now."

"Okay."

Glady concentrated like a pro. She'd had a long career writing mysteries while sharing a house with her brother. True, he was a career librarian, but according to Glady, librarian doesn't equate with quiet, organized, or willing to let other people be quiet and organized. The two of them took some getting used to, but I liked them.

She'd stuck a pencil behind each ear but picked up a pen to write up the sale on the receipt pad. The shop was still old-school in that regard, despite having an electronic cash register.

The other customers, two couples, seemed happy enough browsing on their own and not terribly serious about it. Picking up shells, putting them down, sticking their fingers into any shell with an opening meant for its original critter.

There were no signs of a ghost or a cat. Maybe the rampant seagull spooked them, too. Maybe they were napping.

I went looking. Not far and wide. There is no far or wide about the Moon Shell. The shop was in the house's original living room—fifteen feet by twenty at the most. Also on this floor were a small office and a larger storeroom, neither one with an overload of nooks and crannies. Not that a ghost needed a hiding place. Even so, if Emrys or Bonny didn't want to be found, they wouldn't be. I opened the storeroom door, glanced around, and called softly. No luck. Same for the office. That left me with the apartment upstairs.

"Don't disappear, Maureen," Glady called. "Almost done here. There's important news."

Her customer, a woman not much younger than Glady, murmured, "Two more, I think," and swirled a finger through a basket of impulse-buy cowrie shells next to the cash register. She picked out one and went back to swirling.

Standing against the wall, between the doors to the office and the storeroom, was a tall glass display case. Emrys sometimes stood there, too, leaning one shoulder against the side of the case. With his tricorn hat, full-skirted knee-length coat, long waistcoat visible where the coat parted, knee breeches, stockings, and one well-shod foot cocked over the other ankle, he tended to look comfortable and the picture of pirate-casual. That he could lean against the glass *and* pass through it was a mystery to me. Sometimes he sat at the desk in the office, too, in the chair that was an ergonomic wonder no ghost should require. Anyway. (I didn't like the way *anyway* got tacked onto conversations as a way of ending them, dismissing them, but considering this whole haunted situation, the anyway and the dismissal fit.)

I leaned my shoulder against the display case, feeling comfortable and every bit of newly anointed business owner-casual.

Not disappearing, as per Glady's directive, but I did let my mind wander. The case

It was a sturdy case and locked because the shells inside were the shop's most valuable. Some of them weren't for sale at all. One was as big as an over-inflated football and an incredible work of eighteenth-century shell carving—a cameo shell. Allen Withrow's mother had called the shell the moon shell and named the shop after it. The shell belonged to Emrys. He was the artist who'd carved it. I didn't hear him humming as I stood there, didn't hear his clear tenor singing in English or Welsh. I got no sense he was nearby.

It turned out leaning against the case wasn't all that comfortable. I felt conspicuous, too, and useless, so I ducked into the office and dropped my purse in the bottom drawer of the filing cabinet. As I did, the customer's voice floated in behind me, thanking Glady.

"It's been a pleasure," Glady said, giving me a look when I reappeared.

"I have something for each of the grands when I get home," the customer said. "I think." She set the bag with her purchase on the counter and reached a finger toward the cowries again.

"Every last one of your grandchildren will be delighted." Glady deftly waylaid the finger swirl for another shell by picking up the bag and putting it back in the woman's hand. "Have a safe trip home and come see us next time you visit."

The woman thanked her again and thanked me, too, when I opened the door for her. As I closed it behind her, one of the other customers stepped up to the sales desk.

"That's a super whelk or something or other," Glady said, "and Maureen will be with you in two ticks." She grabbed her sweater from somewhere under the sales desk and practically ran toward me. "Glad you're here," she said, opening the door. "I've been run off my feet and I'm taking the rest of the day off."

"Oh. Okay. But you said something about important news?"

She'd started through the door, stopped, and looked back over her shoulder. "Couple of things. Bonny's at our house. I'll send Burt over with her when I see him. There's an envelope for Rob Tate on the desk in the office. He knows. He'll come get it. Got to run now. Catch you later." And, poof, she was gone.

Wondering how Glady had the energy to run if she'd already been run off her feet, I closed the door. But she'd been keeping the business going while I was gone, so how could I complain?

The customer with the lightning whelk waited patiently at the sales desk. The woman with him handed him two Scotch bonnets and said she'd go ride herd on the kids outside. I smiled at the customer, then at the cash register, hoping I remembered the incantations to make it run without freezing. If not, I'd rummage for the manual. That's how Glady and I had learned to run the thing in the first place.

"You picked out a really nice lightning whelk," I said, my fingers surprising me by landing on the right register keys. "Do you know the difference between a lightning whelk and a knobbed whelk?"

"That sounds like the beginning of a bad joke."

I laughed. "It does. It's *not,* but I have plenty of those, too."

"Then tell me the difference, throw in a joke, and you've got a deal."

"Deal. Information first. The opening, that is the aperture, of lightning whelks is on the left. Knobbed whelks open on the right."

"Good to know," the man said. "And the joke?"

I glanced around for joke material—got it. The stuffed gull. "Why do seagulls fly over the sea?" While he thought, I put his shells in a bag.

"Uh, to *see* the other side?"

"Not quite, but not bad." I handed the bag to him. "They

fly over the sea because if they flew over the bay we'd have to call them bagels."

"We'd have to?" he asked.

"No choice. Rules of a bad joke."

He waved, and as he went out the door, three more people came in. And that's the way the afternoon went. Customers came in waves, washing in and out. Some browsed. Some bought. I tried a few more jokes because Emrys liked them and I thought he might come out from wherever. He didn't but that was okay. All was good.

Except that my welcome-back expectations had been dashed to pieces. No doff of a tricorn, no purr with an ankle twine, no open arms. And no time—I'd expected to have an hour or two, preferably the whole afternoon and part of tomorrow—to ease into waiting on customers and running the shop. Time, at least, to get my bike off the back of the car and to haul the groceries I'd bought in Hatteras up the stairs. Good thing I hadn't bought anything that would spoil.

I was being silly. Of course I could have taken the time to run a few things up to the apartment. The business of selling seashells by the seashore was hardly fraught. Or I could have closed for an hour or for the afternoon. I was the boss, after all. The captain of my own ship and every cliché I cared to use.

But I was happy to have the customers wandering in and out. As long as they kept me busy, the unusual feeling that had settled over me after landing on the island receded into the background. I was aware of it but it didn't rattle me. It was just there like a softly tugging undercurrent, like an indistinct murmur, a Greek chorus of itty-bitty crickets. But during the few moments I was alone in the shop? Back that feeling came on the wings of a squawking seagull.

"Sorry," I said to the seagull overhead. "We've hardly met, and I'm already saying rude things about you."

The bird kept its beak shut. The door hadn't opened for

several minutes either. I retrieved my purse from the filing cabinet in the office and pulled out my keys on the way to the only section of shop wall without a display. It looked like every other part of the shop's white beadboard paneling except for the keyhole. I unlocked this cleverly hidden door and ran quickly up the steep staircase to the apartment.

"Emrys?" I listened. No answer. No breath of air. The compact space smelled dusty, disused, and too warm. I opened the dormer that looked out on Howard Street, and a window in the bedroom, left my purse on the kitchen table, and went back down to the shop. Silence there, too.

"Emrys?" I tried in the storeroom and again in the office. Nothing. Like a cat, Emrys didn't always come when he was called, but this felt different. I dumped myself in that lovely ergonomic desk chair, and would have settled in comfortably for a good grump, but the front door opened and several chatting, laughing people came in. No wonder Glady had to take the afternoon off. No rest for the grumpy and ghostless.

I slapped my hands on the desktop, telling myself this was the life of a shopkeeper and this was the life for me, and pushed myself to my feet. And there, in front of me on the desk, was the envelope with Rob Tate's name on it that Glady mentioned on her way out the door. Rob Tate, Captain of the Ocracoke station of the Hyde County Sheriff's Department. Stand-up guy. But why would anyone leave an envelope for him here instead of taking it to the station—all of, what, a half mile away? I looked closer at his name, at the handwriting. There was something familiar about it, and it made me uneasy.

Chapter 3

Two forty-something men in cargo shorts, Hawaiian shirts, and loafers with no socks came into the shop. They did something I'd seen more than a few customers do that afternoon. Hands in pockets, they made a circuit of the room, glancing at the displays the way people do who aren't seriously shopping. They made a second circuit looking at the walls. The shorter, balder of the two stopped to say "boop" and tap the seagull playfully on the tip of its beak. I made a mental note to take the bird down or hang it higher. Then they both stared at the ceiling for much longer than plain white plaster should have held anyone's attention.

I caught the eye of the lankier, hairier guy. "Except for a few cobwebs, what are you looking for on the ceiling?"

"Nah, don't mind me," he said. His hands went deeper into his pockets and his shoulders did a little up and down move that said, "Aw, shucks, ma'am."

His buddy, the beak booper, snickered and mimed a potshot at the seagull. "Got him. Rats with wings."

This gull was now my friend and I would defend it to its dying . . . no. That ship had sailed. I would defend it to *my* dying day or see the dear thing retired from shop life with dignity. I might tell the gull that when we were alone, but it wasn't worth explaining to these false customers. Emrys would call them varlets and louts. I missed him.

Then the louts, Aw Shucks and Beak Booper, both looking parboiled from unaccustomed time in the sun, went further than other browsing customers had. They didn't just look at the walls, they studied them and zeroed in on the section with the concealed door. Aw Shucks sidled over and stood with his back to it. Beak Booper feigned interest in a pair of delicate, blown-glass Christmas ornaments—pretty little crabs. He took them from the driftwood Christmas tree and held them to the light. I proved to myself that I could run the cash register and keep an eye on two suspicious so-and-sos at the same time. Aw Shucks rocked on his heels and nonchalantly rapped on the wall with his knuckles. He gave a little nod and both of them looked at the ceiling again.

"No one's home upstairs." I smiled from Aw Shucks to Beak Booper. "In case you were wondering."

Beak Booper twitched, making the crabs clink against each other. He hastily rehung them on the driftwood and put his hands back in his pockets.

Aw Shucks stepped closer to me. "Is it true? What I mean is—" His face morphed from avid curiosity to something... more serious? Worried? Concerned? His eyebrows couldn't seem to make up their minds. Whatever the expression was, once the eyebrows settled, it didn't play well with the riot of tropical flowers and parrots on his shirt. Or the whiff of beer on his breath. The pause he took after saying *what I mean is* went on long enough that I thought he'd forgotten he'd had a meaning. But then he spoke, pitching his voice low. It didn't sound naturally low. It sounded like he'd decided a deeper voice complemented his newly arranged eyebrows.

"The old guy who ran the place," he said. "We met him a time or two when we were on the island. We were sorry to hear he'd passed."

I nodded. Tipped my head.

He raised an eyebrow.

"If you know he's gone," I said, "what did you think would happen when you knocked on the door?"

The eyebrows went into shock, slid through surprise and into guilt, then skidded to a stop at affronted. Aw Shucks took a step back as if to prove it.

Beak Booper snickered. "You're as subtle as snakebite, Clay."

They finally left, and a woman stepped up to the sales desk. "Sorry to keep you waiting," I said.

"Not a problem." She laid a selection of native North Carolina shells in front of me. "For my daughter. She's a brand-new high school biology and zoology teacher in High Point."

"Mixing it up with high school students? More power to her."

"She says shells are her jam. She's always loved them, and the creatures that make them, and now she loves coaxing her students out of their own shells."

"Fantastic. Congratulations on having a wonderful daughter with a great career ahead of her."

The proud mom took the bag I'd put her carefully wrapped shells in and then leaned closer across the desk. "I saw those guys who just left drinking their lunch at the Bar & Grill on the harbor. I'd say the two of them have fewer brains, total, than a single barnacle, and the few brains they do have they're wasting."

"I think you're right and also poetic."

"I taught high school English for twenty-five years." She had a dimple when she smiled.

Before the next pair of customers came to the cash register, I jotted down the proud mom's quip about brains and barnacles. Emrys would get a kick out of it, he being a big fan of both poetry and insults. There was still no sign of him, but I wasn't worried.

After selling a conch, a small horseshoe crab, two sea stars, and half a dozen sand dollars, I idly sketched an idea for a new display case. One that could be attached to the concealed door, with just enough space under the case, so the door would still swing open freely. In this small shop, why not take advantage of every possible display area? Also, what was the point of having a concealed door if it wasn't better concealed?

Customers kept coming right up until Allen's usual five o'clock closing time. Neither Emrys nor Captain Rob Tate did. Tate could be busy riding herd on tourists out driving golf carts after drinking their lunches.

Most of the customers seemed to arrive with a purpose. For some, that purpose was admiring, choosing, and buying shells, before heading off to the next shop, or an eatery, or a well-situated deck or dock to wait for the sunset with a drink in hand. I knew these plans because the couples and family groups chatted among themselves as they shopped. A few solo customers shared their plans with me, in lieu of a shopping partner, and asked when the last ferry ran back to Hatteras or my opinion of a restaurant.

That pattern and purpose was only true of some customers, though. For a surprising number of others who opened the door and walked in, their purpose seemed to be less about shells than about the building. As though, after gazing around and being nosy enough to peek into the office and storeroom, they could mark off another historic house on a self-guided tour. Odd, because although this was a good example of an old Ocracoke house, circa 1930, there wasn't anything historic or architecturally significant about it.

A few of these oddball tourists tut-tutted over Allen Withrow's death when they came to the cash register. Some of the tut-tuts actually sounded sincere.

Other oddballs were as blatant about their curiosity as Aw Shucks and Beak Booper had been, though not as annoying.

And most of them ended up browsing the shells, anyway, because why not? The shop, in my proudly biased opinion, was up to its gunwales, up to its crow's nest even, in enticing seashells giving come-hither winks. Their browsing and buying were afterthoughts, though, like coins dropped in a donation box for upkeep of the site. Another difference between these customers and the first set—they didn't chat among themselves. They whispered (but not as quietly as they thought).

"It doesn't *feel* like anything happened here," said a woman to the man with her. She rubbed her upper arms as though she did feel something.

"I keep telling you," the man said. "It didn't happen here."

"But it wasn't a *random* death." With a bit of a start, the woman glanced around, as though realizing someone might be listening. "He lived here and worked here," she said in a breathier voice I could still hear because her tour of the shop had brought her closer to the cash register. "His death, his *existence*, must have left traces."

"The exto phlegm you keep talking about?" he asked.

"Ectoplasm. And I don't feel it here and I thought I would. I'm disappointed." She gave me a quick, tight smile.

"Can I help you find what you're looking for?" I asked.

On a sharp intake of breath, her eyes lit with hope.

I doused it with an apology and a smile. "I'm sorry I can't help you with ectoplasm, but shells make nice souvenirs."

"Maybe another time," she said. "We're running late."

"Thanks for coming in."

I'd worked part time at the public library, back in Johnson City, Tennessee, and that had conditioned me not to roll my eyes or make other faces in front of or behind a customer's back. We'd called them customers at the library, too, and while good customer service could strain a person's mental health, it paid off. Generally.

None of the customers, Aw Shucks and Beak Booper included, discussed the graphic details of Allen's death, or asked me what I knew about *any* of the details. For that I was grateful, because it would have strained my mental health more than smiling and letting customer behavior roll off my back. But had business been like this for Glady the whole time I was gone? If so, I owed her more than an afternoon off.

The last customers, a mom, dad, and their ten-year-old son from Montreal, stayed late and made it worth my while. The boy, Jacques, had an itch to spend all his birthday money. He had a good eye, choosing a few rare and a few showy specimens, and then examining whelks, scallops, olives, augers, Scotch bonnets, periwinkles, and oyster drillers. His dad kept a running tally of how much he'd spent, and his mom ferried the precious booty to the sales desk.

"Shells are Jacques's new hobby," she said. "More of a passion."

"I am going to be a conchologist. That is the scientific study of shells," Jacques told me. They both had French accents. Jacques's, I was sure, would someday leave knees weak wherever it went. "Most seashells are made by mollusks," he continued. "Do you know how many species of mollusks there are living today?"

"Anywhere from fifty thousand to two hundred thousand, and I think two hundred thousand is closer to the truth."

"You *do* know," he said.

"I do, because I'm a malacologist, a zoologist who studies—"

"Mollusks! You see? I know this." Jacques squinted at me. "Then why are you here in this shop?"

"My specialty is freshwater mussels," I said. "I used to wade in the creeks and rivers of Tennessee studying them. It was a great job, but it didn't last. Now I live here, and this is my shop, and I'm surrounded by shells all day long. Like a happy hermit crab."

"I will have my own ship and study mollusks off the coast of North and South America," Jacques said.

"Cool. Will you be like Jacques Cousteau with his ship the *Calypso*?"

"No, mine will be a submarine, and when I have studied the coasts, I will travel around the world like Captain Nemo in his *Nautilus*."

"Even cooler."

The most expensive shell he picked out came from the locked case—a handsome nautilus as big as a dinner plate. The label with the shell said that Allen Withrow's mother had brought it home from a collecting trip to the Philippines in the sixties. Jacques had obviously received serious birthday cash. As the family left, Jacques promised to navigate his submarine to Ocracoke and stop by for a visit.

I waved goodbye from the porch, happy to end the day on a positive note. Otherwise, given the amount of business, the odd nature of some of it, and the occasional strain, I might wonder if the shopkeeper's life *was* for me. But that was what this time on the island was for. To find out if I wanted this. I wondered how long that would take. A matter of weeks? A couple of decades?

"Emrys?" I called after going back inside and closing the door. "Everyone's gone home and I've *come* home. Aren't you going to blip in to say hello?" *Blip* was a word I'd taught him. He liked it.

No answer. No pirate humming chanteys in the background. No shimmering or blipping into view. A knock at the door, though, and that made me jump. How loudly had I been talking to no one? More importantly, why hadn't I locked the door?

Chapter 4

The unlocked door opened, and Rob Tate stuck his head around the edge. "All right if I come in?"

"Sure. Glady said you'd stop by. Nice to see you."

"Welcome back. I saw your car. Looks loaded to the gills. Want any help unpacking?" Tate usually had a clear, calm voice. It mirrored his personality. Both were assets for law enforcement anywhere, but especially in a tourist town. He was about ten years younger than me. So roughly the age of Aw Shucks and Beak Booper. Tate's way of moving was calm, too, and his eyes were clear, unlike those of his loutish contemporaries. Tate's calm stepped into the Moon Shell along with him, but his voice sounded frayed around the edges, and he looked more run-down than I felt after my day-and-a-half drive and long afternoon on my feet. It wouldn't be fair to ask this guy to make trip after trip from the car much less up the steep stairs to the attic.

"Thanks, but I'll just do the bare minimum tonight and get the rest in the morning."

The starch in his khaki uniform shirt looked relieved.

"Still shorthanded?" I asked.

"Matt's in the office a few days a week. Anxious to be back full-time."

Matt, Tate's deputy whom I hadn't met and whose last name I'd forgotten, had fallen off a roof he was fixing after the hurricane I'd blown in on. He'd broken his leg in two places. That made Tate still down one and a half deputies and Matt somewhat lucky. Tate's other deputy, Frank Brown, had died by the hand of the same person who'd killed Allen Withrow.

Tate eyed the seagull. "Min's bird?"

"Could be. Who's Min?"

"Min Weaver. Glady and Burt's mama. You should feel honored to have it hanging here."

"When I first saw it, I have to say, I wasn't thrilled. Please don't tell Glady and Burt that, though. Then a guy in a loud shirt pretended to shoot it, and I suddenly felt protective. My inner seagull mother coming out. But why should I feel honored?"

"You'll have to ask Glady and Burt. No other trouble from that loud shirt?"

"Not trouble, but interesting behavior from him and his buddy. From a lot of people who came in." I told him about the customers who seemed to be looking at the building more than the shells. "When my husband and I brought our boys to Ocracoke, we did plenty of browsing through stores, but we looked at the pirate souvenirs and T-shirts and whatever else was for sale. We didn't go into shops and look around like they were historic house museums. We didn't try to feel the essence a murdered man left behind." I'd gotten a little worked up.

Tate had listened with either polite or pretended interest until the part about the essence of a murdered man. At that, one eye twitched.

"Sorry," I said. "It was a long trip, and I didn't expect to be thrown into full shop owner mode as soon as I got out of the car." I stopped jabbering and then jabbered again. "I also didn't mean to complain just now."

"No need to apologize. If any of your lookie-loos become a

problem, let me know. They're probably thanks to Irv Allred's post on Facebook."

"Irv Allred." I suppressed a shudder. "I think I saw him fishing at the dock when I came in on the ferry. Is the fishing any good there?" I wondered if I should add "fishing in unlikely places" to my list of Allred's unusual hobbies. Add it to his claim that he saw tokens of death before people died, his interest in ghosts, his desire to see one, and, according to Emrys, his very strong desire to catch one. I, who'd never believed in ghosts, didn't know if catching them was possible. But if it was, it wouldn't happen to Emrys if I could help it. Then the rest of Tate's words registered. "What did he post on Facebook?"

"Details about the murder case last month and this latest case. Glady mentioned that kind of weird foot traffic in the shop when she told me you were on your way back. She called them 'murder tourists.'"

"Murder tourists." I suppressed another shudder. "Wait, what do you mean by *the latest case*?"

"You haven't heard?" Tate asked. "Glady didn't tell you? Or Burt?"

"Glady flew out of here with barely a hello, so, no, I haven't heard."

"The customers weren't talking about it?"

"A lot of them were whispering, and only some of them whispered loudly or closely enough for me to hear. So, if they were whispering about whatever it is you're talking about, then I didn't catch it. How long are we going to go back and forth like this?"

Tate filled his lungs and looked almost cheerful. Cheerful enough to ignore the snark in my question. "I'm glad you haven't heard. That means the story's losing steam. Unless." He said something short and sharp under his breath. "They could've been talking about it and you didn't realize what you were hearing."

"We'll never know the answer to that unless you tell me what you're talking about." My increased snark snapped him back to communicating clearly.

"Two days ago the body of an adult female, as yet unidentified, was found in a tidal inlet. The death was not accidental."

"That's . . ." It was horrible. Shocking. To say that things like that didn't happen in Ocracoke was a cliché, but true. "I'm so sorry."

"Yeah. Well." Tate wiped the back of a hand over his forehead. "I want this thing cleared up before we're overrun with people here for the Jamboree."

"Do you think you can do that?" The Pirate Jamboree was a bit less than two weeks away.

"The initial work is done. Forensics at the scene. Inquiries here and in the wider area for anyone missing a relative, friend, or work colleague."

"No leads?"

"Not yet."

"Do you have to treat the whole island as a crime scene? No. Ignore that. Obviously not. Dumb question."

"Not dumb," he said with a quick smile. "More like wishful thinking. Believe me, I *wanted* to declare the whole island a crime scene. But now I've taken up too much of your time. Glady left word there's an envelope here for me."

"There is, but can you stand one more question?"

"Sure," Tate said.

"Or call it a hope. I hope you were able to call in more deputies."

"Had to," he said. "Initially."

"Initially?"

"They came, they collected evidence and statements, they decamped for the comfort of the office in Swan Quarter."

"Wow. That doesn't sound ideal for a murder investigation."

"There's nothing ideal about a murder investigation." His unexpected bark disappeared behind the hand now rubbing his face. His mother should have warned him his face would look permanently run-down if he did that too often. "They'll be back if I need them or if they need me. The focus of the investigation is now off-island, the preliminary theory being that the victim had no connection to the island. Other than being left in the inlet."

I hesitated to ask my next question, but only for a nanosecond. I'd never been good at saying no to my curiosity. "You aren't as sure about that theory?"

"Can't be." That answer came clipped but calm. Calm enough for me to ask another question. I'm a fairly calm person, too. "In emergency situations, like a hurricane or a murder, can you deputize people to give you a hand?"

That raised a smile. "You mean let the amateurs loose?"

"They could be trained amateurs."

"In some circumstances that could be helpful. Valuable. Not in a murder investigation. But if you were offering, thank you." He gave an almighty yawn. "Do you know what the biggest headache in this job used to be?"

"Drunken tourists in golf carts?"

"Close. Until now it's been tourists letting their children drive golf carts. Anywhere and everywhere. Some so young their feet don't reach the gas and brake pedals, so the parents let another child crouch on the floor to push them."

"No. I don't believe it."

"Swear on my badge." Tate solemnly put his hand on his badge. "Now my biggest worry is murder."

"Ugh."

"And a—" He looked like he swallowed another word, rather than say it. From the twist of his lip, it felt nasty going down. "And a trio of amateur sleuths."

Well, slap my face. He meant Glady, Burt, and me. As though we hadn't solved his last *incident* for him. Pffft. "The envelope's on the desk in the office." I pointed with my thumb and enjoyed picturing icicles dripping from it.

Tate ignored the ice or didn't notice. He ducked into the office. I didn't follow and crane my neck to read the letter along with him, but I watched him study the front and back of the envelope, lift the flap, unsealed, and remove a single, folded sheet. It couldn't have taken long to read. He turned around almost immediately.

"Is this your idea of a joke?"

"I like jokes. . . ." My voice petered out. If the note was a joke, Tate didn't think it was funny.

"Don't touch it." He held up the note. "Read it but don't touch it."

I read the single line, *The dead woman is Lenrose*, and then the signature, *Maureen Nash*. No wonder seeing Tate's name written on the envelope had made me uneasy. It was my handwriting, and that was my signature.

Chapter 5

"Whoa." I backed away from Captain Tate. Away from that note. "I don't know anything about that and did not write it." But it sure looked like I had.

"You knew it was on the desk."

"Because Glady told me."

"Who's Lenrose?"

"I don't know." I shook my head, couldn't make myself stop shaking it, couldn't take my eyes off the paper in his hand. Started babbling and couldn't make myself stop that either. "I've never heard of her. I've never heard of anyone with that name. I've never heard the *name* before. I can prove I've been on the road for the past day and a half. I've got receipts. I arrived this afternoon. Ask Glady."

"I intend to." His words and the searing look in his eyes stopped my babble mid-spate. Tate took a plastic bag from one of his pockets, refolded the note, and slipped it and the envelope into the bag. His black pants, black shoes, black belt with its holster and various cool-looking leather pouches attached, and his shiny badge looked more official now. The award for most official going to the badge and the holster.

If he'd been wearing a cowboy hat, Captain Tate wouldn't have tipped it to me on his way out the door. He didn't invite me to go across the street with him to Glady and Burt's either. I went anyway. Not by his side but not cravenly skulking after him. A crow on the Weavers' porch roof lifted off and flew silently away as I followed Tate up the front walk.

Burt answered Tate's knock, opening the door only a crack. "Hey, Rob. Not a good time."

"That's fine," Tate said. "I'm here to see Glady."

"She isn't home," Burt said. From the little I could see of him through the crack, his beard was growing back in nicely. He'd shaved it off as part of a disguise when he, Glady, and I— the trio of amateur sleuths Tate maligned—had been developing a suspect. Burt's face was so tanned, and he'd worn the beard for so many years, that without it his face had suddenly looked two-toned like a brown and white saddle shoe.

"Her golf cart's home," Tate said.

"I am not my sister's golf cart's keeper." Burt started to close the door.

Tate put a brave hand between the door and the jamb. "What do you know about a note left for me across the street?"

"It might not be the longest street," Burt said, "but can you be more specific? What note and where across the street? Really not a good time, though, Rob."

The smell of something chocolatey baking slipped past Tate's hand still bravely keeping the door ajar. Burt's baking must have progressed beyond breakfast muffins.

"A note left for me at the Moon Shell," Tate said. "On Allen's desk in the office."

"You mean Maureen's desk?" Burt asked. "Nice to see a bit of you standing there, Maureen."

I waved.

"The note," Tate ground out between his teeth. "What do you know about it?"

"Sorry. First I've heard of it."

While Tate had been abusing his teeth, he'd moved his hand

from the door to massage the back of his neck, which he vigorously kneaded. A mistake that Burt took advantage of by closing the door.

Tate pivoted, the hand at the back of his neck working harder, and gave me a terse parting shot. "I'll be in touch."

Chapter 6

After trekking most of my stuff from the car up to the apartment, the back of *my* neck needed a good massage, too. And the small of my back. Maybe my calves. I'd only planned to unpack half the stuff, but this was "stress unpacking." The note and Tate's reaction to it had unnerved me and made me nervous at the same time. I puffed and panted, dragging boxes, bags, and piles through the back door, through the storeroom, and up the steep staircase—with barked shins, for the last half of my edgy marathon, because I banged into the recycling bin in the dark.

Exhausted, I left the last box of books in the car, climbed the stairs, and opened the wine and a box of Goldfish crackers I'd bought in Hatteras. It was all the supper I could muster the energy for, and delicious. I took a glass of wine and a small bowl of yellow, cheesy fish to the window seat in the living room. Sat with my back to the deep window casing.

"Emrys?"

No answer. No ghost. I wondered about going across to collect Bonny, but the window where I sat looked out onto Howard Street, and the lights were off at Glady and Burt's. I drew in a deep, calming breath that didn't live up to the hype of deep breaths. A gulp of wine helped. It was an unassuming red, perfect for the understated, mellow look of money all around me in the living room of Allen's—my—apartment. My feet were as tired as the rest of me, but I'd landed on them with this inheritance.

Gene Kelly belted out "Singin' in the Rain" from my phone. That was the ringtone for my older son, Kelly—as prone to unease and nerves as I am. Which isn't really all that prone, but I'd promised to call both boys to let them know I arrived. They were nice boys. They proved it every time they didn't complain when I called them "the boys." Kelly was twenty-nine and O'Connor twenty-seven.

"You promised to call," Kelly said.

"That's true. I didn't want to interrupt you at work. Or myself. I didn't expect to be thrown into the lion's den my first afternoon. Make that the lion's mane's den."

"Was it like that? Highly poisonous jellyfish?"

"Metaphorical," I said. "The shell-buying public was out in force. *You* promised not to worry."

"That's true, and you can tell I didn't because I waited until this evening to call you. How's the weather?"

"I hardly noticed. Warmish, though." I glanced out the window. "Clear tonight. Lots of stars."

"Have the police returned the golf cart?" asked the son who'd always been into vehicles.

"Not yet." Allen's golf cart, now mine, had disappeared the night he died. It became part of the ongoing investigation when it was found. "I forgot to ask Captain Tate about it. He's the top cop in the sheriff's office here, not a boat captain. He stopped by to welcome me back."

"Good. That sounds friendly. Does the cart have a name?"

"I don't know. Allen might have had a name for it. I'll ask Glady and Burt. She calls hers Dorothy Parker because she can park her. Burt's is Minerva. Is naming a cart standard practice?"

"Ask your ghost." Kelly laughed. "I can't believe I just said that." I pictured my seeing-is-believing son shaking his head at himself. He was coming around to the idea that Emrys existed and admitting it was stretching him in ways I loved seeing. His dad would have loved to see it, too.

"Surely between the three of them—Glady, Burt, and Emrys—I'll get a straight answer on the naming issue." I drained my wineglass and reached for the bottle. Then didn't open it. More than one glass was almost always more than I wanted.

"If names turn out to be *de rigueur*," Kelly said, "you could call it the Mussel Cart. You know, like a TransAm or a souped-up Mustang, but spelled *M-U-S-S-E-L*."

"Perfect. I'll call it that whether names are the done thing or not."

We chatted a bit more. I said nothing about murder, strange notes, or the absence of ghosts. After promising to call him again in a couple of days, we said goodnight, and I called O'Connor. Jeff, my dearly departed, had been the director of the theater department at East Tennessee State University, a great fan of stage musicals, actors Gene Kelly and Donald O'Connor, and our own Kelly and O'Connor. The boys were great fans of their dad.

"Mom! About time you called. How's everything there? How's Bonny? And Glady and Burt? And Emrys! Is he there now? Say hi to him for me. Does he mind if people say yo-ho-ho to him?"

I laughed at the spate of questions. He and Kelly had worried about me being on the island after the hurricane, then worried more after reading about Allen Withrow's murder in the paper. O'Connor had been able to take vacation on short notice and came to see for himself that I was okay. Then I'd worried them even more by telling O'Connor I had a new friend, and the friend was a ghost. That was a lot to ask anybody to believe, much less sons still grieving for their father, sons who suddenly had to wonder if their still grieving mother was going around the bend. The look on O'Connor's face when I told him about Emrys—I never wanted to see that look on either son's face again. Then Emrys had spoken to O'Connor and shimmered into view in front of him. The revelation of the revenant. Talk about eye-opening.

"Mom?" O'Connor said.

"Sorry, Con. What were you saying?"

"I asked how Emrys is."

Saying nothing to Kelly about the missing ghost had been easy. He hadn't asked a direct question about Emrys. But answering a direct question from either of my sons with a lie? Nope.

"I'm not sure he's here, Con. The shop was busy, and that meant I was busy, and I haven't seen or heard him."

O'Connor didn't say anything at first and then quietly asked, "Nothing at all?"

"Not a woo-woo or a peep or a yo-ho-ho," I said, trying to lighten the situation.

"Are you worried?"

I said, "Hmm," trying for a noncommittal noise.

"So, you are."

That was why I didn't lie to the boys (besides the fact that lying to one's children was generally a rotten thing to do). I was no good at it. "He might be lying low until after the Jamboree," I said. "Although it's almost two weeks away, and that seems like an overreaction."

"Do you really know how ghosts react or overreact?" O'Connor asked.

"We probably can't lump all ghosts together like that, but you're right. I don't really know that much about how *he* reacts or overreacts. Huh. Okay."

"Feel better?" he asked.

"Yes. A bit. Thank you."

"Call me if you see him, okay? Or text. You can always text."

He and Kelly reminded me of that every so often. I don't have any problem texting other people, but I haven't liked texting them since the day Jeff died. That day he sent me a text asking if I'd like to meet him for lunch at our favorite café. I'd said yes and waited for him there. He didn't make it. There was an electrical accident backstage and, as I'm sure he would have joked, he'd had his last curtain call. "I'll call you in a few days, one way or another."

"Love you. Night, Mom."

After I disconnected, my stomach growled something rude about people who think small bowls of tiny crackers are supper. I agreed with it and made a peanut butter sandwich on sourdough rye, grabbed a banana and a glass of water, and went back to the living room.

Thank goodness my car, a Volkswagen Golf, didn't hold a ton of stuff. That meant the main room—kitchen at one end, living room at the other—wasn't now wall-to-wall boxes and I wasn't facing endless days of unpacking. Just days of trying to shoehorn the things I'd felt I couldn't live without, from the house in Tennessee, into this apartment already furnished with Allen Withrow's beautiful things.

The apartment, occupying the house's half story, had sloping ceilings that met the walls at about my shoulder height. The same beadboard paneling—painted white in the shop and left unpainted in the apartment—covered the walls and ceiling. The bare pine gave the place the feel of a log cabin. None of Allen's clothes, linens, towels, or toiletries remained. Glady had recommended a woman who'd been happy to take them away to keep, sell, give away, or trash as she'd liked. What was left was either antique and valuable or modern, expensive, and useful.

The kitchen appliances were top of the line, including the

kind of stand mixer (cobalt blue!) that I'd coveted for years. The bathroom had an antique claw-foot tub with a shower and shower curtain arrangement and an over-under washer and dryer set. The bedroom had an adequate closet and a more than adequate armoire that could easily have an entrance to Narnia at its back.

It was the living room that still kept me from believing this inheritance could be anything except a dream. By rights, all of Allen's possessions and the business should have been Jeff's. He would have loved the gentlemen's club atmosphere Allen had created up here—the old leather recliner, antique settee covered in deep green brocade, the bookcases crowded with novels (first editions, leather bindings, books in slipcases). The impossibly frail and impossibly valuable-looking desk. The photographs of early Ocracoke and the small, exquisite watercolors hanging over the desk. The woven carpet, almost the size of the room, with its geometric patterns of greens, browns, blues, reds, and golds.

Patterns. It was patterns that worried me. Not the patterns in the carpet, but the phenomenon of ghostly patterns. Shortly after we'd met, Emrys told me a story he'd heard as a child of the gray lady—a ghost who could be seen walking the length of a corridor and then disappearing. She would then reappear, back where she'd started, and walk to the corridor's end again. She did this over and over and never varied. When I explained what a film loop was, he agreed that the poor old gray lady was caught in a never-ending loop.

Emrys's pattern was different, less active as he said, and it centered on the carved shell in the locked display case downstairs. He'd carved the shell as a present for his wife. He'd died before he could return to their mainland home, in Edenton, to give it to her, and the shell became his pattern. Not walking toward it over and over, or reaching for it, but looking at it. He described it as being attached to the shell. Caught in his pattern, the shell became his entire focus. When that happened, he had no conscious awareness of anything else. *As though the shell is my lifeline, my source of breath and heartbeat*, he'd said.

Like a friend who couldn't meet you for coffee because of a business meeting or a doctor's appointment, Emrys wasn't available when his pattern drew him in. Sort of like Glady who'd had to run somewhere this afternoon. Except that, for Emrys, falling into his pattern was never a prior engagement (I wasn't convinced that Glady's abandonment of me had been either). The pattern made Emrys not just unavailable but powerless. He didn't know when the pattern would take over, and he couldn't break out of it when it did.

"Emrys?"

No answer.

So.

I sat in my comfortable, silent, Howard Street aerie, staring out the window through the branches of the live oak. Worrying that Emrys was caught—completely, irrevocably caught—in his pattern. Worrying that I'd never see him again. Wondering if his absence—his possibly permanent absence—was the source of the odd feeling I'd had since arriving on the island. Feeling helpless.

Chapter 7

I wasn't one to give up easily. If Emrys was in the house and caught in a pattern or loop or whatever anyone wanted to call it, then there had to be something I could do to reach him. Calling his name hadn't done the trick, but I had another trick up my sleeve. To be more precise, I had the trick in the traveler's writing box Jeff had given me for my birthday back before the boys were born.

The box was a nifty thing made of cedar and slightly larger all the way around than a ream of paper. The lid could be slid off, turned over, and slid back on—revealing the underside made of a laminate that gave a smooth, hard writing surface. The interior was partitioned into two spaces by another piece of cedar. Paper and notebooks fit in the larger space. Writing implements fit in the smaller one. A carrying bag came with the box so I could sling it over my shoulder and take it on hikes or to creeks and rivers for mussel research. It worked well as a lap desk, too.

The boys and I had packed my stuff in a hurry for this move. "Don't bother to mark the boxes," I'd said gayly. "I'll have everything unpacked and put away before I have to wonder what's in them." That turned out to be *almost* true. The writing box was in the fifth box I opened (and rooted through rather than unpacked). I pulled the good old friend from between two blankets, gave it a pat, and slid open the lid. Inside, an envelope with an Ocracoke postmark stared up at me. The return address was the Moon Shell, and it was addressed in lovely script to Mrs. Maureen Nash.

The letter had arrived in Tennessee on Saturday. A mere two days ago? Mind-boggling. The night before, the boys and I had attended a performance of *Brigadoon* at the university, done in Jeff's honor as the late, beloved theater director. The whole evening was wonderful. Joyful, emotional, and like closing a door I'd been keeping open since Jeff had died. A door kept ajar so he could slip back through and stay with us. Stay where he belonged. It wasn't logical thinking, but when is mourning logical? I'd drifted around the house, my job, my life, but keeping the door open that mere sliver had kept me feeling . . . attached. Attached to listening for Jeff in the next room, looking for him around corners, smelling his head on the pillow beside me. Attached so that I didn't drift away altogether to who knew where.

Kelly and O'Connor were staying for the weekend, so the morning after the memorial performance, I treated the three of us by making French toast. While I did, Kelly brought in the mail, junk except for the letter. Assuming it was from Glady or Burt, I told Kelly to open it and read it aloud. The letter wasn't from either Weaver. It was from Emrys.

The letter nudged me. It elbowed me in the ribs. It got me to move. To pack the car with clothes, books, bike, and rosy expectations and drive back to Ocracoke.

Now maybe I could elbow Emrys in return. He wasn't without a certain amount of vanity, so if calling his name hadn't worked, then maybe reading his own words aloud would catch his attention and snap him out of his loop.

I took the letter downstairs. With the door to the shop open, I sat on the bottom step. Smoothed the letter on my knees.

Picked it up again. Looked across at the locked case and the cameo shell—the moon shell.

The *shell*. What was I thinking? Why just *look* at it? Why not hold it as I read the letter? If he was laser-focused on the shell, then I should be, too. And if he was attached to the shell, then he would come with it when I took it out of the display case and up to the apartment. I got the key from the desk in the office, took the shell from the case, and carried it and the letter up to the living room. There, all three of us—me, the shell, and Emrys (I hoped)—settled in the recliner. What a crowd.

He'd written the letter on Moon Shell letterhead and started it with a quote from Shakespeare. He liked literary quotations, loved Shakespeare. His father, a cobbler in Wales, had told him that sprinkling quotations into a conversation was the sign of a well-read man.

"Okay, Mister Well-Read Man, listen up," I said and started reading.

"*'Words are easy, like the wind; Faithful friends are hard to find. William Shakespeare.'*

Dear Mrs. Nash,

You may assume that I am writing because the situation is urgent. I assure you it is. You must return to the island and soon.

Glady is a good-hearted soul, but she feeds Bonny far too much. Worse, Coquina is learning to whistle. She practices incessantly—on the Moon Shell's porch. She must have absorbed Allen's "talent" for the art. Which brings me to the reason I am writing and why I say that you must return.

I have found a haven where the girl's noise cannot reach me. It is Heaven, or as close to Heaven as I apparently will get, if you will forgive my poor joke. It is not, however, a haven suitable for anyone who would worry about cramped quarters or adequate headroom. The place I speak of is the area above the ceiling of the Moon Shell's half-story and below the rooftree—a sealed-off attic of triangular shape and mean proportions.

Although there is no ready access to this space (except for those of us corporeally unencumbered), there appears to have been a trapdoor, at one time, in the ceiling of Allen's bedchamber closet. The opening is still visible in the attic, but plastered over in the closet, possibly by Allen. At a guess, he did this decades ago after storing a number of boxes in the attic.

At this point I should tell you how lucky you are that I ignored my better judgment concerning small, dusty spaces. There are boxes in the attic that don't appear to have been opened since being squirreled away. I, however, being able to pass through cardboard as well as lath and plaster, have had a look at the contents and received one shell of a surprise.

Mrs. Nash, our conjectures were all wrong. Allen did not bury the spoils of his plunder beneath our feet. Rather, he sealed what he stole from your husband's family in the attic over our heads. The treasure the varlets carried off is far better than coins and jewels. In short, it is time for Plan B. You really must return to the island.

Yours in all sincerity, Emrys Lloyd, Accidental Pirate, Doughty and Ever Loyal.

P.S. There is also the small matter of the gentleman who arrived this morning and whom I overheard say that Allen is expecting him."

I put the letter on the coffee table and listened but heard nothing. "Emrys?" Nothing. I picked up the shell and called his name into its opening, then put the shell to my ear. Nothing but the susurrus that wasn't really the ocean and wasn't the ghost either. I put the shell on the coffee table on top of the letter and flopped back in the chair. The only thing that reading the letter accomplished was to make me feel like I was wallowing up to my armpits in questions.

First—Plan B? What did he mean by Plan B? Did he have one? Was that where he was? Off larking about on a Plan B? In that case, what had Plan A been? The answer to all of that might be simple, though. When he'd been feeling useless, humiliated, and ready to give up because we thought we'd nailed Allen's killer (talk about your prima-donna ghosts), I'd told him how I liked to face the world—prepare for the best, be aware of the worst, and if the worst happens, say with conviction and optimism, "On to Plan B." He thought that was useless and announced that he couldn't trust me because I was an imposter. I threw that back in his face saying that I couldn't trust him because he was a pirate. He'd disappeared in a snit—the ghost equivalent of going to his room and slamming the door. He hadn't reappeared for about twenty-four hours. Huh. Maybe he wasn't caught in a loop. Maybe he was fuming somewhere. But who was he mad at?

And how had he managed to write the letter and mail it? According to him, his ability to manipulate objects was extremely limited. He was proud of himself for being able to turn the pages of a newspaper, press computer keys, and turn deadbolts. When we'd discussed the idea of him keeping a diary, he'd told me he couldn't use a pen. Recently, in an emergency, he'd shakily scrawled a note of four short lines. The letter, though, was several pages of unwavering old fashioned script.

So, what was going on with that? Had he regained his dexterity with a pen, or had he lied about being able to use one? Or had he lied about his manipulation limitations in the first place? But if he *had* lied, did it matter? Whether he'd lied or regained skills, *if* he could move things and use them, that could be handy in any number of ways. I could ask him to swab the deck once in a while.

But those questions paled to the ones I had about "the treasure the varlets carried off." Treasure "far better than coins and jewels." I knew the bare details of the burglary, the who, what, and when. Allen Withrow and a buddy had stolen a valuable collection of seashells and antique shell art from Jeff's great-grandfather back in the sixties. The buddy had gone to prison. Allen had gotten off. But feelings of guilt must have dogged him because he decided to make up for the robbery by leaving the Moon Shell, his possessions, and a piece of island shore property to Jeff or Jeff's heirs. That was a lot of guilt. If the treasure had been up in the attic all those years, why not just give it back? Maybe what Emrys found in the attic was all that was left after Allen sold off bits and pieces over the years.

An old collection of shells, properly labeled, might contain shells no longer found or no longer legally collected. The collection or some of the individual shells could be worth quite a lot. And antique shell art! Some of that stuff was hideous, some gorgeous. Some, like the cameo shell sitting beside me in the recliner, really was treasure. But was Emrys a good judge of "far better than coins and jewels"? He was a deceased pirate who lounged around singing about what to do with drunken sailors. Although, who knew treasure *better* than a pirate? This one in particular. He and his brothers had, in one fell swoop, stolen cargo worth more than the sum total of all of Blackbeard's plunders.

Wading deeper into my questions, would I want to sell all or part of the treasure in the attic if that meant staying comfortably on Ocracoke and keeping the business afloat? Or would I be loath to part with it for any sum? If I kept it, *where* would I keep it? How many boxes in the attic and how much stuff in them were we talking about? Kelly and O'Connor should be in on making decisions about the treasure, too. And the land.

Then there was the question of this man, the *gentleman,* as Emrys called him in the letter. He'd arrived at the Moon Shell looking for Allen Withrow and claimed that Allen was expecting him. Who was he?

I shivered and didn't think it had anything to do with the odd feeling creeping around my edges again. Like a malevolent mist. Why was I scaring myself like this?

I got up and did the few dishes I'd used. Unpacked sheets, blanket, quilt, and pillow and made the bed. Put my pajamas under the pillow. Arranged toiletries in the bathroom. Hung towels and put a bath mat on the floor. Wondered what I really knew about ghosts.

What if they had expiration dates? What if when they reached that date they—poof—disappeared? Would that be any weirder than ghosts existing in the first place? Weirder than being haunted by the ghost of a Welshman with a melodious tenor who'd, incidentally, become a pirate?

Or . . . I stared at the ceiling. What if ghosts could have more than one loop? What if Emrys had a new shell-related loop and he was up there in the sealed-off attic looping away on the splendid treasure? That sounded not only possible but ghostly and thoroughly piratical.

In addition to the splendid treasure, the shore property, the business, his antiques, artwork, books, and fancy kitchen gadgets, Allen left me a broom and flashlight. I armed myself with them and went to the bedroom closet. There was no need to take out the clothes I'd brought with me, still on their hangers, and already hung up. No need to take the plastic bins with sweaters and other cold weather gear I'd slid onto the shelf above the closet pole. I shined the flashlight on the ceiling and looked for any sign of the hatchway. Was there a patch of plaster a slightly different color or texture? A faint outline? Nope.

I checked the bedroom ceiling and then, because the closet shared a wall with the bathroom, I shined the flashlight on that ceiling, too. No signs of a leaky roof, which was good. No signs of an old hatchway. I was sure Emrys was right and there was one, but Allen had either been a skilled plasterer or he'd known someone who was. That presented another question. Did Glady and Burt know that Allen had sealed off the attic and, if they didn't, did that matter? It might if Allen had ever moved out and the Weavers docked his damage deposit.

I took a chair from the kitchen into the closet and stood on it for a closer inspection of the ceiling. So completely smooth.

Everyone should have such a beautiful closet ceiling. I grabbed the broom, knocked on the ceiling three times with the handle, called his name, listened, and heard nothing. I rapped "Shave and a Haircut" but heard no "Two Bits" from the attic in return. Emrys might not know the classic call and response, but I didn't hear any other sound from above either. Not a single boo. I'd actually never heard him say *boo,* though, or heard him sound like anything but a mid-eighteenth-century gentleman. Even when he talked about computer passwords or *The New York Times*.

It was worth a try. I put the chair, broom, and flashlight back and got ready for bed. Crawled under the covers and tried not to feel lonely. Didn't succeed because no cat, no ghost, no friendly greeting from Glady or Burt, and a lot tired. And loneliness and worries made for a restless night and led to another deluge of questions.

Had Emrys found a way to have eternal rest? He'd told me that Allen had promised to search for a way to make that happen. After Allen's death, Emrys hadn't found any evidence that Allen had actually searched. What if Emrys found a way on his own? But would he take that final step without saying goodbye?

Or what if helping to find Allen's killer had fulfilled some kind of requirement that allowed Emrys to rest? But if that was true, why had he lingered in the shop for several weeks afterward?

In the depths of the night I wondered if he'd met someone—meaning another ghost. He said he'd almost never met other ghosts over the decades and centuries, but he read obituaries like they were dating profiles. Would it be so bad if he found a friend?

What if he found his *wife*? But why would that have taken so long—apart from him dying here while she waited for him at their home a hundred and fifty miles north in Edenton?

Then the worst question—what if Doctor Irving Allred, ghost hunter, had surprised everyone who knew him, done what he'd set out to do, and caught Emrys? But wouldn't that be news, even if no one believed him?

Toward dawn, a memory nagged me from fitful sleep—Emrys was a forger as well as a pirate.

Chapter 8

I slunk out of bed at dawn to the cawing of crows and a gnawing feeling of dread. Had Emrys forged my handwriting for that note to Tate? It was the only explanation and not one I'd be discussing with Tate. But why would Emrys do that? What did he know about the murder? Or about the dead woman? And why wasn't he here to answer all these blasted questions himself? This time I shouted his name. "*Emrys!*" And heard not a sound except for the crows.

But if he'd left one note, maybe he'd left another. One for me with explanations. "There's nothing wrong with hope!" I shouted at the absent ghost.

I pulled on Jeff's old University of Kansas hoodie over my pajama top and ran down to search the desk in the office. Finding nothing in any of the drawers, I turned to the lovely seascape on the wall. Until Emrys had told me about the safe behind the painting, I'd never seen a hidden wall safe in real life. This one had a push-button combination that Emrys could probably work, but could he take the painting down? Before his letter arrived, I would have said no. The safe held five books—illustrated, mid-nineteenth-century scientific treatises and monographs on mollusks and conchology so valuable they made my heart stop. I took them out, gingerly leafed through them, and moved on to a wooden box that held two miracles of Victorian excess—foot-tall glass apothecary jars filled with seashells arranged in intricate, fanciful patterns. No note from the ghost.

The seagull hanging over the display table exchanged guarded looks with me, and I trailed up to the apartment. After showering and dressing, I put Emrys's letter back in my writing box, the writing box in the bedroom, and the moon shell back in the locked case in the shop. Then I searched methodically downstairs and up for anything else Emrys might have written. Any clue at all. But if he'd left any kind of message for me, like him, it was missing.

A text from Glady arrived, though.

The lights are on, so you must be up. Will be over shortly with muffins and Miss Priss.

Muffins were good, but who was Miss Priss?

Chapter 9

Miss Priss turned out to be Bonny the sweet brindled tabby that came with the inheritance from Allen. She jumped out of Burt's arms when I opened the shop door. She stopped for a delicate sniff of my stockinged feet and then trotted up the stairs to the apartment.

"Miss Priss the Ungrateful," Glady said with a different kind of sniff. "Notice that she didn't spare a single backward glance for those of us who took care of her the whole time you were gone. Nor did she say thank you the entire time we kept her."

"I'll say it for her—" I started to say.

Burt cut me off. "Give me the—." He cut *himself* off and took a plastic container from Glady that she'd waved around to emphasize Bonny's rude behavior. He handed the container to me. "Bonny's living up to her reputation as a pirate queen," Burt said, "and her species. She's a *cat*. If she were a crow, you'd be all gooey about her."

"I've never been gooey in my life," Glady muttered.

The Weavers were living up to their reputation as eternally bickering brother and sister. Neither of them had said good morning or welcome back. I peeked inside the container—muffins that smelled brown, gingery, and welcoming all on their own. "Come on upstairs," I said. "Let's see if Bonny put the coffee on."

She hadn't, but it only took me a minute. Bonny had more pressing business. She, like Glady, stalked around and between the packing boxes and bags of my assorted stuff still strewn from the living room to the kitchen. Glady wore brown capris and a brown and black striped top, and I wondered if she knew how much she and the cat looked alike this morning. Burt might have picked up on that. He pulled out his phone and took quick, surreptitious photos of the two curiously inspecting a carton I'd left open after my search for the writing box.

Allen had named his cat after Anne Bonny, one of only a few known female pirates, who sailed and plundered during the golden age of piracy in the North Atlantic. There was plenty of documentary evidence for Blackbeard spending time in and around Ocracoke, but none at all showing that Anne Bonny had ever set foot here. From the short time I'd known Bonny the cat, her tendencies leaned more toward snacking and naps than pillaging.

I got out mugs for the coffee, plates for the muffins, and a spoon to give Bonny a welcome-home treat of her favorite canned food—the fishiest, smelliest available at the store in Hatteras.

"I see you haven't gotten much unpacked yet." Glady plopped herself on the settee and looked askance at my moving mess.

"I'll get to it this evening," I said.

"It's not like she was expecting company," Burt said, settling in the recliner.

"For her welcome-home breakfast? She should have," Glady said. "I sent her a text."

I put the plates and mugs on the coffee table and went back for the coffee carafe and muffins. I handed the muffin container to Burt. "Will you do the honors?"

"Ginger molasses," Burt said. "Made with rye flour." He'd become a muffin-baking maestro during the pandemic and had kept up the practice since. That and going out at first light to take pictures around the village.

I poured the coffee and handed a mug to each of them. Still on my feet, I proposed a toast. "To both of you. For taking exceptional care of Bonny, for keeping the Moon Shell open while I was gone, and for your continued friendship." I went to each of them and clinked mugs and then back to the kitchen for a gift bag I'd left on the counter. "Kelly and O'Connor went shopping Saturday night," I said, handing the bag to Glady. "A bit of northeast Tennessee for you."

"There was no need to make a fuss," Glady said. From the gift bag she took a box of candies that included bear paws, turtles, and an assortment of chocolates in the shapes of hearts, groundhogs, and the state of Tennessee. "You were only gone five or six weeks."

"Just three," I said.

"Is that all? Felt like more." She took a jar of chowchow out of the bag followed by a bag of stone-ground grits, a jar of sourwood honey, and a bottle of East Tennessee bourbon.

"Don't worry about wearing old Glady out," Burt said. "She only had the place open three hours a day, three days a week."

"When Maureen left, she and I discussed business hours, and we decided that it wasn't practical for me to keep *all* the hours Allen did." Glady's words crossed their arms and narrowed their eyes at Burt.

"Three hours, three days, three of anything is more than the shop would've been open without you, Glady," I said. "Thank you." It was tempting to echo her *is that all* about the three hours a day and three days a week, and I didn't remember our conversation about business hours exactly the way she did, but I was lucky she'd been able to keep the shop open at all. "I'm glad you didn't try to do more."

"Maureen didn't listen to me," Burt said to Glady. "She's gone back to worrying about wearing you out."

"Not true," I said. "I'm glad you didn't try to do more, Glady, not because you couldn't, but because you have so many other things going on in your life, and I don't want to be the one responsible for cramping your style."

"Unlike this buffoon," Glady said. She'd repacked the gift bag and now bit into one of Burt's muffins. "These are fabulous, Burt. Your best recipe yet."

"Not too heavy on the ginger?" Burt asked.

"Perfect," Glady and I said in tandem.

Burt sat back with another muffin and the bottle of bourbon he'd slipped back out of the gift bag. He took a pair of glasses from his shirt pocket and studied the bourbon's label.

"Well now, this is just like old times." Glady smiled and took another muffin, too. She looked and sounded less stressed and distracted than she had yesterday. Less than she had since arriving this morning. She looked more like the friend I'd expected to find when I returned. She even rubbed Bonny between the ears when she hopped up between us on the settee. Running the shop and keeping Bonny really must have been asking too much of her.

Although, thinking back on our conversations before I left, I'd only asked her to look after Bonny. She'd volunteered to keep the shop open so she'd have a good excuse to get away from Burt. Well, coffee under the bridge. I drained my mug and poured another round for all of us. I couldn't help wondering if her testiness was really from her three-day workweek or if it had anything to do with the note for Rob Tate. Probably not the note, though, or she wouldn't be munching happily on a third muffin now. Still, I decided to bring up Tate tangentially before asking about his note or any others she might have found. Now that she'd relaxed, there was no point ruffling her again.

"Nice seagull over the display table," I said.

"Adds real atmosphere, doesn't she?" Burt asked. "A real touch of class. Been in the family for years."

"Rob Tate said something about that. He said it might be the gull that belonged to your mother and I should feel honored it's here."

"Mrs. Bundy," Glady said.

"Oh, so not your mother's. Did Mrs. Bundy lend it to the shop?" More than one woman had a stuffed seagull? Was having stuffed seagulls a thing around here?

"The gull's name is Mrs. Bundy," Burt said. "After the ornithologist in *The Birds*."

"The movie," Glady added. "Not the Du Maurier short story."

"Now *that* I love. May I ask why your mother had a stuffed seagull?"

"There's no telling, really," Glady said.

"Always hard to say," Burt agreed.

"Is it another of the cockamamie Mama stories you won't tell me? Tate said her name was Min."

"Min's short for Minerva," Burt said.

"You named your golf cart after her? I wondered where the name came from."

"He had to," Glady said. "Mama left the cart to him in her will with the stipulation he rename it Minerva."

"*R*ename it? What did your mother call it?" I asked.

"*Nuestra Señora de Guadalupe*."

"After the treasure ship?" I almost dropped my coffee mug. Almost slipped up and asked if Emrys knew about the cart's original name. If he did, I couldn't imagine he'd been thrilled by it. The *Nuestra Señora de Guadalupe* was the first and last ship he'd plundered in his ill-fated career in piracy. An ill-fated and accidental career, he insisted, bullied into the adventure by his brothers.

"Mama loved local history," Glady said.

"Oh, sure. It's good stuff. Full of surprises." Like the Weavers, I mused, and their mama whose escapades they called cockamamie but about which they only dropped snippets of tantalizing details. "Did either of you find another note? Besides the one for Rob Tate, I mean."

"Were you expecting one?" Glady asked.

"No, just wondered." I raised an eyebrow at Burt.

He shook his head. "Before Rob tried to barge his way into my muffin meditation yesterday, I didn't know anything about notes."

"And that's the first I've heard about any barging." Glady's blue eyes skewered Burt.

"He was looking for you," Burt said.

"Then I'm glad you didn't tell me," she said. "Not that he can drag anything out of me anyway. I found it next to the cash register and don't know anything else about it. I'd love to know what it said, though."

They both looked at me, eyes bright, like birds waiting for me to toss the crust of a sandwich. I didn't see any reason not to tell them. "It was short. Not sweet. A single line. It said, 'The dead woman is Lenrose.' It was signed, 'Maureen Nash.'" Their dropped jaws looked genuinely stunned.

"You weren't on the island when I found it." Stunned or not, Glady didn't say that with enough conviction to suit me.

"When exactly *did* you find it?" Burt asked.

"Before I opened the shop yesterday."

"So, someone left it before you closed the day before," Burt said. "And, as is your habit, you didn't notice them or it."

"Baloney," Glady snapped. "That's for your assessment of my habits. As for not noticing the note—maybe." Then, as though it was a perfectly natural thing to do, she scooted as far from me on the settee as possible.

"Glady?" I waited until she looked me in the eyes. "Why

would I sneak into the shop and leave a note for Tate? *How could I do that without someone spotting me or my car when I arrived on the island?"*

Her left eye narrowed, and I could practically see her brain working out two or three ways I could do that.

"Glady, I have the receipts to prove I was on the road the day before yesterday, receipts for a hotel room in Edenton that night, one for breakfast the next morning, and receipts for gas and groceries in Hatteras."

"You're right. Silly of me." She didn't look like she felt silly. She looked upset. Sad?

"Oh my gosh, Glady. Was Lenrose a friend of yours?"

"Why are you talking about her in the past tense?"

"Because of the note." I'd been underwater with Glady, unintentionally, in real life several times. This conversation was beginning to feel like that.

She shook her head but didn't look any less upset. "A couple named Sullivan came into the shop a week or so ago. They introduced themselves as Victor and Lenrose Sullivan. Nice-looking couple. Retirement age. Pleasant. Victor said Allen was expecting him. I hated, just *hated* telling him that Allen is gone."

"I'm so sorry," I said. In the early sixties, Glady and Allen were briefly married.

"They took it hard. And his wife is the murdered woman?"

"Was," Burt said. He held his handkerchief out to her.

"You're so sympathetic, Burt," Glady said. "Please put that thing away."

"The night we met, you told me Allen was expecting someone," I said. "Do you think it was Victor?"

"If you'll remember," Burt said, "*you* pretended to be the person he was expecting."

"If *you* remember," Glady said to him, "she didn't so much pretend as go along with our assumption that she was."

Their bickering seemed like a sign they were returning to an even keel after the shock of the note. I enjoyed it for a few minutes and then interrupted them. "Did Victor tell you why Allen was expecting him?"

"No, and I didn't like to pry."

"Of course you didn't," Burt said. "Although you had plenty to say about someone who hadn't heard about the murder." He directed the rest of his comments to me. "Got her so worked up she had to close early and practically run across the street to tell me."

"Of course I did," Glady said. "For heaven's sake. What kind of a shell do the Sullivans live under?"

Closed *how* early, I wondered, then told myself to forget it. She'd been doing me a favor. "Do you want to know what got me worked up yesterday?" I asked.

"You mean besides finding out you'd written a note to Rob Tate?" Burt asked.

"This was before he read it." I told them about Tate's amateur-sleuth crack.

"Ingrate," Burt said.

"More so than Bonny," Glady agreed. "And I'll tell you what I think of that note. I think it's someone's poor idea of a joke."

"Any idea whose?" I asked.

"You wouldn't want to know someone like that even if we did know who it was," Glady said.

"What do you know about the victim?"

"Heard or know?" Burt asked.

"Because you know, Maureen, they aren't the same thing," Glady said.

"*You* might have forgotten that," Burt said. "I'm sure Maureen's heard it *and* knows it."

Burt was burly and Glady more petite, but their round faces, and even the creases at the corners of their eyes and mouths, made it obvious they were brother and sister—now more than ever as they sat there, as pleased as cat siblings who'd nudged a couple pens off a table. But I thought these two might be pleased because they'd successfully avoided answering another question. I didn't know why they played that game or where they learned it. Possibly from their cockamamie mama. I tried again, asking for more specific information from just one of them. "Have you seen the Sullivans since they were in the shop that day, Glady?"

"No."

"Wow. Okay." I took out my phone. "That's probably something Rob Tate needs to know. The note didn't give a last name for Lenrose, and he might not know anything about the Sullivans."

"Put your phone away. I wasn't finished," Glady said. "Have I *seen* them? No. Have I seen their *car*? Yes."

"That car is a marvel." Burt set the bottle of bourbon aside, and his hands went to work helping him do justice to the marvel. "It's a 1953 Kaiser Manhattan. Two-tone, green and white. Sleek lines and between the windshield and the other windows, including the rear window, there's more glass than you'd see from any of its competitors. A Manhattan is like a greenhouse on wheels."

"Sure," Glady said. "That's what everybody wants to drive around in—a greenhouse."

"AC," Burt snapped. "Manhattan's came with air-conditioning. I saw it this morning. It's a beauty, but if they want it to stay that way, they should be careful of the salt air. Bad for the paint."

"I'm impressed, Burt. I didn't know you were such a car buff."

"He didn't know any of that before he went into hyper retired-librarian mode." Glady got up. "I saw the car yesterday afternoon at the bookstore and again at the gift shop down the street."

"Village Craftsmen?"

"That's it," Glady said.

"The car is still here, but that doesn't mean Lenrose is," Burt said.

"What *have* you heard and what *do* you know about the victim?" I asked.

"Heard is the extent of it, and that isn't much." Burt paused, possibly for dramatic effect.

Glady pounced and snatched the pause before Burt was finished with it. "Unidentified female," she said. "And that makes me wonder—maybe Victor thinks Lenrose left the island, and he hasn't made the connection between her and the body."

Chapter 10

Before the Weavers left, I asked Glady if she would come back over lunch.

"You could just eat your lunch in the office," she said. "Or next to the cash register."

"I could, but what I'd really like to do is run by the bookshop and Village Craftsmen and ask if they remember seeing the Sullivans."

"Sleuthing. Good plan," she said. "I'd offer to come with you, but *someone* has to watch the store."

I immediately felt guilty for taking advantage of her free time again. Disappointed, too, but I didn't get far down that pity path before Burt fussed at her.

"Don't go messing with her the way you mess with me," he said.

"Why not? She's practically family."

They turned beaming smiles on me and then Burt levered himself out of the recliner.

"Covering for an hour won't be a problem," Glady assured me. "I'll be back at one because I like my lunch at noon and I'm not about to eat *my* sandwich at the cash register."

Burt was already creaking his way toward the door with the muffin box and bourbon. Glady grabbed the gift bag and called, "Wait for me, you old fool." She followed him down the stairs, and I heard them bickering amiably until the front door closed behind them.

"Speaking of lunch hours," I said to Bonny, "what kind of shop hours are we going to keep?" She gave her answer, if you could call it one, by washing her paw. "Is that a sign you spent too much time with the Weavers and their question-skirting ways?" She didn't answer that question either. I fired up my laptop and checked online to see what hours other shops in the village kept. Allen hadn't posted the hours on the door. He hadn't written them down anywhere, as far as I'd seen. No need. He ran the place himself, and he didn't need a reminder. I settled on opening at ten and closing at five and closed on Fridays. That mirrored a number of the shops. "Good enough for starters, Bonny. We'll see how things go and make adjustments whenever we want."

Thanks to the Weavers being early birds, like the crows, it wasn't much later than eight thirty. That gave me a bit more than an hour to work on emptying boxes and finding places to fit my stuff in with Allen's. Bonny found this much more interesting than discussing shop hours. She helped by jumping into each box I emptied and looked annoyed when I flattened them.

"You can't have every box," I told her, "but if you find one you like, we'll keep it. Deal?"

While I decided where to put the coffee, tea, herbs, and spices I'd brought from my Tennessee kitchen, Bonny decided on the small box they'd come out of. She folded herself into it.

"It's a snug fit," I told her, "but not unattractive."

She agreed with the slow blink of a contented, well-satisfied cat.

"You're a good point of reference, too. Now when someone asks me what size box they need to pack up assorted seasonings and whatnot, I can give a precise answer. There's no question about it, I'll tell them, what you need is the Bonny-size box. A box for all occasions and any application smaller than a bread box."

I took a picture of her in the box and showed it to her. She didn't care. She'd closed her eyes for a nap. Instead, I labeled the picture *New and Improved Instant Cat Loaf in a Box* and sent it to Kelly and O'Connor. Next step, tote the flattened boxes to the storeroom to await recycling, get the last box of books from the car, and tote it upstairs.

That done, I called it quits on moving in for one morning. Someday soon I'd have to make decisions about which of Allen's books to keep or which of my own to let go. Or where to squeeze in another bookcase. For now, I wanted another look at the closet ceiling. But standing on the kitchen chair and staring at it didn't change the results. Still no sign of a hatchway.

"Emrys?" I called. "I'm home."

Still no sign of a pirate.

Bonny roused herself shortly before ten. She trotted down the stairs ahead of me, tail up, ready to greet the public. Three steps from the bottom she startled and froze, back arched, hackles raised. The hair on the back of my neck rose, too. Something wasn't right. Had I locked the back door after bringing in the last box? Had someone gotten in? I didn't hear anything. Did Bonny? It didn't matter. She'd taken the situation into her own paws.

Shrinking as low to the steps as possible, ears flattened, Bonny oozed slowly to the bottom of the stairs, stopped, looked, hissed—at Mrs. Bundy soaring overhead. With another hiss she took evasive action, scuttling into the office and under the desk.

"Oh, sweetie." I got down on my knees and peered at her. "Didn't you see that old seagull up there when you came in? She can't come after you. Glady and Burt stuck her up there, and she can't come down. She takes some getting used to, but she isn't alive."

Acknowledging my words with a blink, Bonny turned her eyes back to Mrs. Bundy, freezing the bird mid-flight, her steely gaze all that stood between us and gull chaos.

"Good girl," I told her. "You've got this."

Customers started wandering in soon after I unlocked the door. Most smiled and bid me good morning. Some bought shells. Some toured the shop like murder tourists, but none as blatantly as yesterday. Bonny slunk out of the office and made her own tour of the shop, stalking stiff-legged, proving to herself and Mrs. Bundy who ruled this roost.

Glady came back at one with a small plate covered with a napkin. "Chocolate babka," she said and lifted the napkin. "Gorgeous, isn't it? Burt's branching out. I know you're anxious to be on your way, so I did you a favor and didn't bring a piece for you."

"Thanks. Kind of you."

She slid the plate onto a shelf under the sales desk. A sandwich might be out, but she had no qualms about eating dessert behind the cash register.

My nose wanted to follow her, sit up, and beg. I made it behave. "Tell Burt his babka smells amazing."

"I will. I won't gush and say *amazing* the way you did, but I'll pass along your compliments. Now, you need to run, but before you do, I have something important to tell you." She paused, looked serious.

Uh-oh. I glanced quickly at the only customer—humming to herself as she compared olive shells.

"Maureen," Glady said. "Pay attention. What I'm about to say could make or break this jaunt of yours. I'm going to pass along to you expert tips."

"Tips?"

"On how to ask questions without giving away your real motive for asking them."

"Ah. Thanks."

"You'll thank me later," she said. "Above all, be pleasant." She immediately scrubbed that tip away with a wave of her hand. "No need for that one though. You've got pleasant covered in spades. You're even pleasant when lunatics point guns at you."

"Just one and just once. I was probably in shock."

"Trust me when I say most people don't handle shock as well as you. Back to the tips. Be circumspect. Circuitous. Size up your mark. Pass the time of day. Browse the merchandise. Slip your questions in and then get out of there."

"Act natural?"

"Don't make fun. I'm drawing on my crime background here." To say she had a crime background was a bit of a stretch. Glady had written several long-running mystery series—mysteries on the cozy end of the crime-fiction spectrum.

"How's the idea for the new series coming?" I asked.

Another scrub of her hand. "No time for that now."

"No time to write or no time to tell me about?"

"Dearie me," she said, looking at her wrist, "is *that* the time? Don't dillydally another minute. I can't stay more than an hour. So, off you go. The sooner you do, the sooner you'll be back."

I let her shoo me out the door. It wasn't worth pointing out that she wasn't wearing a watch on her wrist.

Village Craftsmen was a mere hundred or so hops, skips, and jumps down Howard Street from the Moon Shell. Or, because I rode my bike, a short pedal between the lichen-crusted picket fences on either side of the unpaved lane. The pickets were so much a part of the street's shady, shadowed landscape, they might have sprouted from the thin soil. They might have been a long line of ancestors standing watch with weathered, worn faces, watching with the same sense of purpose Bonny had in keeping her eyes on beady-eyed Mrs. Bundy. Did the pickets ever pull themselves up after dark and stalk down the street keeping malevolent spirits at bay? If I ever saw Emrys again, I'd have to ask him.

Large, weathered shells hung from the tops of the fence pickets at Village Craftsmen. Jeff and I had loved this place and touches like that. We always stopped in on our visits to the island. An Ocracoke staple for over fifty years, most, if not all the handcrafted items inside were produced in North Carolina. When the boys were very young, we took turns watching them outside and browsing inside. Jeff always came out with a bag and a story about the marvelous thing inside it that had insisted on following him home. Once it had been a handmade kaleidoscope that looked like an antique spyglass. Back home in Tennessee, he'd helped the boys make their own kaleidoscopes with cardboard tubes and mirrors.

I parked my bike in the rack near the stairs. Planks, like signposts, were nailed to the newel at the bottom of the stairs. And they *were* signposts of a sort. Each plank had a line marking the height of the storm surge—the high water—from a hurricane that tried to sink Ocracoke and failed, including Sandy, Gloria, Allen, Isabel, and Matthew. Then along came Dorian who, in 2019, looked at the other storm surge lines and said, "Hold my beer, losers." The Dorian plank wasn't nailed to the newel post at the bottom of the stairs. It was nailed to the side of the building, well above the top of the stairs and several feet above the store's floor. The planks were a stark and sobering reminder of how precarious life on a barrier island was, even on one so enchanting and seemingly enchanted as Ocracoke.

The Village Craftsmen was several times larger than the Moon Shell but still not a huge place. It was well laid out with an eye for displaying as many attractive things in the available space as possible. It wasn't a place for a quick browse, but neither the merchandise nor the display furniture looked crowded or crammed in. I dutifully followed Glady's tip and enjoyed admiring glazed pottery, polished wooden ware, metalwork, glass ornaments, knickknacks, decorative tiles, and on and on until I came to a display of handmade pens. There were ballpoints and fountain pens. Barrels made of wood, stone, abalone, and both white and black mother-of-pearl.

Black mother-of-pearl was amazing stuff that came from shells found only in the warm waters of the South Pacific, more particularly the waters of French Polynesia. The black or dark gray came from the background color of a shell and was overlaid in a whole aurora borealis of iridescent colors.

I picked up a ballpoint with a black mother-of-pearl barrel and saw that I held a galaxy in my hand worthy of being photographed by the James Webb Space Telescope. The gleaming black barrel appeared infinitely deep, hiding subtle blues with swirls of green and glimpses of deep purple. Past those colors, even farther in, were sparks of bright peacock. Weighing the pen in my hand, feeling its balance, gave me an idea—an expensive idea, given the pen's price. Worth it? I wouldn't know unless I bought it. I held it up to my ear. Sure enough, it whispered that it wanted to follow me home.

A woman with a set of nesting wooden bowls, the largest big enough to hold salad for an army, beat me to the sales counter. The bowls were an armful, so I didn't begrudge her. While I waited, I read a poster advertising Ocracoke Ghost and History Tours. That could be fun. Also fun was a display of books—*Howard Street Hauntings and Other Ocracoke Stories*, by Philip Howard. I needed another book like I needed... who was I kidding? Of course I needed another book. Of course I needed this one.

There were ten or twelve other people shopping, but the woman behind the counter had the relaxed manner of someone who knew the magic of good retail service. She chatted unhurriedly and pleasantly with her bowl customer, kept an eye on shoppers floating around the store, and warmly invited the bowl customer to come back again before she left.

She turned her smile on me when I set the book and pen on the counter. "Great stories in that book. Is it for you?"

"It is. And the pen's for a friend who writes."

She held the pen to the sunlight. "Lucky friend."

"Definitely. I'm Maureen Nash, your new neighbor at the Moon Shell."

"Oh! Great to meet you! Glady Weaver said she was expecting you." She introduced herself and tapped the book. "Philip is my dad."

"Cool."

She tapped the book again. "If you're interested in ghosts, and when you've got your island legs under you, you should take our Ghost and History Tour."

"Does anyone ever see ghosts of pirates? On the tour or"—I waved a hand—"anywhere on the island?"

"No guarantees, but no one goes home disappointed. Did you know that we Howards are descended from pirates?"

"Wow. No."

"William Howard was Blackbeard's senior officer, his quartermaster. He escaped hanging by an Act of Grace from the King in 1718. In 1759, he bought this island for one hundred and five pounds sterling. The Howards have been sterling citizens ever since."

"1759—so was he living here when the *Nuestra Señora de Guadalupe* incident happened?"

"He might have been, but we don't know. He doesn't appear in any records between the Act of Grace in 1718 and the date of purchase. That was the crime of the century and written up in papers all over the world, though, so chances are he heard about it whether he was here or not."

"Say," I said, trying for Glady-approved casual, "Glady saw a green and white classic car here yesterday. Did you happen to see or talk to the couple who drive it?"

"I've seen it around the village but noticed the car, not the passengers. If they were in here yesterday, I didn't know who they were. Can you describe them?"

I laughed. "No. Glady described the car but not the couple." I should have asked her for a description and hadn't even thought of it. What an amateur.

"Did you want a ride in that car?" she teased.

"I wouldn't say no, but really we were wondering how to get hold of them. Their name is Sullivan. Glady said he was a friend of Allen's and came into the Moon Shell looking for him."

"Aw, it's still hard to believe Allen's gone. I'm sorry I can't help."

I thanked her and put the pen and book in my backpack. Then I hopped back on my bike for an even shorter ride around the corner onto School Street. There, set back from the street and tucked under live oaks and cedars, was Books to be Red in a little old cottage with a blue front porch. If anyone had dreams of finding the perfect beach bookstore, this was it. A sandwich board with *OPEN* written on both sides stood close to the street.

My primary objective in the bookshop was to find out if Lenrose Sullivan had been in yesterday. But now I had another—to hunt down and buy a blank book worthy of being written in with the mother-of-pearl pen. The hunt took me past a display of local books. An Ocracoke cookbook caught my eye. It joined me, and together we found exactly what I'd been looking for. It wasn't just a blank book. *Blank book* was too pedestrian a term for what I picked up and found myself stroking as if I held Bonny in my arms. It was a journal bound in soft black leather, with an indigo ribbon marker and crisp white pages. The endpapers were marbled in plum, indigo, white, and peacock. The pen and the journal would make a handsome couple.

As I paid for them, I introduced myself as the new owner of the Moon Shell to the thirty-something woman behind the counter. She reciprocated and welcomed me to the island and the neighborhood, giving me a friendly and curious once-over. I thought about doing a slow twirl so she could form a three-hundred-sixty-degree impression but opted for smiling and complimenting the bookshop. It was a sincere compliment and earned a beaming smile in return.

"I have kind of an odd question, though," I said. "There's a classic car in town, green and white—"

"I've seen it! Doesn't it make you long for a poodle skirt and a jock's letter jacket?"

"I'll let you know. I haven't seen it yet."

"Bummer."

"But Glady said—do you know Glady Weaver?"

"Who doesn't?" She leaned her elbows on the sales counter. "I was at a potluck last week and someone said, 'Glady and Burt are hard to miss and, if the world is a just place, no one will ever have to.' I couldn't agree more."

"Same," I said. "Glady told me she saw the car parked here yesterday, and we wondered if you saw the couple or happened to hear how long they'll be in Ocracoke."

"If I saw them, I didn't know it. After a while, the memory of one tourist blurs into the memory of forty-seven others. And I didn't see the car here." She made a wry face. "Unlike right now, yesterday was way too busy for staring out the window. Sorry."

"No big deal. Glady just hopes she'll see them again before they leave. She said Mister Sullivan—that's their name, Victor and Lenrose Sullivan—Victor told her that Allen was expecting him, and then he asked if Allen was in or when he'd be back. Poor Glady had to break the news about Allen's passing."

"Oh, that had to be tough. Poor, poor Allen. He should have lived to be a hundred. He'll be missed." She stared at nothing for a moment and then quietly swore. "But here you are. It really is nice to meet you, Maureen. Everyone is glad you're keeping the shop open. *We're* glad you are, and not just because having another popular shop within easy walking distance is good for our business. Business might even be better with you there. Allen ran the place more like a hobby for the past ten or fifteen years."

"Really?"

"He kept fairly regular hours."

"That's good."

"But only when it suited him. He called himself a casual capitalist who liked the laid-back approach to business. I took that to mean he didn't need to do much more than cover expenses and didn't have to worry about making enough during the busiest months to cover the lean ones."

This was more information than I'd gotten out of Glady and Burt, or from Allen's lawyer when he told me the shop was mine. It was more information than I'd gleaned from Allen's own records. "Was it a retirement gig for him?" I asked.

"At his age? Probably." She called hello to a family coming in the door and then turned back to me. "It was a gig he loved and that's why he kept it going. He loved Ocracoke, too. And books. He'd close at lunchtime, more often than not, and stroll down here to browse."

I started to slip the journal and cookbook into my backpack with the pen.

"Hang on. Let me wrap the journal in tissue paper. It'd be a shame for it to get scuffed." She swaddled the baby and handed it back. "I hope you love the gig as much as Allen did."

"I'm here on my lunch hour, so I'm off to a good start. Thanks. See you later."

I had one more stop to make before heading back to the Moon Shell. This one I didn't look forward to—the sheriff's station. But I wanted to check in with Tate and find out whether he believed me when I'd said I didn't write the note identifying the murder victim. I wasn't *really* worried that he didn't believe me, I kept telling myself as I pedaled slower and slower. Glady could tell him she found the note the day *before* I arrived. And I had the receipts for the trip.

The Hyde County Sheriff's station was out on the highway, in the direction of the ferry dock. Not far though. Only about a half mile from the bookstore. If I pedaled any slower, I'd be in danger of tipping over.

I also wanted to tell Tate about Victor Sullivan's visit to the Moon Shell and how he'd expected to meet with Allen. I wasn't sure why I thought that was important. But there'd been a question about Allen expecting someone, and now we had a someone. The information about Victor was secondhand, but Glady could give Tate the firsthand version. We also had the weird note. Not to mention we had the murder. I reminded myself not to say *we* when I talked to Tate. There was no point in giving him another opportunity to slam amateur sleuths.

I checked the time. Darn. Still plenty of it to make it to the station and get back before Glady blew a gasket. The sun felt warm on the top of my head and shoulders. Not hot, though, and I sure wasn't pedaling like a fury. Even so, I began to sweat. What I really wanted to ask Tate was whether the unidentified body could possibly be Lenrose Sullivan.

Chapter 11

The young guy who glanced up from a computer screen when I opened the station door had to be Deputy Matt Kincaid. Figuring that out took no skill whatsoever. Tate only had one deputy. That deputy had a broken leg. Here was a deputy in a regulation khaki shirt, rising to greet me on one leg, with a hand on the desk to steady himself. Also, dead giveaway, a pair of crutches leaned against the wall behind him.

"Good morning!" He had an engaging smile and looked wobbly.

I waved him back down. "Don't stand on my account."

"Okey-doke. Thanks." He eased himself back down. He looked younger than Kelly and O'Connor. Brawnier, too. Like a brawny surfer—blond with a fading tan. "You know, time doesn't exactly fly when you're stuck here like a dam—like a desk jockey—but I can at least get it right and say good afternoon instead of good morning."

"Good afternoon." Did people still talk about desk jockeys? Did young deputies say okey-doke? "Are you Deputy Kincaid?"

"Yes, ma'am."

"Nice to meet you. I'm Maureen Nash."

"New owner of the Moon Shell," he said promptly. "You

could've knocked me over with a feather when I heard about Allen—if I'd been on my feet instead of flat on my back because I fell off a roof."

"I heard about that. How are you doing?"

"Busted my leg but good. I'll be in a full leg cast for at least another few weeks." He knocked on the cast with his knuckles. "I'm back here part time. Only at the desk, but at least it keeps me from going stir crazy, and it gets me out from under Gram and Gramps's feet. It was their roof I fell off, and they felt so bad they wouldn't hear of me going back to my own place until I'm out of the cast. It's hard to argue with Gram and Gramps."

"I can imagine. How are the crutches working out?"

"You've heard of people with two left feet?" he asked. "With the crutches I have *four* left feet. But being clumsy's nothing new. That's why I fell off the roof."

"Maybe stay off roofs in the future?"

"That's the first thing Captain Tate said when he came to see me in the hospital. Gramps, too."

"Not your grandmother?"

"She said it twice." He grinned. "*You* aren't clumsy, though. I've heard all about how you and Ms. Weaver took a soggy midnight hike a few weeks back. I'm danged impressed."

"Probably only half of what you heard is true. Less than half, depending on who you heard it from."

"From Captain Tate, so I believe every word of it."

"In that case, feel free to call on Glady and me anytime you need further impressing. Speaking of Captain Tate, is he in?"

"No, ma'am. He's out interviewing people. *Again*. Because some dingbatter passed him a note supposedly identifying our dead body and that caused all kinds of shi . . . shellfish to hit the fan. Pardon my language."

"Don't worry about it. You combined two of my favorite things—euphemisms and shellfish." Interesting. Matt didn't seem to know I was the dingbatter—the person not from Ocracoke—in question. "You said supposedly identifying the body. Is there any chance the note is right?"

"That's what the captain's trying to find out. I told him I can help. I can do more than sit here. See the crutches there?" He pointed over his shoulder. "I've been practicing this move. Watch." Excitedly, he rolled his chair backward, the excitement possibly giving the roll more oomph than he'd used in his practice runs. He slammed into the crutches. They clattered to the floor and, from the shock on his face, I wondered if he'd given himself whiplash. How would he explain *that* to Tate?

"Matt? Are you okay?"

"Captain Tate doesn't call me the ox of the Outer Banks for nothing." He burst out laughing and then spluttered, "Was that great or what? Oh." He sobered. "Wonder if I broke the crutches or dented the wall?" He twisted the chair around and caught his foot in one of the crutches.

"Whoa, there, cowboy." I picked up the other crutch and stood it upright against the wall again. "This crutch looks fine. The one *you've* got has a deputy tangled in it. The wall is cinderblock, so it should hold up to a few more collisions. How about you, though? Are you sure you're okay?"

"Just *bored*." He chuckled again. "Big, active, bored, clumsy guy with a broken leg is another accident waiting to happen." Matt stood the second crutch against the wall. "I'm fine. And I will be fine. I might be clumsy and bored, but I don't have a death wish. Do you want to leave a message for Captain Tate?"

"It's not really important. I'm sure I'll bump into him sometime."

But bumping into Tate didn't happen before I bumped into several other people.

Chapter 12

"About time," Glady said in greeting when I walked back into the Moon Shell. She looked at her wrist, which still wore no watch. "If you'd been gone another fifteen minutes, you'd have been late. Any sightings?"

"None."

"Are you sure you asked the right questions?" she asked.

"Pretty sure. The problem is that people see the car and then that's all they see. They don't pay any attention to the passengers."

"Interesting."

"Let me put something away and then I'll be right—"

"Shush. I need to get this down."

I left her feverishly scribbling on the back of one of the shop's paper bags and went into the office. "Emrys?" I whispered. No answer. I took the journal and pen from my backpack. Now that he could write again, he might like a journal and pen of his own. *This* journal and *this* pen, I hoped. I laid them on the desk for him to find, wondering if they might attract him from wherever he'd gone, something like catnip. Ghost-nip.

The Moon Shell had settled into the same kind of lazy afternoon the bookstore was having. Glady grunted when I scooched her out of the way so I could ring up two customers. She shushed me, groped for a tall stool, and sat on it when I quietly suggested she go on home. Two things surprised me by that reaction. She was no longer frothing at the mouth to leave, and I'd never seen the stool before. Maybe Mrs. Bundy had swooped out and back in with it.

Between customers, I walked around the shop, straightening here, flicking a dustrag there, getting into the swing of feeling like someone who sells seashells by the seashore. I was just wondering if either Glady or Mrs. Bundy could offer worthwhile care and maintenance tips for stuffed seagulls when Burt walked in. With him came another plate covered with a paper napkin. My heart leapt.

"For you," he said and handed it to me.

"Thank you!" The bottom of the plate was warm. I lifted the napkin and inhaled the scents of fresh bread, warm chocolate, and spice.

"I added a few things to the recipe to make it my own," he said, pulling off an amazing feat—sounding both off-hand and *Top Chef* proud. "I waited until I saw you come back. Then I waited until the customers left. Then I gave the babka a nuke to bring out the cardamom and give the chocolate a boost."

"It's awfully nice of you to put the extra effort in," I said, "and to make a special trip over with it."

"I wasn't about to make the rookie mistake of sending it with Glady in case she ate her piece and yours."

"I would have, too," Glady said. "You can trust me on that."

"It's still in danger because you're still here," Burt said. "Guard it with your life, Maureen. Better yet, gobble it."

"Aye-aye." I took a bite and closed my eyes. "Aye-yiy-yiy-yiy-yiy."

Burt saluted and took a tour around the shop. Like the murder tourists, he paid more attention to the room than the merchandise, almost like he was taking measurements. His appraisal made me nervous. He and Glady owned this house. They were glad to have a tenant. But what if they wanted a more lucrative business here so they could raise the rent? According to them, they'd only ever had a verbal lease agreement, first with Allen's mother and then with him. I'd told them I would feel more comfortable with a written lease, but so far, we'd let it slide. Had I made a mistake thinking I could move in and stay? That might explain Glady's brusque attitude since I returned. That might explain why they were both here now—Burt surveying, Glady still writing on the back of the bag. The beauty of the babka palled. Time to change the subject in my head.

Last month, Glady had been excited about planning a research trip to Scotland. Years ago, she'd spent time there. Ever since, she'd kept a spark of an idea for a mystery series set in the Highlands tucked away, gently glowing like a peat fire in the back of her mind. I tried for some of the offhand manner Burt had carried off so well and asked, "Do you have dates for your research trip, Glady?"

Burt snorted. Glady either hadn't heard my question or ignored us. Writing could be a touchy subject for her. None of her books sold terribly well anymore. There were so many of them though—a whole slew, as Burt said—that the royalties brought in enough to throw a party once or twice a year. Or as Burt also said, enough to cover her funeral and a wake someday. Burt's opinions, and his willingness to share them, was one reason writing was a touchy subject. Glady knew I'd had some success with picture-book retellings of shell-related folklore, though, and I thought we'd bonded over our ideas for future projects. Now I hoped the bond would hold if I pressed a wee bit harder. I hated the idea of her giving up or falling into a depression over how to continue. "Glady, how *is* the idea for the Scottish series coming?"

"Meh."

"So, no research trip?"

"I've lost steam for that series. I wouldn't mind taking the trip, but the series—" Looking annoyed, she shook her head. "I wouldn't feel comfortable writing it. I'm not sure I—no. Not true. I *am* sure I couldn't do a Highland series justice. It wouldn't just be a case of imposter syndrome. I would *be* an imposter."

"I think you could find a way to avoid that," I said.

"I already told her that, but she got cold feet," Burt said. "So, I told her to knit herself a pair of warm socks, grow up, and start pecking away at the keyboard."

"And I told you I will," Glady said. "But first I'll knit something for you. A gag." She motioned me over. "I have a new idea. Mysteries for children."

"Good move. Mysteries for kids are hot." I made the mistake of putting my plate of half-eaten babka on the sales desk. Glady broke off a piece and ate it. I reclaimed the plate.

"I've been reading a ton of them," she said. "There aren't many murders in middle-grade mysteries, and I find that appealing. I'd never have to kill anyone again. Either in a book or in real life. Not that I ever have in real life."

"Pshaw to that," Burt said.

"To which?" I asked. "She *hasn't* killed anyone, has she?"

"Hard to say. She pretended to be a nurse for that speck of time back in her wild youth."

"I did not pretend," Glady said. "I just wasn't cut out for the caring life."

"So, she came back home and started killing people on paper," Burt said. "She's an interesting case, our Glady. She needs the outlet of thinking about murder to stay sane."

"Not true."

"You're right," he said. "You're one of the sanest people I know. You need that outlet so *I* can stay sane."

"How's that working?" I asked.

Glady shrugged. "Mixed results."

"The notes you were—" I mimed her feverish scribbling. "Are they for your children's mystery? Or something to do with the shop?"

Glady put the pen down. Her lips folded into a thin line as she folded the paper bag and jammed it in a pocket.

"Sorry," I rushed to say. "I'm being nosy. Pay no attention to my questions. Except one more. Do you feel like you're putting a jinx on your stories if you talk about them too soon?"

"While it's true I don't like to talk about stories in detail when I'm writing them, it's not because I'm superstitious. I got over the idea of jinxes a long time ago."

"Right about the time Irv Allred started dropping warnings through the letter slot," Burt said.

"*Allred.* Yeesh. Wait—" I said. "What kind of warnings? Could he be the one who left the note here for Tate?"

Glady and Burt gave that serious thought.

"It's possible," Burt finally said. "We should be careful about saying so, though. Last week he threatened to sue a tourist who called him a quack. The tourist told anyone who'd listen that Allred asked him if he wanted to try an experimental poultice made of toasted sand mixed with ground olives for his sprained ankle."

"The man's a nuisance," Glady said. "One of the notes he put through the mail slot warned me not to sign my books in red ink because, if I did, I'd be guilty of committing suicide. Total and utter hooey. He based it on a Korean superstition. The tradition in Korea has been to write the names of the dead in red ink. And so the belief arose that writing the name of a living person in red ink will lead to their death. Burt found that out for me."

"The kicker," Burt said, "is that Allred wrote the bloody note in red ink, addressing Glady by name."

"But signed his own name in black ink," Glady said.

"I told him the note was one of his death omens, plain as day," Burt said, "and that if anything happened to Glady, I would take it to Rob Tate and call it what is was—a death *threat*."

"Has anyone ever threatened to ride Allred out of town on a rail?" I asked. "Or keelhaul him with the ferry?"

"Easier to ignore him." Glady dug the paper bag out of her pocket. "These notes are primarily for the new book, but if we need to tackle the case of the unidentified female, they might be useful there, too. Was that really all you learned on your reconnaissance mission? That people are dazzled by the car and ignore the people in it?"

"What do you mean *if* we need to tackle the case?" I asked. "We're already tackling it, aren't we?"

"What do you mean *reconnaissance mission*?" Burt asked. "Don't turn me into the sleuth left out in the cold here. Two amateur sleuths do not a trio make." He looked from Glady to me and back again.

"I would have told you about Maureen's mission before I came over here after lunch," Glady said, "but I didn't dare interrupt you. You were making indecent cooing noises to your babka." She summed up where I'd gone and what I'd learned, finishing with, "You didn't miss much, Burt. She was gone for most of an hour with paltry results to show for it."

"Why don't we call them paltry *preliminary* results," I said. "Not every line of inquiry bears fruit immediately, or at all, but some lines of inquiry plant seeds for later harvest."

Glady wrote that on her bag.

"Besides," I added, "that isn't all I learned." I told them about talking to Deputy Kincaid. "He said that because of the note, Tate is out interviewing people again. That doesn't get us any further forward, either, but it's information."

"Information is power," Burt said.

"Here's to preliminary power, paltry or otherwise," Glady said. She raised one hand in a power salute and raised the other after filching the last bite of babka from my plate. A babka pirate if ever I saw one.

"Told you she was dangerous around that stuff," Burt said. "Oh, Glad, I almost forgot. I found something for you." He patted the many pockets of his cargo pants and then started on his shirt pockets. He took something shiny from one of them and tossed it on the sales counter.

"Ooh." Glady held up a broken metal watch band. "Thank you. They'll love it."

Her *ooh* sounded sarcastic, but the rest was clearly genuine.

"For her bird brains," Burt explained.

"Don't ruin it by calling them names. It's for the crows," she told me. "He made a platform on a fence post in the backyard for me. Like the feeder at the little place you rented last month. I leave trinkets on it for the crows."

"Do they take them?" I asked.

"Some they take and some they leave. There's a mystery for you," she said. "How do they choose?"

"I thought they'd go for the bling—the shinier and more useless, the better," Burt said. "For the most part they do, but not always. Once it was a little plastic dinosaur They've taken small shells, the cap from a pen, a foot-long shish-kebab skewer. I've started taking pictures of the platform every morning and evening to track the inventory."

"Have you taken a shine to them, Burt?" I asked.

"Still up in the air," he said. "No *cause* to rush it."

"No reason for *ravin'* about them?" I asked.

"You'll never get him to admit it," Glady said. "He *says* he built the platform for me. He really made it for himself. Every morning on his walks he looks for things they might like. It's his way of thanking the crows for leading him to us that awful night last month."

"So she likes to think," Burt said. "It's really just another way to recycle the jetsam people can't be bothered to hold on to until they find a garbage can."

"It's his peculiar way of having fun," Glady said.

"I believe it and it reminds me of something my husband and the Cat in the Hat liked to say. 'It's fun to have fun, but you have to know how.'"

"She's got your number, Burt," Glady said. "Which reminds *me*. I can't let you hold me up any longer this afternoon, Maureen, but I'll send you Yanira's number. You should ask her about working a few weekend hours. Holidays, too."

"That's a great idea. Thanks. Thanks for covering lunch, too, and for bringing babka. See you guys later."

They left with Glady muttering to Burt about nosey parkers and naps. I had no idea what that was about but looked forward to getting Yanira Ochoa's phone number. Yanira Ochoa taught first grade at the Ocracoke school. Up until recently she'd also worked part time at the Fig & Yaupon Bakery & Beer Garden. With that business closed now, she might be looking for extra hours. Her daughter, Coquina, was a petite third grader who twirled in tutus and fanciful headbands. She liked seashells, too, and I liked both the Ochoas.

Doctor Allred, though? Not so much. Glady had said he was a nuisance, and that tallied with my feelings. For the most part. But how big a step would it take to go from nuisance to menace? And from menace to something far worse?

Chapter 13

The meaning of *nosey parkers and naps* became clear as afternoon shoppers and murder tourists started wandering into the Moon Shell again. From their conversations, more of them had enjoyed long lunches than had taken naps. But however they'd spent the last few hours, I was happy they now chose to spend time admiring and buying shells. Even if some of them whispered comments like "the dead guy owned this place," and "nope, no way would I be caught dead working in a dead man's shop," and "we're walking in a murderer's footsteps." Ah, the pitter-patter of little murder tourist feet with money to spend. After the third pair of those feet paused at the open office door, I pulled it shut.

It seemed obvious to me that the office wasn't part of the shop. There was nothing on display and no extra stock in boxes, bags, or bins waiting to go on display. But my years at the public library had taught me to never count on anything being obvious to members of the public. Even the reading public, whom I'd always thought should show more signs of intelligence.

The reason for the pauses at the office door and the few hesitant steps through it might have been the attraction of the contrast between the shop and the office. The doorway was a portal between two almost jarringly different worlds. Facing the shop, you saw the airy seaside colors, sunny windows, the dive-bombing stuffed seagull, and seashells of all descriptions inviting you to pick them up and shell out for them. Turn to face the dim office, and you stepped back a century. You looked for the studious soul who must be reading or writing at the antique desk or sitting with elbows on the arms of the chair, hands together and index fingers resting against the lips—a person so deep in contemplation that you stood there unseen and unheard. You might not have existed. You might have been a ghost.

And I might have imagined all those thoughts running through people's minds. The office wasn't entirely antique anyway. The desk chair gave that away. And Glady had it right. The people stopping by were either customers who'd walked through the shop's door to look at and buy stuff or they were ghoulish tourists on a pilgrimage. Give shoppers and tourists another open door and in they would invariably go, following their nosey noses for more of whatever they'd come to find.

Glady's text with Yanira's number arrived. I debated between calling and texting Yanira and decided on the more personal touch of calling. The call went to voicemail. She was probably still at school. That was just as well. I was still at work, too, and should call her when we'd both have time to talk. I left a short but cheery message and went back to greeting customers and ringing up sales. I also congratulated myself every time my jaw didn't drop at the murderish questions a few people got up the nerve to ask. Some of them asked their questions breathlessly as though they'd come to worship in the shrine of crime. The most outlandish question came from a heavily tanned woman in sherbet-colored clothes. She looked about Glady's age but less healthy. She asked in a quavery voice, "Why did you rename the shop?"

I smiled. "The shop's had the same name since Dottie Withrow opened it in the late sixties. People called her Mrs. Seashell."

"That's not what I heard," the woman said.

"What did you hear?"

She pointed to the cameo shell in the locked display case. "That the shop is named after that big fat shell."

"It is."

"Then why doesn't the sign out front say the Murder Shell?" she asked accusingly.

"The . . ." I couldn't repeat her words. Couldn't reduce the fabulous shell or the shop to that tasteless name. Couldn't turn them into something from a B movie or a social-media meme. "Dottie Withrow called that shell the moon shell because of the moon in the picture carved on it," I said with a smile to cover my feeling of ick. "Dottie named the *shell* and then named the shop after it. Did you get a chance to look at the shell? The carving is an amazing piece of eighteenth-century art. But I'm sorry, whoever told you the shop's been renamed was either mistaken or pulling your leg."

She looked flattened, as though her disappointment in that information, or in me, or in a world that lacked a shop called the Murder Shell, weighed her down. Still, I didn't know why I'd felt the need to apologize. She left without buying anything. Her loss, I told myself. Then I had to keep myself from shooing everyone out the door and locking it. It would never do to fall prey to a full-blown, retail-hell-induced huff so soon after arriving. What a wimp.

A pair of grinning teens who looked like brothers were next through the shop door. The younger one turned to the older and gave his shoulder three quick jabs. "We're finally here," he said in an excited whisper that wasn't really a whisper. "You think they caught the guy?"

"Dunno." The older brother moved out of jabbing reach, his face going cool-teen blank. "I haven't heard the whole thing yet. But they might not. Hey, better be careful or the gull will peck your eyes out."

"*You* be careful or it'll pick your nose."

"Dweeb."

"*You're* the dweeb. They might not what?"

"Catch the guy. The episodes end in cliff-hangers. Last week it was some kind of quote. Something like you can't catch killers. You can only catch bad planners."

"Huh?"

"Think about it."

The younger brother didn't show any signs of thinking about that cliff-hanger. He dashed over to the horseshoe crabs that caught his eye. *I* thought about it, though. What if the person who killed the unidentified woman was a better planner than the one who'd killed Allen? Plenty of murders went unsolved. There was a whole subgenre of true-crime books and TV shows tackling unsolved murders. Podcasts, too. Hmm.

The proud mom who'd bought shells for her biology-teaching daughter, the day before, came to the sales desk, and I dragged my thoughts away from podcasts. The mom laid a fleet of Scotch bonnets on the desk. "One for each of my daughter's students," she said. "I've also been beachcombing and picked up a small bagful of shells for them to sketch and identify."

"If your daughter is ever interested in hooking her students up with freshwater mussel biologists, as a field trip or an online program, I might be able to help. Shells are my jam, too." I told her about my years in the field (and in the creeks and rivers) as a working malacologist. "She can reach me here at the shop."

"She'll love that. May I ask a crazy favor? Will you take a picture of me with the seagull? I'll send that to her, too."

"My pleasure. That's Mrs. Bundy," I said and explained where the name came from. As I took the picture, I had a brainstorm. "If you send the picture to me, too, you can be the first member of the Mrs. Bundy Fan Club on our social-media sites. That's if you don't mind if I post the picture online."

"I'd be honored," she said.

"Great!" I made a note to myself to get this fan club up and running.

When she left, my mind snapped back to thoughts of murder tourists and podcasts. *Someone* had to be feeding tourists this idea that the Moon Shell was a must-see destination for true-crime enthusiasts. Irv Allred had spilled information about both murders on Facebook. How many people read his posts, though? It was hard to believe he had many followers. Enough to account for the unsettling number of people coming to gape, anyway. But what if the story had been picked up by a podcaster?

"These are living fossils." The younger brother put a small horseshoe crab on the sales desk.

"Not yours, dweeb," his brother said. "It's dead."

"You're right about them being living fossils," I said. "Horseshoe crabs date back as far as the Ordovician."

"Four hundred and forty million years ago!" This brother had a sweet smile and, on closer inspection, he looked like a tall nine or ten instead of twelve or thirteen. "Does the seagull really have a fan club?"

"Yes. I just invented it a few minutes ago."

"Can I be in it? Will you take my picture?" he asked.

"You can and I will, but if you want me to put your picture on social media, I'll need a parent's permission."

"I'll bring them back here," he said.

"Dweeb," his brother said. "I'll be waiting in the golf cart. Don't take forever."

"Hey, before you go . . . ," I called after the older brother. But he was out the door.

The younger brother sighed. "Selective hearing. That's what Mom calls it. Dad says it comes with acne and occasional whiskers."

"And what do you say?" I asked.

He held up a finger, gulped a huge breath, and then belched. "Excuse me," he said and grinned.

"A prodigious and amazing talent." I rang up the horseshoe crab for the kid and took his picture with Mrs. Bundy. "I heard you and your brother talking about episodes of something. Is he listening to a podcast about a crime that took place—"

"Here!" His eyes grew huge and he whispered, "Were you here when it happened?"

I shook my head. "What's the name of the podcast?"

"He won't tell me."

Nuts. I was tempted to call the older brother a dweeb. But if *he* could find the podcast, so could I. The dweebish horn of a golf cart beeped out front.

"I'll bring my mom and dad," the boy said and dashed out the door.

In between customers, I hunted around for the podcast online. No obvious search terms found it. Neither did less obvious terms. None of the best true-crime podcasts listed by *Vogue* or *Town & Country* magazine sounded likely. No one on true-crime forums was talking about murders on Ocracoke. I hadn't known what a huge fascination true crime held for so many. It'd be easier to ask the next chatty murder tourist what they'd heard and where. Except that the steady drip, drip, drip of them had dried up, and the only people coming through the door were run-of-the-mill vacationers. Oh, the tragedy of people with money to spend and fresh sunburns.

The rest of the afternoon I spent going back and forth between the office and the sales desk with piles of files from the two three-drawer cabinets. Allen kept track of the store's inventory in a program on his laptop, but I'd yet to find records showing where he'd bought that inventory.

It shouldn't have been hard, but the best word I could come up with to describe Allen's filing system was enigmatic. For instance, what version of the alphabet had he used? If Emrys had been around, I could've asked him. So much for depending on wayward pirates.

Most of the files contained pages and clippings from newspapers and magazines. They were articles about shells and human-interest stories about people who collected shells. Dates and publications were neatly printed in the margin if an article had been clipped from the center of a page. These weren't business filing cabinets. They were a set of three-drawer scrapbooks whose organization I couldn't decipher. Judging by the earliest dates, Allen's mother started this vast collection. I wondered how many times she or Allen had reread them after sliding them into folders. Had they ever? I wished I could ask Dottie Withrow about the files. I knew I would enjoy reading my way through them and wished I could do it over many cups of tea with Mrs. Seashell.

Instead I had Glady and Burt, whom I liked. A lot. But who didn't always answer direct questions, who gave indirect answers, who'd been oddly cranky (Glady), and who'd walked around the shop as though measuring the space and appraising it (Burt). I needed sound plans for the Moon Shell and keeping it in tip-top shape to prove to Glady and Burt that I was serious about running the business and running it well. To keep them from finding another tenant if that's what they were doing. Suggesting that I hire Yanira for part-time help could be a sign they thought I was shaky.

Thinking along those lines could also be a sign I was shaky. If Jeff were here, he'd tell me not to borrow trouble. Then he'd probably break into "Pack Up Your Troubles in Your Old Kit Bag and Smile, Smile, Smile." He'd loved singing and never let it trouble him a minute that he couldn't carry a tune.

If Glady and Burt had concerns, they could sit down and tell me. And if I had concerns about them having concerns, then I could stand up for myself and ask them. So there.

I grabbed a clean cloth from under the sales desk and went

to polish fingerprints from the locked display case. The murder shell's case. It was a horrible name for the shell but sadly apt. That shell, the moon shell, was involved in Emrys's death in 1750 and Allen's a month ago. People only knew about the connection to Allen's death though, so that hardly made it the murder shell. Unless the new case of the unidentified female was somehow connected with the shell, too. Ugh.

Glady and Burt told me Allen's mother had never had the shell on display, that Allen changed that after she died. He'd put it front and center in the display case on a pedestal draped in midnight-blue velvet. The shell was fabulous enough on its own. It didn't need that kind of pomp, so it hadn't bothered me when the velvet met a watery end. I'd replaced the velvet with a piece of watered blue silk that had the look of the sea and waves about it. The shell didn't need to bask on silk any more than it needed to preen on velvet. The height the pedestal gave it was good, though, and the pedestal was a glass cake stand, chipped from careless handling. Big enough around that it didn't cramp the football-sized shell's style, the silk-draped cake stand would do until I came up with a better idea.

Speaking of ideas . . . my plan to attract Emrys with ghost-nip wasn't working. So far. Time for new, improved ghost-nip. Ghost-nip enhanced. During a customer lull, I went into the office, took the seascape down again, and opened the safe.

One of the rare books inside was a first edition published in 1839. In fine condition, it had a green leather spine, marvelous illustrations, and a delightful mouthful of a title. *The Conchologist's First Book: or A System of Testaceous Malacology, Arranged Expressly for the Use of Schools, In Which the Animals, According to Cuvier, Are Given with the Shells, A Great Number of New Species Added, and the Whole Brought Up, as Accurately as Possible, to the Present Condition of the Science* by Edgar A. Poe. It was the only one of Poe's books to go into a second printing in his lifetime. It was an updated version of the original book, and he'd written it because he needed the money. He was falsely accused of plagiarism for his efforts. I took Poe, closed the safe, and rehung the painting.

Poe and I ran upstairs to the apartment. He stayed behind on the coffee table when I ran back down to the shop. If *some* ghost-nip was good, more had to be better. Allen had briefly shown the book to Emrys once but snatched it back and locked it in the safe. Surely the triple whammy of the shell, the journal and pen, and the Poe he longed to read would lure him from . . . from wherever. My mind really didn't want to wander down that path. The longer Emrys was gone, the more I didn't want to think about the options presented by *wherever.*

So, between customers, I gave my mind a break by indulging in socially acceptable nosey parker-ing on Facebook. I hadn't posted anything about the shop or the move. I hadn't posted anything much at all since Jeff died, but I lurked and hit *like* often enough to prove I hadn't given up or faded away.

Today I hit *love* on something amazing that popped up. Kathleen Thomas had just posted that she was in Ocracoke on "a fig expedition." Kathleen and her husband, dear Tennessee friends, had moved to Maryland seven years ago, and we hadn't seen each other since. I immediately messaged her using way too many exclamation points.

Chapter 14

Bike pedals whirling, I screeched around corners like a Porsche 911 Turbo on two wheels. Bounced through a pothole, caught air, and became Mrs. Bundy with the wind whistling past my ears, my hair straight out behind. I streaked past the street where I should have turned. Corrected with a bicycle pirouette of Baryshnikovian beauty. Destination? The cottage Kathleen Thomas and two friends were renting for a few weeks.

"You're here!" Kathleen yelled when I rode into view. "You're here!"

I careened into the short gravel drive, braking in a cloud of dust and the reek of melting bicycle tires.

"*You're* here. I can't believe it." I dropped my kickstand. What a good old bike. If I'd asked it to, it would have flown me here like a fiery bat out of shell plus any other similies or exaggerations I threw at it.

"*I* can't believe that you haven't changed a bit. No fair." Kathleen flipped her now silver hair over her shoulders and held out her arm. "Come over here. I need to hug your neck."

I met her at the bottom of the accessibility ramp where she sat in her wheelchair and leaned down to hold her tight. "Oh, my goodness," I whispered in her ear. "Just like that, neither of us is a day over thirty-two."

"And the world is our oyster."

"And our purple wartyback mussel," I added.

"Mark sends his love. I wish we'd been able to make it to Jeff's funeral."

"I don't remember much about it, but I've been told it was lovely."

"Tissues," Kathleen said. "We both need tissues."

I'd come prepared, pulled a couple from my backpack, and handed one to her.

"Now come on in and meet Paula and Roberta," she said. "I told them we'd need a minute out here."

Kathleen maneuvered the chair in a tight circle, and I walked beside her as she drove it up the ramp. Eighteen years ago, addressing an auditorium full of parents as the president of the PTA, she'd had a stroke. It had been a pretty good place to have one—better than behind the wheel of the family van, anyway, or alone at home. Some of the parents at the meeting were doctors, and she'd gotten the help she needed as fast as anyone could react. The stroke was devastating, though. It left her right side paralyzed so that using a walker, while possible, was a struggle. She moved more easily and safely, and much faster, in the motorized chair. That she was left-handed was a blessing. She'd had to learn to talk again and worked hard at it. You could still hear the stroke in her voice, though, the way you can hear a cold in someone's head. People who didn't know her sometimes thought she sounded a wee bit drunk. For instance, *fabulous* came out as *fablious*. Her senses of humor and adventure remained intact and, in her words, *fablious*.

The gently sloped ramp we climbed had the fresh-lumber smell of being new or newly rebuilt. A piece of driftwood hung over the door with *Fig Follies* painted on it. The faded green clapboard of the cottage, looking weather-weary with spots of lichen, hinted at a damp, musty interior, possibly with overtones of fish. Not so, I discovered. When I opened the door, we were met by two smiling women and the herby, cheesy, tomatoey aromas of supper.

"Surprise!" Kathleen said. "Look who I found wandering down the street. Paula, Roberta, I want you to meet my friend Maureen Nash. Maureen, meet my friends Paula Román and Roberta McLaughlin." Kathleen wiggled her fingers first at a woman with a streak of magenta in dark hair she'd pulled into a clasp at her nape, and then at a woman with more salt than pepper in her short waves. At a guess, Paula was younger than Kathleen's and my early fifties, and Roberta came in at a decade or so older. She wasn't exactly tall, but taller than the rest of us, which didn't say a lot.

"Nice to meet you," I said. "And very nice of you to invite me for supper." I pulled the bottle of wine I'd opened the night before from my backpack. "One glass is missing so I can vouch for it being unassuming but tasty."

"Unassuming like our humble abode." Roberta took the bottle.

I glanced around the room. Nautical charts and a life ring hung on the cedar-paneled walls. The love seat and two armchairs were each a different shade of toast, from light to dark. The faux hardwood floor tipped quietly toward the outer wall, making me think this had once been a porch. "It has nautical charm," I said and sat in the chair nearest to Kathleen. It was the same color as my chinos, so my legs faded into the upholstery. Ooh, I was half-ghost.

"We made plans at the last minute," Kathleen told me. "So, we're lucky we got this place."

"No question." Roberta opened the wine, took a sniff, and nodded her approval. "We're not exactly in a prime location, though."

"Because the island is already pretty much booked up for the Pirate Jamboree," Paula said, sounding like a mother patiently explaining something. Again. "And there's no location in Ocracoke that isn't at least *close* to being prime. Besides," she said, looking at me, "the cottage is clean, comfortable, and it's called Fig Follies. How can you go wrong with a name like that?"

"The mosquitoes think it's a prime location," Kathleen said with a laugh.

"The mosquitoes think we're prime rib," said Roberta. "You can hear them singing about it in your ear at night, their tiny nasal sopranos whining on and on and on about your blood being unassuming but tasty."

"Unassuming like us," Paula said. She stretched the waistband of her sweatpants and let it snap back. "Life is too short for tight waistbands and sore feet while on vacation."

All three of them were dressed for comfort—Paula and Kathleen in sweats, Roberta in yoga pants. Neither Paula nor Roberta made a move to be more comfortable by sitting down with Kathleen and me.

"Something smells awfully good." I lifted my nose toward the kitchen.

"Roberta made lasagna," Kathleen said.

"By 'made,' she means I took it out of the freezer and popped it in the oven," said Roberta. "Paula made parmesan rosemary rolls."

"Following the same recipe," Paula said. "Buy. Heat. Kathleen's making dessert."

"I open a mean package of cookies," Kathleen said. "We are all excellent cooks."

Then, as if on cue, all three declared, "We are the Fig Ladies!"

"Because we're all about figs," Kathleen said. "Remember my fig tree back in Johnson City?"

"Your fig jam, too." I rubbed my stomach and licked my chops to show her how well I remembered her fig jam. "And you said you're on a fig expedition. Cool. Um, what happens on a fig expedition?"

"We'll get to that." Kathleen waved the question aside. "First, there's so much more to tell. And it's *show* and tell. How are we doing for time on the lasagna, Roberta?"

Roberta looked at her phone. "We're A-OK. The timer will go off in twenty minutes."

"Haul yourself back up, Maureen," Paula said. "We have places to go." She grabbed my upper arm. "Do you have a strong stomach?"

I looked at the three of them. The concern between their eyebrows didn't match the light breezy tones of their voices. "Where are we going?"

"Just across the yard," Kathleen said, "and there's nothing to worry about."

"Not now," Roberta said under her breath. Not under enough for my liking.

We followed Kathleen down the ramp and around the corner of the cottage to where she stopped in front of a tarp-shrouded hump—a tarp, like a shower cap, with elastic around the bottom.

I reached down and snapped the elastic the way Paula had snapped her waistband. "I like this. To keep it from blowing off?"

"Works, too," Kathleen said. "Help me get it off, will you?"

We uncovered another motorized wheelchair, this one with a wider base and four oversize balloon wheels.

"My all-terrain vehicle," Kathleen said. "Good on the beach, good in loose sand, excellent speed, and it's my favorite color—purple."

"More of a blue violet," Paula said.

"Purple," Kathleen said. "Don't burst my bubble." She transferred to the all-terrain chair and motored across the sandy yard to the larger of two fig trees. Both figs were ringed by piles of oyster and other shells, a familiar sight around Ocracoke.

"We had no idea we'd be lucky enough to have a fig tree at our rental," Kathleen said. "But you know what they always say—two figs are better than one."

"Do they?" I asked.

"Aren't you the gullible one," Paula said. "When we saw the trees, we booked an hour with the island fig expert. We wanted to hear straight from the fount of fig wisdom about the pros and cons of piles of shells for fig health because, frankly, these shells smelled." Paula held her nose.

I took a sniff. Didn't smell anything.

"The expert was great and gave us a crash course in Ocracoke figology," Roberta said.

"Do they call it that?" I asked.

Paula sniggered.

"Not officially," Kathleen said, "but I will from now on. The expert told us his theory of shells as fertilizer. That shells all on their own don't do the trick. But back in the day, people poured the water they'd used for cooking seafood and shellfish under the fig trees in their yards, and they tossed their oyster and clam shells there, too."

"Don't forget the fish guts," Roberta said,

"Right," Kathleen said. "So, it was the nutrient-rich water, and the bits of meat still clinging to the shells, and all the fablious fish guts that fertilized the figs."

"And that solved the mystery of the malodorous shell mounds," Paula said. "Or so we thought."

I looked from one to the other of them. "Why didn't it?"

"Do any of these shells look recent enough to have bits of meat sticking to them?" Roberta asked. "Do you see any fish guts?"

I shook my head.

"So, I was all set to dig around in the pile," Kathleen said.

"To see if someone had buried more recent shells under old ones. To see just how much leftover meat is involved."

"But Roberta and I didn't want to," Paula said.

"Because we don't want to be listed as bad renters in case we get together like this again," Roberta said.

"Then." Paula looked at me during an unnecessarily long dramatic pause. "Then we realized the smell was coming from somewhere else."

"See, it was calm the day the fig expert was here," Kathleen said, "and none of us smelled a thing."

"The next morning, we smelled it again," Paula said. "But the way the breeze wafted through the yard, it was hard to tell where it came from."

"Or where it had been," Roberta murmured. "Much like my first husband. Sorry. Tasteless." She crossed her arms tightly over her chest and rubbed their gooseflesh.

"The smell was worse," Kathleen said.

This story was getting worse, too. I didn't want to know, didn't want to ask, but the words came out anyway, rising from the certainty growing in the pit of my stomach. "What happened next?"

"We tracked it down," Paula said. "Like three sniffer dogs."

"To the tidal creek," Roberta said.

"And we found a body," Kathleen said quietly. "Submerged and almost hidden by a mass of honeysuckle vines."

Chapter 15

I felt my mouth open to say something. But to say what? What came out was a small, round sound like a stone dropped into a well so deep the eventual kerplunk barely registered. "Oh."

Kathleen nodded as if to say *I know*. Not given to sighing, she lifted her left shoulder and let it fall. Roberta, still hugging herself, tipped her head back and stared into the gathering dusk. Paula squinted at the ground, then over her shoulder, then toward a tangle of scrub and trees at the far edge of the yard.

Tate had described his amateur sleuths as a trio. Glady, Burt, and I fit that description. If he'd called us a bumbling trio, I wouldn't have liked it, but I wouldn't have argued. Much. What if he'd been talking about these three, though?

Kathleen watched me, using the x-ray vision of an old friend to see the thoughts turning over in my head. Roberta continued staring at the sky. Wishing she could fly away from this?

"Is the inlet over there?" I pointed toward where Paula still squinted at the scrub and trees.

"There's a decent path through there," Kathleen said.

I blew my cheeks out. "I'm so sorry this happened. It's horrible. And I'm sure this is going to sound callous, but I hope it doesn't put too much of a damper on your fig expedition."

"We won't let it," Kathleen said. "If for no other reason than the expedition gives us a good cover story."

"Oh?" This time my *oh* was less of a deep-well kerplunk and more of a substitute for *uh-oh*.

"We *are* all about figs, and that's why we came to Ocracoke," she said. "But—"

Paula cut in. "But after our discovery, and over a few necessary après discovery-of-a-dead-body drinks, we had a light-bulb moment." She quit looking at the scrub and looked at me. "We realized that all the best teams of detectives have names. So, we're now the Fig Ladies."

"Oh." That *oh* stood for *oh, dear*.

"You know what I mean," Paula said, her voice getting animated, "like *Cagney and Lacey* or Shawn and Gus in *Psych*."

"You're dating yourself," Roberta said. "Let's be like Mabel, Oliver, and Charles in *Only Murders in the Building*."

Paula narrowed one eye at Roberta. "Mabel, Oliver, and Charles don't have a name, and I don't think—"

"It's okay. I get the idea." I got both ideas. The one about cute names for detective wannabes and the one that these two might spat as often as Glady and Burt. "When did you find the body?"

"Was it three days ago?" Kathleen said. "Four?"

"Five," Paula said. "On Thursday at, or about four fifty-two p.m." She'd produced a pocket-size spiral notebook from somewhere. "I called nine-one-one at four fifty-four. Roberta took pictures. Would you like to see them?"

"Let's look at the incident scene, first," Roberta said. "We looked at it through seriously shocked eyes," she explained to me. "If we visit the scene now, we might notice something we missed in the rush of adrenaline."

"Are you okay about going over there, Maureen?" Kathleen asked.

"Should we?" I asked. "Are the police finished with it?"

"I saw someone taking down the crime scene tape yesterday morning," Roberta said.

"You didn't tell us you saw that," Paula said.

"Slipped my mind," Roberta said.

"We need to share *all* information." Paula tried to make her point by snapping the flimsy cardboard cover of her spiral notebook shut.

"Kids, kids," Kathleen said. "We'll make more progress if we try to get along. Let's go see what our refreshed eyes and Maureen's new eyes spot."

I tried to look enthusiastic as we traipsed across wispy grass toward the trees. This wouldn't be like tripping over a body in a dark wood with more substantial trees, I told myself. I was an old hand at that and didn't want to repeat it. And wouldn't. Couldn't. There wasn't a body here anymore, and all was good. And yet . . . I had trouble making my feet move fast enough to keep up with Kathleen's all-terrain chair.

A ruckus of crows kicked up. They circled from the trees, out over the yard, and back to the trees, cawing as they flew. There might have been a dozen, or it might have been the same four or five lapping each other like middle-distance runners.

Ahead of us, Kathleen turned her chair and drove along the scrub edging the trees. When she stopped, she waved us forward. "Here's the path. You guys go first. I'll bring up the rear." To me, she said, "It's about thirty more feet to the inlet."

We went single file, Roberta in the lead. Between crow caws, I heard Paula counting steps to herself and assumed Kathleen's "about thirty feet" wasn't cutting it with her. As we got closer, I began to smell the brackish water of the inlet, a smell I associated with wading in creeks, come rain or come shine, in the name of mussel research. Good times.

There wasn't much room for the chair and a person side by side, but I stepped to the edge of the path so Kathleen and I could walk next to each other. "We might want to check for ticks after trekking through here. Or I might. You might be tick-proof in that chariot."

"Ticks," Kathleen said. "Ugh. But not as ugh as the smell we were tracking. We thought it must be an animal. We wanted to find the animal and bury it. Bury the smell."

"Did you have a shovel?"

"We were going to buy one if we found anything. Quicklime, too, if we could find that."

"Any idea how long the body was in the water?"

"No. We've asked Sheriff Potato Head to come fill us in on whatever he can. As a way of getting closure."

"Potato Head?"

"Tater or whatever his name is. He's ignoring us."

I bit back a smile, sure that Tate *was* ignoring that request. I was also sure Kathleen wouldn't call him Sheriff Potato Head to his face. Neither would I. Paula or Roberta, though? I didn't know them well enough. Tate didn't deserve that, so I hoped not. Those two unknown quantities waited for us on the inlet's bank.

"Instead of a secret garden, it's like a secret creek back here," Paula said. "If you cleared the weeds and brambles, it might even be pretty. That is, if you didn't know there'd been a decomposing body in it."

The inlet's water no doubt rose and fell as the tide came and went. For now it rested quietly, the color of strong tea. Some of the trees straggling near the banks leaned toward the water as though looking at their reflections. Water striders navigated around floating leaves. I stepped closer to the edge of the bank, taking care in case it had been undercut. I couldn't judge the water's depth, wondered what critters lived in it. The inlet didn't need our help to be pretty. It was that and more already.

I looked at the path behind us and then across the inlet where a narrower path disappeared into more trees. "It feels secret back here, but there are two paths, and the inlet's a path, too, if you can get in with a canoe or kayak. Easy enough access for a killer. Did you find the body right here?"

"That would be a dumb killer," Roberta said. "If you're going to hide a body in a secret creek, you wouldn't do it at the foot of an easy access point."

"Not all killers are clever," I said. "Some of them are, though, and they wouldn't have left a body within smelling distance of a rental cottage."

"Good point," Roberta said. "And a killer who makes one mistake might make more. Although I don't know how that's going to help us."

"I'll write it down anyway." Paula pulled out her notebook and scribbled in it.

"We walked a short way along to the left," Kathleen said. "Toward the mouth."

"And lost the scent," Paula said. "Not entirely, but the breeze came from that direction."

I nodded. "From Pamlico Sound. So, then you backtracked and walked upstream? Can your chair make it, Kathleen?"

"This thing? It's practically a trailblazer. The police weren't too happy with us. If there was any evidence on this side of the inlet, they must have thought the three of us did our best to obliterate it."

"The smell got stronger the farther upstream we went." Paula picked up a stick and slashed it back and forth like a scythe. "We spared no foliage in our search for the stink."

I started upstream and heard them fall in behind me, with the hum of Kathleen's chair in the rear. The crows continued in their big, cawing loop. A caw-cophonous loop. I'd have to remember to tell Glady and Burt that one. Then I heard something else. It was . . . someone singing? Softly, though. So softly I might be imagining it.

"Stop there, Maureen!" Roberta called. "That's where we found it. Found her."

"Located where in the water?" The inlet was narrower here, maybe six feet across. "In the middle? Against the bank?"

"The bank. Yeah," Roberta said. "We saw the flies first."

"I'm not going any closer," Paula said. "If I do, I know I'll see it all over again." She stepped backward, bumped into Kathleen, and gave a little scream.

"Were you able to tell it was a woman?" I didn't listen to the answer. The singing—where was it coming from? I rubbed my ears but then only heard the crows.

"Maureen? Are you okay?" Kathleen asked.

"She's smelling the ghost of the stench," Paula said.

That's sort of what I was thinking. Not about smelling the stench. The ghost part. "I'm fine, Kathleen. Thanks. With this whole little wild area to search"—I swept my arm at everything around us—"how did you think you'd find the source of the smell?"

"When you put it like that," Kathleen said, "it makes you wonder if we thought at all."

"I'll tell you what *I* thought," Paula said. "That if we didn't find that stink, then I didn't care why we'd come to Ocracoke—I was out of here. I couldn't stay with that smell."

"The smell wasn't so bad at the cottage," Roberta said.

"So, call me a wimp."

"Not a wimp, Paula," Kathleen said. "Sensitive."

"Anyway," Roberta said. "That's why we went looking. Not because we wanted to get closer to whatever it was. We went looking so we wouldn't have to run—" She looked at Paula and then quickly looked away. "So we wouldn't have to pack up and leave the cottage."

"You didn't call the rental company about it? Ask them to take care of it?" I asked.

"You're so practical," Kathleen said. "That's one of the reasons I've always loved you."

"She sounds like Sheriff Potato Head," Paula said sourly. "We found the path. We followed our noses."

"We got lucky," Roberta said. "Or not so lucky. But we found her, and we feel responsible for her."

Responsible. That was an interesting reaction. "Responsible how?"

"She isn't just an unidentified female," Paula said. "She's a woman. She's somebody's daughter. Maybe a wife or a mother. Someone is guilty of killing her and taking great pains to hide her. The least she deserves is to have someone else take great pains to find that person."

Kathleen powered over to Paula and took her hand.

"Finding her body was horrifying, to coin an understatement," Roberta said. "But *our* horror might be nothing compared to whatever she experienced."

Roberta went to stand with Paula and Kathleen, and all three looked at me. It might have been pain and resolve that I saw in their eyes, a clear opposition to getting any closer to the place they'd found the woman. But I thought I also saw the simple question: *Can you understand?*

I nodded, pretty sure that I could understand.

And then I heard the singing again. Barely. What the . . .

I wanted to look around wildly, cock my ears in all directions to hear it better, shake my head like a horse bedeviled by flies to knock it out of my ears. I didn't do any of that. Didn't so much as flinch. I turned away from the Fig Ladies. Scanning as I turned. Saw no one. It was impossible to tell where the lilt, now more like a sigh, came from. A grating caw sounded overhead, and a crow swooped low over the water. Its wings brushed away the last notes of the song.

"I'm just going to look . . ." I tipped my head toward the inlet.

"Take your time," Paula said. "Better you than me."

On the pretense of getting a better look at the place in the water where the Fig Ladies had found the honeysuckle-shrouded body, I moved closer to the bank and sank into a crouch. If the bank gave way, it would be a surprise but not a big drop into the drink. Hunkered there, I did a more careful survey of the area, in the water, above it, and across. Nothing. Until the crow, or a different one, landed on a half-submerged tree trunk across from me. Something blurred my eyes, and I blinked to clear them. But it wasn't my eyes—it was the air beside the crow, the air moving as though it reflected the surface of the water. I blinked again because how could *that* be? And in that blink, perched beside the crow, Emrys shimmered into view.

Another kind of *oh* escaped before I could stop it.

"What?" Kathleen called. "What is it?"

"Nothing. It's okay. I just thought I saw . . . but it's nothing." It wasn't nothing, but it wasn't anything they could see. Or hear. Emrys started to sing again.

He sang quietly to himself and gave no indication he was aware of us. I didn't understand the words of his mournful song and wondered if they were in Welsh. They seemed to skim across the inlet toward me, but just before they reached me, just as I might puzzle out their meaning, they'd slip under the water and sink.

I tried giving him a tiny wave. He didn't react, so I looked around my feet for something small to toss that way. I found an empty snail shell and lobbed it at the dead tree on the other side of Emrys, the side away from where the crow sat. My aim was off, and the shell went straight through Emrys to land on the soft bank behind him. He broke off singing, though, and shook himself. Had the snail shell ruffled his . . . ectoplasm?

He didn't look up, but he spoke. "Too much of the water hast thou, poor Ophelia, and therefore I forbid my tears."

The crow stopped polishing its beak on the dead tree and looked at Emrys. It flapped and flew off, the tip of one wing brushing the side of Emrys's face. Was it a coincidence that he looked up just then?

I waved again. He startled, stared, and almost fell off the tree into the water.

"Mistress Nash?" A hand went to his chest. "Mistress Nash. Thank heaven." Hope and relief filled his voice. "I believe I've discovered a new type of loop. I appear to be trapped in it and stuck here on this log. Can you help?"

Chapter 16

I couldn't very well call across the inlet to let Emrys know I'd do my best to get him out of the loop. But does an eighteenth-century ghost know what it means to get a thumbs-up? I gave him one, anyway. I added an A-OK sign and put a finger to my lips for good measure, and then I held up one finger and hoped he read that as *Hold on, I'll be back, be patient*. I looked at him, took a deep breath, and did each sign again.

Emrys answered with a slashing motion across his throat.

What was that about? He didn't need to use sign language. I narrowed my eyes and raised empty palms to him.

He gave a dramatic sigh. "Be*hind* you."

"Maureen?" Roberta said. Be*hind* me. "Hey, are you okay?"

"I tried to warn you," Emrys said. "I'll wait here, shall I?" He faded away as his gaze returned to the water.

After peeling my shoulders from around my ears, I stood and brushed off whatever might be on the seat of my pants. Roberta put a tentative hand on my arm. I only jumped a little. "What were you doing?"

"Um, just looking—"

"For clues?" she asked dubiously. Dubious was better than an outright scoff.

"Well, you know, when you've read a lot of mysteries."

"Honey," she said, "if the police did their job right, then they crawled all over both banks and the creek bottom and took away every tiny clue there was and more crap besides."

"Let's get out of here," Paula said. "Maureen looks creeped out."

That was a good enough story to go with, so I didn't deny it. Kathleen made a tight circle and led us back along the bank of the inlet. Silent, we walked behind her in single file. The sound of Emrys's crooning song floated after me, blending with the hum of Kathleen's chair, and then was lost. I hated leaving him there.

When we reached the wispy grass in the yard with the fig trees, I moved up beside Kathleen and leaned into the story of being creeped out. "Would you . . . Kathleen, would you all mind if I . . . Can I give you a rain check on supper?"

Kathleen stopped and grabbed my hand. "Of course we don't mind."

"You really are upset," Paula said.

Kathleen ignored her. "It's Jeff, isn't it?"

"But *she* didn't see the body," Paula said.

"She didn't, but she lost her husband last year in an accident." Kathleen kept her grip on my hand. "It was too soon to throw something awful like this at you. I'm sorry."

I shook my head. "It's okay. I'm okay. Really. But there's more to it, too. Beyond Jeff. I'm not usually in this much of a . . . muddle." A flitter of black caught the corner of my eye, and I turned to watch a crow land in one of the figs. I turned back to the three Fig Ladies who were watching me. "I really would like a rain check, and I promise I'll tell you what else has been going on."

"What about it, ladies?" Kathleen said. "Lunch tomorrow?"

Paula nodded, and Roberta said, "Lunch here so we don't have to worry about being overheard."

"Perfect," Kathleen said. "Because there's more to our fig

expedition story, too. Beyond figs." She wiggled her left eyebrow at me. "Isn't that how our escapades always went? You and I got up to some crazy things back in Tennessee."

I gave her another hug. "See you tomorrow."

Back at the Moon Shell, I took the shop's namesake from the display case and carried it upstairs. I sat in the recliner with it and ran my fingers over the nighttime seascape Emrys had carved. He'd cut down through the shell's multiple layers, using each slightly different, pale color for his palette. The result was an intricate scene teeming with life *under* the waves, a three-masted ship plying *through* the waves, and a full moon, high above, shining on them all. I especially loved the underwater creatures—jellyfish, sea anemones, other fish of all kinds (though thankfully no sharks), and an assortment of shells on the sea bottom. Including a tiny helmet shell, like this one, that I hadn't noticed before. I imagined a minuscule scene carved on it with tools no bigger than a cat's whisker.

Bonny came to sniff at the shell and then looked around as though expecting to see someone.

"He's stuck out there in the wilds of Ocracoke," I told her. "I'll go out later and bring him home. I hope."

The water in the inlet, this evening, had been like glass. I wondered if Emrys could see his reflection in it. Would that be any different, for a ghost, than looking in a mirror? Could he see his reflection in a mirror? So many things I didn't know about my friend the ghost.

I turned the shell over and felt the glasslike surface of its aperture—its opening. Here, the shell shaded from creamy white to a sunset of pale and then darker salmon disappearing into the interior. The shell's teeth—raised ridges along the exterior edge of the aperture—were brown as though the original inhabitant had had a wicked tobacco-chewing habit. A shame that customers never saw this part of the moon shell. The carving was the most amazing part of it, of course, but shells this shape naturally rest on their apertures. Maybe I should change that—somehow display the shell above a mirror so people could see the aperture, too. It wouldn't be basking on watered silk anymore, if I did that, but the moon shell didn't need fancy fabrics to be totally fabulous.

Now the fabulous shell and I had a job ahead of us. I wrapped it in a cushy bath towel, making a neat bundle. Bonny supervised as I packed the bundle into the box she'd found to be just right for her snooze that morning. The box turned out to be the perfect size for transporting a valuable piece of eighteenth-century shell art, too. Bonny rubbed her cheek against a corner of the box, giving it her seal of approval.

We ate supper—Bonny's deliciously fishy, mine like cardboard because of nerves—and then we waited for decent folk to be in bed. Bonny waited calmly and watched as I kept my mind busy by tackling the last of the unpacking, flattening boxes, and doing a bit of fitful bookshelf and cupboard rearranging. I finally dumped myself back in the recliner and nerve-scrolled through kitten videos. Bonny joined me, but neither of us fully engaged with the videos.

"If you'll hold the fort until I get back," I told her at midnight, "I'll go get our pirate."

I put the Bonny-size box and a flashlight into the metal market basket attached to the handlebars. Then, under a full moon, I headed back to Fig Follies, going more quietly than a ghost because I didn't sing.

The cottage was dark when I rode past, as though on tiptoe, across the wispy grass. When I found the path into the scrub and trees, I dismounted. After a quick debate, I wheeled the bike into the woods with me. Not for a quick getaway, but in case someone in the cottage woke up and chanced to look out a window facing the woods. No sense in leaving my trusty steed glinting in the moonlight and raising difficult questions. The flashlight would stay off until I was farther from the house.

In amongst the trees, the moon struggled to find us. *I* struggled to breathe evenly. A rhyme the boys had dreamed up to scare each other, on a long-ago Smoky Mountain camping trip, started repeating itself in my head.

Beware the rustles and chitters,
of sly woodland critters,
and who knows what else all around.
They'll follow and watch you,
and laugh when they've got you,
and carry you deep underground.

Not the earworm I'd choose for an after-midnight slink through the woods. The bike's familiar handlebars gave me comfort, though. They also gave me something to hang on to in case I stumbled over a root or branch.

When I reached the inlet, a lazy tide rippled upstream. Splinters of moonlight captured by the ripples transformed Paula's secret creek into a bewitching one.

Could a tide like this carry a body so far from the inlet's mouth? A surging storm tide might. I should ask Glady and Burt about the weather for the past week or so. It would also be interesting to know if the pathologist had been able to determine how long the body had been in the water, and if it had spent time in the clearer water of Pamlico Sound as well as the tannin-stained inlet.

Emrys might be able to answer my weather and tide questions. Depending on how long he'd been sitting on the half-submerged log. Depending on how deeply he'd been in thrall to his new loop. That log appeared ahead of me now, ghostly in the moonlight, but with no obvious ghost.

The small crunching and scrunching of my feet and bicycle tires seemed magnified by the late hour. I stood still for a moment, hoping to hear—and there it was. The mournful song came like a prayer across the inlet. I leaned the bike against a tree and took his shell from its wrappings.

"Emrys?" I called quietly. No answer, and I still didn't see him. I took the flashlight and the shell and sat on the bank where I'd crouched earlier. "Emrys? I brought the shell." I held the shell in one hand, turned the flashlight on it, and waited.

The song faltered and then abruptly stopped. As ghost-nip, the shell was the cat's pajamas. The next thing I knew, Emrys flickered into view beside me and put a hand on the shell. Even for him, he looked pale.

"Ready to go home?" I asked.

"Yes."

"How do you ... uh ... how do you travel from here to there?" He didn't float around the shop. He walked. But he also disappeared and then reappeared in other locations. "Do you go like"—I snapped my fingers—"in an instant?"

"How do you transport the shell?" he asked.

"Well wrapped, in a box for extra safety." I patted the basket. "In here."

"Excellent. Then shall I ride here?" He sat on the back fender with one leg crossed over the other and a fist propped on one hip. "Mistress Nash, I am surprised. Your mouth hangs open much the way it did when we first met. Have you never seen an eighteenth-century gentleman ride sidesaddle on a bicycle?"

"Mr. Lloyd, I'm glad you're coming home. I've been dispirited without you." I packed the shell and flashlight back into the basket and then turned the bike around. "Can you tell me what happened?"

"Are you going to walk the bicycle the entire way?"

"Only through the woods. Why?"

"I'm rather excited. This is my first bicycle ride. To answer your question, where would you like me to start?"

"Tell me how you ended up at the inlet." We'd reached the end of the path, and I got on the bike and started pedaling.

"This is lovely," he said. "I might be having the time of my life if I were alive. How did I end up at the inlet? Quite simply. I was drawn by the scent of death."

I braked and turned around to stare at him.

"Your mouth is open again. Anyone abroad who catches sight of you might question your sanity."

"Anyone else abroad at this hour is also insane, but I see your point." I started riding again. "Tell me about the scent of death."

"It wasn't an animal. I knew that, as I've become used to those odors over the many years. It wasn't obvious to the living, as yet, but I knew it was wrong. It was a scent that should not be. And then a pair of crows arrived and I followed them. They led me to the inlet, to that log, and there I found the body of a woman."

"That must have been awful. I'm sorry."

We rode quietly for a short way before he said, "I was surprised by how it affected me. Seeing her abandoned like that, under a shroud of vines, and with another vine knotted around her neck. I've wondered if that's what caused the loop."

"I can see how it might."

"Although I think meeting her ghost must be what did it. The ghost of Lenrose."

I gulped. "She introduced herself?"

"No, she wasn't exactly feeling herself. But I know it was Lenrose because I also met her *before* she died. Before Allen died, for that matter. In the shop."

"Did she meet *you* in the shop?"

"No. But I sat vigil for her sad body there at the inlet. It seemed the polite thing to do until someone else found her. I found the experience humbling."

"Did her ghost talk to you?" I asked.

"She spoke once, but not necessarily to me. She said, 'What on *earth* am I wearing?'"

I stopped the bike and stared at him. "You're not making a joke, are you? She really said that?"

"She did."

"What was she wearing?"

"As far as I could tell," he said, "knee breeches."

Chapter 17

We argued amiably the rest of the way home over the likelihood of the ghost of Lenrose wearing knee breeches. We concluded we were both right. She *had* been wearing knee breeches but, in modern parlance, her trousers were called capris or pedal pushers.

"I still have a question about the pants, though," I said as I rolled the bike into the storeroom. "Why was she surprised? What was odd about them?"

Ever one to argue, Emrys pointed out that I'd asked two questions.

"Two. You're right. Do you have an answer for either of them?"

"No. The fact I saw and heard a ghost took most of my attention. The situation rather stunned me."

"I know the feeling." I yawned, rather stunned myself by the day's events and length. By then it was past one.

Emrys supervised as I put the moon shell back in the display case. He admired the watered silk and wished he could feel it as he ran it through his fingers. Bonny came to say hello. He greeted her like an old friend and told her he'd missed her.

"Are you ready for bed, Miss Cat?" I asked as I locked the case. "I know I am."

"Never," Emrys said.

"Easy for you to say. I'm beat."

"You cannot possibly mean to say that you'll waste time in sleep before looking at the treasure I found."

An affronted pirate is an amazing spectacle. A spectacle not unlike a thwarted teenager in costume.

"Unless . . ." His indignation faltered. "Did you not receive my letter?"

"I did. Thank you! That was so much fun. It came Saturday morning while Kelly and O'Connor were there."

"Saturday." He rubbed his jaw. "I've lost track of time, what with one thing and another, and having no experience with how quickly letters travel in this century. I wasn't sure it would find you, or how soon you would arrive here, or *if* you would. What day is it now?"

"Early Wednesday morning. I'll show you just how early." I yawned. "The first night I was here I looked for a way into the attic. When I couldn't find you anywhere, I thought you might be up there."

He looked stricken.

"I've been worried about you. When you weren't—"

"You didn't wait for me?" he asked.

"What do you mean?"

"You looked at the treasure *without* me?"

Oh, for the love of histrionic. . . . "Keep your tricorn hat on, Emrys. I didn't look at the treasure. I couldn't get into the attic."

"Too large to get through the hatchway, eh?" He looked me up and down. "Interesting. I wouldn't have thought so."

Histrionic and annoying to boot. "I couldn't find the hatchway." Then, trying to be the adult in the room, I explained my search and disappointment. "Disappointed not because I wanted to look at the treasure without you. Because I couldn't find *you*."

"Well. I believe you. But—" He stopped and scowled at Mrs. Bundy. "But if you had been able to get into the attic, would you have looked at the—"

"We'll never know," I said over him, "because it didn't happen."

"Then let us not mention it again," he said as though I'd been the irksome one.

"Fine with me."

He looked positively avuncular. "Now, if you will be so kind as to bring the ladder upstairs, I will show you the cunning trick Allen used to conceal the hatchway in the closet. Then we can look at the treasure together."

I yawned and . . . gave in. "Where's the ladder?"

"Against the wall in the storeroom. Burt left it there after hanging the dead seagull. Thank goodness seagulls don't have ghosts that linger and loiter. Can you imagine having one of those creatures flying about your ears? They cry, they complain, they—"

I tuned out his complaints and went to find the ladder. Found it, closed my eyes, asked for patience, and then I moved my bike from in front of it. Then the folding table and stack of plastic chairs that were behind the bike. And the vacuum cleaner, a mop and bucket, and several large boxes of extra bags for the shop in various sizes. Why had Burt wedged the ladder behind all that? Probably because why not? How often did anyone need it? I tuned out my own complaints and schlepped the ladder up the stairs, adding another thing to my to-do list—inventory and rearrange the storeroom.

"Emrys?"

There was no immediate answer, and then he cleared his throat. "Up here."

I looked up. He'd stuck his head down through the living room ceiling. He'd never done something like that before. I'd seen him reach through the glass of the display case, but a disembodied head still wearing its hat had a different vibe to it. A vibe that for the briefest nano of a nano second threatened to feel nauseating. His smile swept that problem away.

"Meet you in the closet," I said.

"I hope you know that I would insist on carrying the ladder if I could," he said, appearing beside me. "Do you know that I may have never carried a ladder in my life? Climbed them, of course. This one looks unwieldly."

"Only in confined spaces," I gritted out between my teeth, struggling to maneuver the ladder through the bedroom door and around the corner to the closet.

He opened the closet door for me and bowed.

"Thanks."

"The least I can do. The most as well, in the way of manual labor." He sighed an unnecessarily theatrical sigh. "My talents now lie in other areas that were interesting and entertaining for only the first decade or two of my afterlife."

"So sad."

"I find I am quite good at offering suggestions, however."

"Amazing." *I* found I had a talent for peeved answers.

"For instance," he said as I stared at the closet pole and the shelf above it. "I suggest you remove whatever you have hanging from the pole and the boxes from the shelf and then remove the pole and the shelf. Otherwise we won't be getting anywhere fast. Best remove the clutter of footwear from the floor as well."

I bit back a couple more peeved words. They might also be classified as rude words. I could have closed the closet door at that point. I could have left the ladder leaning against the closed door. I could have crawled into bed and slept like the dead guy I'd stayed up until this extremely late hour to rescue. But I didn't do those things because I'm no quitter when I've reached the pigheaded phase of being peeved. To save my sanity, though, I tuned out the rest of Emrys's suggestions or whatever he was prattling on about.

The contents of the closet pole and shelf went on the bed. That "clutter of footwear"—two pairs of shoes and one pair each of hiking boots, sandals, and slippers, all neatly lined up on the closet floor—was now neatly lined up beside the bed. I studied the pole and the shelf and thought I might need to unscrew something somewhere—but no, I didn't. They were held in their clever brackets by gravity, and the weight of whatever someone put on them, and each lifted out of the brackets with ease. I brought them out and leaned them in a corner of the bedroom. Now the empty closet had almost enough room to swing a stuffed seagull and plenty of room for the ladder. I moved it in and opened it, and while I stopped to swipe my sleeve across my forehead, Emrys climbed it.

"Judging by the ease with which we removed the closet pole and shelf," he said, "and because I know there is a hatchway above us in the attic, may I suggest that Allen did, indeed, plan to reenter the attic from time to time. That means the hatchway exists in this ceiling in some fashion. A ghost hatchway, do you think?" Enjoying his joke, he chuckled. I didn't. "My best guess is that you did not look hard enough to find it."

I didn't grind my teeth as he studied the ceiling and then rose up *through* the ceiling and disappeared into the attic. A moment later he was back.

"I see now where you went wrong. If you had looked at the hatchway from the other side, you would have seen—"

I didn't slam the closet door on him. I was tempted. Sorely tempted. "Stop," I said. "No more condescension. No more belittling remarks. No more *we* when it's me. I couldn't have looked at the hatchway from the other side, could I?"

"No." He looked contrite. Then his eyebrows and the corners of his mouth lifted in a tentative smile. "I will admit that until we've found a way to open the hatchway, only those of us who've passed over to the other side are able to look at it from the other side. Still friends?"

"Still friends. This one's just tired."

He peered from the closet to the bed. "Then we should get busy and finish this so you can clear your bed off. No one could sleep with it in that state."

"You're full of good suggestions. In your letter you said Allen plastered over the trapdoor on this side. Did he?"

"That was a guess on my part. I now have a different theory. Are you ready?

"Yes."

"Just as Allen masked his thieving nature, lo these many years, so it appears he masked the hatchway. Good, don't you think?"

"That sounds a lot like plaster," I pointed out reasonably.

"It's completely different," he said unreasonably.

"Then please explain."

"There is a metal loop, as big around as a silver doubloon, here." He made a circle the size of a silver dollar with his thumb and index finger and then touched the center of the near edge of the closet ceiling where it met the wall above the door. "Attached to the loop, by a clasp, is a short cable. The other end of the cable is anchored here." He touched the ceiling six or seven inches in from the wall and the loop. "There are also discrete hinges here and here." He touched the edge of the ceiling in two places at its edge along the back wall, each about a foot in from the corners at either end. "And two more, opposite those, on either side of the loop."

"How do we open it?" I asked.

"An interesting problem, isn't it? It could well keep us up all night."

"Then why don't I take a turn on the ladder?"

"By all means," he said gallantly.

"Oh no, wait, wait."

"Please make up your mind."

I shushed him. Bent my head and bounced my fist against my chin. What did this setup over our heads remind me of? It was that short cable . . . like a . . . what? And the hinges. The *hinges*. "Hop down." I waved Emrys out of the way and climbed the ladder. "Why would there be hinges on the far edge and this edge? What sense does that make?"

"I can assure you my eyesight is excellent. There most certainly is hardware on each edge."

"But the two on this edge with the loop and cable are probably—" Where I judged the bogus hinges to be, I quickly pushed up on the ceiling and then lowered my hands. That edge of the ceiling swung down—six or seven inches before being stopped by the cable. "They're *latches*," I said. The whole ceiling is a concealed door to the attic."

"How did you guess?"

"I've seen cupboards that open with a touch this way. And we babyproofed some of our cupboards with safety catches inside that acted like this cable. It can only open so far until—" I unhooked the short cable from the loop and let the ceiling swing down and open. "Voilà! Coming up?"

"You'll need a light."

Triangular and of mean proportions Emrys had said in his letter to me. He'd been right on both counts. Still standing on the ladder, I shined the flashlight around. It made the triangle shadowy and the proportions even meaner. The space was long, though, going from end to end of the house, like a tunnel, or an incredibly long pup tent. It had the attic smell of sun-baked wood and dust that I knew from attics in other houses I'd lived in. A smell of secrets and long summers. Emrys now sat cross-legged between two rows of assorted cardboard boxes. The rows stretched from the hatchway to the far end of the triangle. In some places there were boxes on top of boxes. I looked over my shoulder at the little bit of attic behind me and saw more boxes.

"These can't all have been stolen from Jeff's family, can they?" I asked. "Do you know how many boxes there are?"

"I didn't count them, no."

Dozens, at least. Too many to go through in one night. Way too many for what was left of *this* night.

"Open one." Emrys smiled like a well-pleased cat surrounded by an acre of catnip.

I stepped off the ladder, and he scooted back to make room. I chose one in front of me, the kind of box college students collect for moving from one apartment to another—sturdy and not too big or too small—a liquor carton, this one for rum.

"Good choice," Emrys said. "I miss rum."

The rum carton held smaller boxes with wads of yellowed newspaper filling empty spaces between them. The two boxes on top were red with Christmasy designs in white and gold. Each bore the name of a business. Carson Pirie Scott I recognized as a defunct department store. The other name, Wieboldt's, meant nothing to me, but I guessed it might be another department store. The Carson's box was about the size of a shoebox. The Wieboldt's box was maybe eight inches square and four inches deep. Their cardboard felt brittle, and the Christmas designs and script had the look of bygone decades. I'd begun to feel brittle, too, but when I lifted the Wieboldt's box out of the carton, excitement nudged me in the ribs. Here I sat, with a ghost, in a secret attic full of treasure. Christmas morning to the max.

After an engulfing yawn, I lifted the Wieboldt's lid to find a layer of cotton wool. Under that was tissue paper. Under the tissue paper—a miniature dresser, complete with a mirror in a swivel frame, stared up at me. But this was no ordinary dresser. It was a miniature dresser duded up to gaudy Victorian extreme. The entire piece, except for the glass of the mirror, was encrusted with small, exquisite shells.

"Beautiful," Emrys breathed.

It was, and at the same time it was ugly as all get out. It blew me away. I loved it. I couldn't imagine how much it must be worth.

"Open the next one," Emrys urged.

"It's exciting, isn't it? Just one more, though, and then I really need to get some sleep." I settled the miniature dresser back in its protective cocoon and returned the Wieboldt's box to the rum carton. The Carson's box was deeper and a bit heavier. "Do you know what's in here?" I asked.

Emrys shook his head. I lifted the lid and again found cotton wool followed by tissue paper. Folding back the tissue paper, I found a shallow tray holding six egg-shaped shells.

"This is . . . these are . . . holy cow. I think these are golden cowries. Do you know how rare they are?" The shells ranged from three to four inches long and from yellowish brown to reddish orange and oh-so-shiny. Golden cowries were among the largest of the cowries.

"How rare can they be? We have six of them right there." He looked at the Carson's box. "Maybe more."

I lifted the tray with the cowries and nearly dropped it when I saw what was below. "Not more golden cowries," I told Emrys. "Eight cone shells. Big cone shells. Five-inch–long cone shells that, if I'm not mistaken, are *Conus gloriamaris*—'glory of the sea' cone shells. Once considered the rarest shell in the world and still revered and highly prized."

"Treasure."

I nodded. I didn't know how much "glory of the sea" cone shells, golden cowries, or miniature furniture decorated to Victorian-excess with perfect, tiny shells went for in a shop or on the Internet. We'd only looked at the contents of two of the small boxes inside a bigger box in a sea of other boxes, though. "Are all the boxes full of shells like this?" I asked.

"I believe so. However, very little light comes in through the louvered windows at the gable ends, and so I was not able to see everything clearly."

"Did you come across any notes or papers or letters or lists in any of them?"

"Being a conchologist, amateur though my status is, the shells took my full attention."

He loved throwing around the word *conchologist* almost as much as he loved shells. I shined the flashlight over the cartons again. Yawned again. How much of all this had belonged to Jeff's family? And if not all of it, then where had Allen gotten his hands on the rest? How much of this was booty he'd pirated and squirreled away up here?

"Is there anything as extraordinary as your shell in the boxes?" I asked. "Anything worth looping over?"

"Many remarkable shells and examples of artwork worth contemplating but not looping."

"Shells are amazing creations, aren't they? Small miracles of animal architecture."

"Your contemplations, like you, are rosy. Mine?" He shrugged one shoulder.

"You aren't exactly sour. You just said the shells are amazing, and you call the whole collection treasure."

"I do because those are facts," he said. "But my contemplations of the shells lead me to another fact—everyone involved with them is dead. The people who collected them, the creatures who made them, the men who stole them and"—he doffed his hat—"the ghost who found them in this hiding place."

"You, though, aren't dead in the same way as the creatures and the men because, somehow, you're still here."

"And at the same time not here."

"For a very long time, too," I said softly. "*That's* a lot for anyone to wrap their mind around. I think mind-wrapping is probably the kind of contemplating that ties a person's brains in knots. Emrys, if you don't mind one more fact—I think we should make an inventory of everything here. I'll ask Burt if he can help me move the boxes out of the attic or recommend someone who—" I stopped because Emrys was shaking his head vehemently.

"Absolutely not," he said. "The collection and its location are a secret. We should keep them that way."

"I'd like to know exactly what we have, though. To know what we're dealing with. So I can research values."

"We can do all that up here."

Beginning to feel ticked off, I ticked off my objections on my fingers. "Too hot, no head room, not enough space, I don't want to use my bed as a closet. And I'd like some help moving the boxes down the ladder. You can't do that. Burt can, and I trust him."

"My answer is still no."

"I don't recall asking you about it, and I'm not sure you really have a say in the matter."

The cold stare of a ghost was like nothing I'd ever experienced. Emrys let the chill linger until I thought my eyelashes must be coated with frost. And then he vanished.

Chapter 18

Glady offered to cover the lunch hour for me again the next day. She smiled as she did, but I detected a challenge lurking in her eyes.

"You're awfully kind." Seeing the challenge ratchet up a notch, I continued, but going in a different direction. "But I've been taking advantage of your time and good nature." The challenge took a step back. "I think I'll experiment with closing over lunch. Not every day, but I might as well start today."

"I'd suggest staying open Fridays through Sundays," she said warmly. "Shorter hours on Sunday. Open at one."

"And I'll be fine eating lunch at the sales desk on the days I stay open."

"It will be a wholesome, homey touch."

Challenge met and overcome, and I really had been taking advantage of her.

Shortly before my date with the Fig Ladies, I taped a sign on the shop door. Customers hadn't exactly flocked in during the morning but, if they suddenly flew into a shell-buying frenzy over the next hour, they would know when I'd reopen.

By now my bike and I felt like old hands riding to Fig Follies. The temperature hovered in the low seventies, and sunlight sparkled on passing golf carts. The day felt positively rosy.

The only sour note was the wee-hours tiff with Emrys. Thinking of it as a tiff instead of a blowup made me feel better about it. I hadn't seen or heard him all morning but assumed he was moping rather than looping. Having a moody resident ghost was an adjustment for me. *Being* a ghost, of any description, had to be hard for anyone to adjust to. Even after two hundred and seventy-four years.

"You're here again!" Kathleen said when I knocked on the cottage door. "Isn't this fun? Go on ahead of me so I have room to get turned around. The gals are in the kitchen." She motioned me closer, before I made a move, and whispered, "The others don't like it when I put this thing in reverse. They're afraid I'll crash into something."

"Right. Like *that's* ever happened," I whispered back.

"Ah, the memories," she said.

We snickered, and then I followed the smell of melting cheese to the kitchen. Roberta looked up from a griddle with four sandwiches grilling to golden perfection. "Hello again," I said and handed Paula my contribution to lunch. "Dessert. Fresh from the Ocracoke Variety Store first thing this morning."

Paula opened the bakery bag, said, "Ooh," and took a deep sniff. "Croissants?"

"Fig croissants. It seemed like the right choice. Sorry about taking off like that last night. Thanks for having me back."

"Don't even think about it," Roberta said. "We've had time to get over the initial shock of finding her."

"I'll never forget it, though." Paula shook herself, and that seemed to restore her smile. "Let's not bother with a plate for your croissants. Straight out of the bag is the way to go."

"Same with the chips," Kathleen said from the doorway. "No standing or sitting on ceremony here. Grab those croissants from Paula, Maureen. Put the bag of chips in my lap. Ladies, we'll meet you on the porch."

I followed Kathleen to a large screened-in porch at the back of the cottage. A picnic table, already set, sat at one end. A group of Adirondack chairs painted in primary colors sat at the other. Paula and Roberta came on our heels with a pitcher of iced tea, the sandwiches still sizzling on the griddle, and a hot pad.

"Spinach and fig grilled cheese," Roberta said. "A complete meal of protein, dairy, veggies, fruit, and carbs in one humble sandwich."

"Not so humble," Kathleen said. "They're so good we've had them every day since we've been here."

"Then lay one on me." I passed my plate and Roberta obliged. "So, are you Fig Ladies old friends?"

"We'd never met before this trip," Roberta said. "Up until then we were strictly online friends."

Paula poured tea for each of us. "We're three of only four members of a small and exclusive fig appreciation society."

"I sense a story here," I said.

"Definitely," they said in unison and with feeling.

"But first," Kathleen said, "Mark says hi, and he wants to know if you heard about the guy who broke into the library up near us in Ocean City last week."

"No." Indignant, I put my sandwich back on my plate. "What kind of a rat breaks into a library? What was he looking for?"

"He carted off a bunch of books."

"What, borrowing isn't good enough for him?" Roberta asked. "Did they catch him?"

"Yep," Kathleen said. "They caught him at the end of the pier right after he threw the last book in the water."

"That's terrible!" Paula said.

"What happened next is worse," said Kathleen. "There was a *title* wave."

I snorted. "Tell Mark his joke is *swell*. These sandwiches are, too, by the way. Now, while I eat and your sandwich gets cold, tell me the story of the Fig Ladies."

"Nope," Kathleen said. "The Fig Ladies decided that you will pay for your lunch and abandoned supper with the story of why you're suddenly living in Ocracoke. You haven't posted anything about it on Facebook."

"Here's the short answer. A woman walks into a shell shop."

"Cryptic," Roberta said. "And it sounds like the setup for a joke." She turned on Kathleen. "You said she's a storyteller."

"She is. When Mark was the director of the library, back in Tennessee, he hired Maureen as the storyteller. That's how we met."

"Except I didn't recognize Kathleen the next time I met her," I told them, "because the first time she was dressed up as the library's mascot, Freddie the Firefly."

"Forget Freddie," Kathleen said. "Are you talking about the shell shop on Howard Street? I haven't been in it because there's no ramp."

"And it's hardly ever open," Roberta said. "That's no way to run a business."

"That it's hardly been open is part of the story," I said. "And building a ramp is on my to-do list. You should be able to come in the back door, though, Kathleen."

"*Your* to-do list?" Roberta asked. Her eyebrows were skeptical, her tone scathing.

"All mine." I checked the time on my phone. "I'm on my lunch hour, so I'll give you the main story line and save the subplots for another day."

"Good," said Paula. "More to look forward to, and in the meantime, we can finish our sandwiches and beat you to the croissants."

The capsule summary of how I ended up owning the Moon Shell touched on a few of the low points and enough of the high points to satisfy and even impress the Fig Ladies. Paula loved the idea of moving to an island. Kathleen loved the idea of jumping into something new. Roberta decided I was too young to be a widow.

"Maureen," she said, "It's time for you to get out there and strut your stuff for the rich, tan, island-hopping bachelors."

"Hmm, probably not." I smiled, hoping that made me look less appalled.

"Roberta tends to project," Paula said. "How many times have you been married, Roberta?"

"Three and counting, and proud of it," Roberta said. "Maureen, forget I mentioned strutting and rich bachelors. I can see they aren't your thing." She took a big bite of her croissant, licked flakes of golden pastry from each fingertip in turn, and said, "That leaves more of those tasty, tan bachelors for me."

I checked the time again.

"What time do you need to leave?" Kathleen asked.

"Fifteen minutes. Twenty at the outside. But I want to hear about this expedition of yours that goes beyond figs."

"Ah," Paula said. "Yes. We came here because we were worried. Remember I told you we're a small group?"

I nodded. "A group of four."

"Right," Kathleen said, "and we're worried about our fourth. We only know each other through our Facebook group, but we've been together for seven years and interact almost daily."

"Sometimes several times a day," Paula said. "But we've noticed a growing sadness in her posts."

"And memory issues," Kathleen said.

"I blew it off at first," Roberta said. "For heaven's sake, she and her husband retired five years ago and they're planning to uproot and move for the third time since then. That would be enough to depress me. But Paula and Kathleen are right about her memory."

"Last month she told us she and her husband were coming to Ocracoke, a fig lover's mecca," Paula said.

"We all live within a day's drive of here," Kathleen continued. "And we'd always said we'd meet up someday. Ocracoke seemed like a perfect place to make that happen. The kind of place to have an annual getaway. So, we decided to surprise her."

"We wanted to meet before it's too late," Roberta said bluntly. "Her presence online has been more absent in the last six months. Absent from the group and absent from—" She waved a hand around her head. "Absent from herself."

"We thought we might be able to find out what's going on in her life that's making her so sad," Kathleen said. "All that moving, or maybe one of them is facing a medical crisis. You can ask Mark about how that kind of stress can cause depression and memory issues."

"She's kind of private, though," said Paula. "She's always struck me as being more comfortable leading an online life."

"For a private person," I said, "and with all that moving around, online connections might be easier."

"Or for an older person?" Paula asked. "My mom—"

Roberta slapped the table. "Bite your tongue. Lenrose is no older than I am. Age does not automatically equal infirmity or idiocy. But a question like that one *does* automatically equal irritation."

Kathleen and Paula had jumped at Roberta's outburst. I did, too, but for a different reason.

"Her name is Lenrose?" I asked.

"Unusual, isn't it?" Roberta said. "What do you think—were her parents Leonard and Rosemary? Good thing her mother's name wasn't Tilda, or she would've been Lentil."

None of the rest of us said anything. Kathleen and Paula were too busy picking at their croissants. And like an unleashed puppy galloping into a flock of seagulls at the beach, my brain was chasing after the questions suddenly flapping around in my head.

Roberta looked at the three of us and blew out a heavy breath. "Yeah, yeah. You three are right and I'm wrong. I *shouldn't* make fun of her name. I *shouldn't* slam the furniture. I *shouldn't* jump down anyone's throat for making blanket statements full of moth holes. So, I'm *sorry*."

"I'm sorry, too," Paula said. "It was insensitive—"

"*No.*" Roberta jumped to her feet. "You aren't the one who ruined lunch." She grabbed her plate and glass. "*I* am, so I'll leave and let you enjoy the rest of your party." She stalked off into the house.

"Don't go." Paula started to get up, but Kathleen put a hand on her arm.

"Let her," Kathleen said. "She needed to blow off steam. I think she's more worried about Lenrose than both of us combined. Maureen, *I'm* sorry we're ending your visit on another downer note."

"Don't worry about it." I checked the time again. I really should get back to the shop . . . but no. A few more minutes wouldn't matter. Right now the flapping questions were more important than selling a peck or even a bushel of Scotch bonnets. I poured myself another glass of iced tea. "Executive decision. I'm giving myself a longer lunch hour because I want to hear more about Lenrose. What else is going on that has you worried? Not just worried, but *that* worried." I pointed to the door Roberta had stalked through. "Have you seen Lenrose since you've been here? Have you talked to her?"

"Both," Kathleen said. "Our first day here."

"What day was that?" I asked.

Kathleen looked at Paula. "Tuesday?"

Paula nodded. "The three of us met in Hatteras and came the rest of the way in Kathleen's van."

"We stopped at the Pony Pens on the way into the village here," Kathleen said.

"And there were Lenrose and Victor," Paula said. "We were so excited. We thought for sure it was a good sign."

"Except it wasn't," Kathleen said. "Lenrose was stunned speechless. Speechless and blank, like we didn't compute."

"How could we compute?" Paula said. "We sprang up out of nowhere."

"And grinned at her like demented stalkers. It isn't how we planned to let her know we were here," Kathleen said. "But she rallied and acted happy to see us. But I think it really *was* an act because then she leaned against Victor and said she wanted to sit in the car. We felt terrible. We didn't mean to upset her."

"Victor was wonderful with her," Paula said. "Put his arm around her. Walked her to the car. Then he came and told us she's in the early stages of dementia and sometimes has trouble processing new situations. They'd stopped to look at the horses because she learned to ride bareback when she was a girl and trained horses until they got married. He hoped seeing them would be calming and bring good memories."

"Oh, geez," I said.

"We've seen her since then, and we think the sea air must agree with her," Kathleen said.

I sat up straighter at that news. "When was the last time you saw her?"

"This morning," Paula said. "At the beach. We even invited her for lunch today, but they already had plans."

"Since meeting her at the Pony Pens, her memory seems better," Kathleen said. "Victor thinks so, too. She asked if we were having fun seeing all the different kinds of figs on the island."

"We're feeling a lot better about her," Paula said.

"Then why do you think—" I pointed at the door again.

"Bees in the bonnet," Kathleen said. "Sometimes she calls herself Roberta the Rager."

"She calls me Paula the Pollyanna," Paula said.

"Does she have a name for you?" I asked Kathleen.

"Kathleen the Confident."

"Lenrose?"

"Lenrose the Laureate," Kathleen said. "Because Lenrose is always writing odes to figs."

"She hasn't written any lately, and that's good and bad," Paula said. "Good because they were so bad, and bad because they made her happy and it's another sign that something is going on with her. Since we've been here, Roberta's been calling her Lenrose the Lost."

On that note I thanked them, said my goodbyes, and invited them to come see me at the Moon Shell. On the bike ride back, I wondered if Emrys was still miffed. And whether or not he was, I wondered how he'd react when I told him his tidal creek ghost couldn't have been Lenrose because Lenrose, although not well, was most assuredly alive.

Chapter 19

A shadow on the Moon Shell's porch shifted and took shape when I drew nearer to the shop. As I pulled into the gravel drive, the shadow coalesced into a glowering ghost, arms crossed over his indignant chest. He wasn't the only one on the porch. That is, he was the only ghost but not the only person. A woman sat on the railing at the far end. She smiled and waved as I braked.

"Hi," I called. "I'm running late. I'll be right with you." I rode around back, hopped off the bike, and went through the storeroom to open the front door. "Sorry to keep you waiting. Come on in."

"No worries," the woman said. "I'm on vacation. But you could use a bench or a couple of rocking chairs on your porch for people who don't like sitting on rails or steps."

"Good idea," I said.

"You would have no need of bench or chairs if you kept to your posted hours," Emrys growled. "Even if those hours are but a hastily scribbled note affixed to the door." He stalked in behind the woman.

"Are you looking for anything in particular?" I asked.

"Just another way to kill time while my husband and kids are deep-sea fishing."

"Browse to your heart's content." I reached for that offensive and hastily scribbled note still affixed to the door. Before my fingers touched it, the note fluttered to the floor. *Not* because the tape gave up. Because of the interfering, now invisible busybody ghost. I snatched up the note and, feeling petty, almost crumpled it to smithereens. Then I went one step pettier. With a smile for the note, I smoothed it and laid it carefully on the sales desk like a delicate flower, like the most fragile of sand dollars, like a valuable document that I intended to keep and use forever. Should I pat my heart and blow the note a kiss? Even I couldn't go that far. But I did align it more perfectly to the edge of the desk.

Emrys hovered somewhere nearby, and I knew he'd seen my petty pantomime. I knew because he made a rude noise. And I knew the noise came from him and not the customer because it had come with a distinctly piratical tone and Welsh accent. If a rude noise could be said to have an accent. Pfft. I took calming breaths to get my temper under control.

The customer, blithely unaware of the drama in the air around her, hummed to herself as she browsed. She stirred through bins of shells, and when she found any in the wrong bins, she put them in the right ones. A lovely, calming kind of customer. She brought half a dozen egg-sized Scotch bonnets to the sales desk.

"One North Carolina state shell for the toe of each Christmas stocking," she said. "As near to identical as I could find, as if that will stop the squabbles and comparisons."

"Six shells for six stockings—does that mean six children?"

"Mm-hmm. And all out on the boat with their father for the day. Isn't that about the nicest thing you've ever heard?" She took her bag of shells after I rang her up.

"Absolutely."

"You'd actually be wrong, though. He's also taking them out for supper, and I'm taking a long, soaking bath in the spa tub in our rental. With a glass of wine and a good book." She turned as she went out the door and said one more word. "Bliss."

Emrys appeared when she closed the door. "She isn't the only customer you kept waiting. Two or three others knocked on the door. The cat and I found it quite disturbing."

I channeled the blissful mother of six and apologized. Bonny, holding no obvious grudge, came from the office and twined around my ankles. "I ate lunch with the women who discovered the body in the tidal creek."

"I beg to differ," Emrys said, holding his grudge with a death grip. "I don't know who these women are who claim they found the body of Lenrose first, but they didn't. The crows discovered her first."

"Oh. Sure, that makes sense," I said. "To be more accurate, then, I had lunch with the women who *reported* the body."

"The crows also reported her body."

"Well, not really—"

"They reported it to me."

I was proud of myself for not asking how well that turned out for him. After all, I was almost old enough to be his mother (not counting the two hundred seventy-four years since his death when he could have worked at developing at least a *bit* of maturity), so I should be able to rise above his mood. It also seemed like a good idea to postpone springing on him the news about the body's identity.

"*And* I reported her name to Sheriff Tate," he said.

"By forging my handwriting and signature in a note."

He winced. Slightly. He didn't apologize, but he didn't disappear again, and he looked a little less like a stuffed shirt. A little less like a stuffed frock coat. I smiled at that thought, and he retreated to lean against the display case and gaze at his shell. If his shell had ankles and he were a cat instead of a ghost, he would twine around them making happy cat eyes.

I liked the calm mother's idea of a bench on the porch. A woodworking friend of Jeff's, back in Tennessee, made rustic wooden benches. Maybe one of the boys would bring one when they came for a visit. In the meantime, I took three dark green, plastic patio chairs from a stack of them in the storeroom—the storeroom that kept on giving. Allen had kept an amazing assortment of stuff in there. The plastic chairs weren't an elegant solution for weary or waiting customers, but they'd do until I convinced one son or another to make a trip over the mountains to visit their dear old mom.

A few customers later, Yanira Ochoa called me back about the possibility of working part time in the shop. "It isn't standard for interviews," she said, "but is it okay if Coquina comes with me?"

"I'll be disappointed if she doesn't. In fact, if you don't take the job, I'll offer it to Coquina."

Coquina, the eight-year-old shell fanatic, probably knew more about my stock than I did. Yanira laughed, told me to be careful what I wished for. "We'll stop by after school tomorrow."

When I disconnected, Emrys stood in front of me, arms crossed. "I suggest you make a condition of the child's employment that she not whistle either in the shop or on the porch."

"Thank you for your input. I'll take it into consideration." I didn't roll my eyes, but boy, was I tempted. As if reading my mind, Emrys narrowed his and then returned to his post at the display case. Fine with me. Yanira's interest in the job put me in a curmudgeon-proof mood.

In between more customers, I thought more about stocking the shop. My conscience wasn't going to let me buy shells unless I knew they were ethically collected—no shells collected with their owners still in residence, whether those owners were the original builders or new inhabitants. No killing of my friends the mollusks, no evictions of any species, and nothing from the endangered list.

Had Allen felt that way about the business? Not every shell collector or seller did. He'd been in his eighties when he was killed, but age didn't mean he'd been indifferent to the problems and ethics of over-collecting. Then again, as a young man he *had* been indifferent to the ethics of stealing. Indifferent to the problems, too. *He* hadn't done time for robbing Jeff's great-grandfather. His buddy, his accomplice, did. And then Allen had hidden the loot here in the attic and, as far as anyone knew, lived the life of a model citizen. But what if he'd learned from that "mistake"? Learned there was an untapped, if risky, source for fine old shells in the houses of unwary collectors? Learned how to break into houses without getting caught?

Better business through burglary. Yo-ho-ho. A modern-day pirate. Yikes.

I said goodbye to the latest flock of customers. And there, scowling at them as they went out the door and then at me, was the current shop pirate still looking cross-grained. Emrys had introduced me to that phrase after I'd described Bonny as cross-*eared*—ears back in irritation. He'd been cross-grained when a family had driven their golf cart, achingly slowly, the length of Howard Street, letting their child beep the horn the entire time. He'd said that Glady and Burt were often cross-grained with each other and would probably flatten their ears if they could.

"You're just the guy I need to talk to," I said, hoping to cajole him out of his uncharacteristically long dugeon. "Allen and his mother did a great job with this shop. It's survived for decades. You must have seen a lot about how they ran it, and I'm kind of at sea. Any details you can share will help."

"What manner of detail?" he asked.

"Day-to-day activities and routines. Frequent customers. Oh, and the animal-rights activists who marched in front of the shop with their signs. In case they come back."

"There was only one," Emrys said. "He of the pasty white thighs."

"I'm glad I never saw his thighs. But see? You notice details, and where there's one protestor, there might be more."

"I don't know why you worry," Emrys said. "He was not a genuine animal-rights activist, just as he was not a genuine vegetarian."

"Fair enough. What about Allen's routines? For instance, did he have a cleaning schedule? Because I probably need one—otherwise it'll be too easy to put off dusting and straightening and glass polishing. Housework has never been my favorite thing. It's possible I could hire it out, but I'll need to understand the shop's finances before I spend too much of them. And thank goodness there's no public restroom to keep clean." That was a lot to spew at him, but we were having a normal, nonconfrontational conversation, and that made me feel good. I smiled at him.

"You're asking me about the day-to-day mundanity of a shopkeeper?"

"Um, yeah." I kept smiling even as the good feeling started slip, slip, slipping away.

"As I am extramundane," Emrys said, "I pay little or no attention to the mundane." A ghost in a tricorn hat, looking down the length of his piratical nose, was as overly theatrical as it sounded. Especially when he huffed and disappeared.

I huffed and made a mental note to look up the definition of extramundane. Then made another to look up how to rid oneself of ghosts. And then felt bad for thinking that and sighed. The poor guy had been through a lot in his life and afterlife, he was harmless, and I should cut him some slack.

In 1750, at age thirty-seven, Emrys died. That made him thirty-seven going on three-hundred-and-eleven. If he'd lived to be seventy before becoming a ghost, he'd have lived almost four and a half lifetimes by now. Existed, anyway. He was in a peculiar situation that was enough to turn any sane person *more* than peculiar.

I'd read the bare facts of his pirate story in a display at the Ocracoke Preservation Society museum. Owen and John Lloyd, born in Rhuddlan, Wales, were respected merchants in the American colonies. In September 1750, they happened to be in Ocracoke with their younger brother, Emrys, when a hurricane-battered Spanish treasure ship, the *Nuestra Señora de*

Guadalupe, limped into port. The Spanish captain, worried that his ship would break up and the treasure lost, hired Owen and John Lloyd to remove the cargo to their sloops and ferry it to safety. The Lloyds, with the help of their younger brother, transferred spices, silks, and fifty-two (some said fifty-eight) chests of silver doubloons to their ships. And then they fell prey to temptation. The Spaniards had no way to follow, so the Lloyds decided to sail for the West Indies with the treasure—more plunder than Blackbeard and all his brethren had ever laid their hands on. It was an audacious caper, a true "crime of the century," and written up in newspapers all around the world.

Not an entirely successful caper, though. Owen got away safely. John didn't. His ship ran aground not far from Ocracoke. And then there was Emrys—the only fatality. He told me he'd objected to turning pirate. That Owen changed his mind for him.

Emrys had asked me to hold the cameo shell when I was on the island the month before. I'd held it and then had an extremely odd experience. I *saw* Emrys standing by the sloop's rail, as it rode at anchor near the galleon, and *he* was holding the shell. Another man—Owen, Emrys later told me—became visibly enraged, grabbed the shell from Emrys, and dropped it overboard. Emrys leaned over the rail, watching the shell sink, when a Spaniard on the galleon yelled "*pirata*" and fired a gun. A musket? I didn't know, didn't care. What mattered was that he hit Emrys in the shoulder, sending him overboard, and I watched him drown as his brothers sailed away.

So, yeah, I gave the guy some slack, hoping the line between slack and enough rope to tie me up in knots wasn't so thin that I couldn't see it.

Chapter 20

The next time the shop door opened, Mrs. Bundy's second fan-club member bounced in, followed by his big brother and a couple of smiling adults.

"Told you I'd bring my mom and dad." The kid bounced toward me and then stopped and pointed at the seagull. "See, Mom? That's Mrs. Bundy."

"Named after the bird expert in *The Birds*," the older boy said, sounding a tad too bored to be real.

"Very cool," his dad said. The older boy reacted to that with a slouch.

"Thanks for offering to let Dex be in the fan club," their mother said, "but we don't want his picture online."

"Completely understandable," I assured her. "I took his picture but haven't done anything with it. I'll erase it right now." I took out my phone.

Dex piped up. "Dad said maybe I can be in the fan club, anyway, without the picture."

"Sure," I said.

"So, can she send the picture to you before she deletes it, Dad?"

"Send it to me," his mom said.

"Great. And I'll send a club membership certificate, too, as soon as I design one. With no worries about any other emails arriving to clutter your inbox."

The parents were fine with that, and the mom gave me her email. "Gav, how about you?" she asked the older boy.

Gav lifted a corner of his lip and shook his head.

Dex wrote out his full name, and I made three more mental notes—to design the membership certificate, to announce the club online, and to start making notes on paper or in my phone. Dex bounced back out of the shop, followed by his family.

A minute later, Gav hurried back in. He darted his eyes around as though checking for eavesdroppers and then came to the sales desk. "Can I still join the club?"

"Sure."

"And have a picture?"

"It'll be my pleasure." I snapped his picture with Mrs. Bundy, and he was all smiles, looking as sweet as his brother.

He asked to see the picture, studied it like a connoisseur, then asked for one more. He put on his cool blank teen face for the retake and grinned the sweet smile when he saw it.

"Hey, Gav," I said. "You and Dex were talking about a podcast last time you were in. It sounded like something I'd be interested in."

"You know it happened here, right? I mean, like, *right* here." His eyes were huge.

"Crazy, isn't it? What's the podcast's name?"

"'Croaked on Ocracoke.' Kind of dweebish. But it disappeared. Got taken down."

"Well, darn."

"I know. Real stupid. It was supposed to have two more episodes. I don't even know if they caught the guy."

"They did."

"Good. Who was it? No. Don't tell me. Maybe it'll show up again."

The dweebish honk of the golf cart sounded outside.

"I'm going to be a profiler for the FBI," he said.

"Excellent. You look cool enough to do the job right."

Gav dashed for the door, nearly bowling over Burt, who nimbly stepped aside.

"Refreshing to see a kid that age with a smile on his face," Burt said, "and without a phone like an extra appendage. Gives me hope." He plunked a box on the sales desk.

The box gave me hope for more babka or something babka-like. Babka and something more? The box was big enough for a bonanza of baked goods. None of which I needed. I sniffed the air. No aromas tickled my nose. Burt rested an arm on the box. He looked protective and something else. Uncomfortable? "Glady hasn't been in since you got back from lunch, has she?" He looked oddly pleased when I said she hadn't.

"What's in the box, Burt? Fan mail from some flounder?"

He chuckled at the Rocky and Bullwinkle reference and then looked away. The space above the tops of the display shelves and the ceiling caught his eye. Allen had added decorative touches up there—a couple anchors and a ship's wheel on one wall and enlarged photographs of shells, as beautiful as the best celebrity portraits, on another. I'd never seen this side of Burt before. I didn't know what side of him it was, but it reminded me of when he'd come in with Glady and looked like he was surveying the shop and the possibilities of this valuable property.

His gaze moved to the locked display case, and he cleared his throat. "I brought some of my ships in bottles. I've been—" He cleared his throat again. "I've been wondering where they could go. On top of the shelves is too high to see. Any lower and someone will pick one up and drop it. But in the locked case—"

"To display or to sell?"

"Sell. If you like them."

I knew he made ships in bottles but hadn't seen any. "Show me."

He folded the flaps of the box back, and we bent our heads over it. Four clear glass bottles with corked ends sat nestled in the folds of a beach towel. Burt lifted one out and held it for me to see the ship inside—a sailboat with one mast, two sails, and other details and touches I couldn't name.

"A sloop," he said. "Eighteenth century. Accurate and to scale."

"Burt, I'm in awe."

"All I seem to make is sloops. Hold this one." He put the bottle in my hands and took another from the box. "Here's one with two masts. Sloops had one, two, or three. Back then they were the best small ships in the world. People called them leopards of the sea. Pirates loved them."

"They're works of art." The bottle in my hands held a ship like the one I'd seen when Emrys had me hold the moon shell—like his brother's ship. "Will you let me sell them? They'll look great in the case with the moon shell."

"Deal. Let's start with these four and see how they do." He tucked the two he'd taken out back in the box. "Now, I want my picture taken for the Mrs. Bundy Fan Club before too many of the tourons in golf carts catch on."

"The what?"

"Fan club," Burt enunciated.

"I mean the *what* in golf carts?"

"Tourons. You haven't heard that yet? I bet you've met some, though. Tourists? Morons? Mash them together and what do you get? Tourons."

"I met two of them in Hawaiian shirts on Monday."

"You don't want to go around calling them that to their faces, though. Not good for the island's image." Burt left the box on the sales desk and went to stand so the seagull looked over his shoulder. "How's this?"

"Perfect. How did you hear about the club? I haven't advertised it yet."

"Word gets around."

"I guess." I snapped his picture. Then he wanted another with him holding one of his ships. That done, I shook his hand and congratulated him on being fan-club member number four.

"Who're the first three?" he asked, a sharp look in his eye.

"Tourists who aren't tourons. Hey, you know who I bet would like to join? Noah Horton." Noah was the easily impassioned young man who'd experimented with being an animal-rights activist by picketing the shop while Allen was still alive (with his pasty white thighs on display, according to Emrys).

"He's gone," Burt said. "Flew away on the wings of his next fancy. He realized his strength isn't in one-man protests."

"Or riding out hurricanes, investigative journalism, or veganism," I said. "What is it this time?"

"Catchy slogans. He relocated to the family place in Key West to start a T-shirt company."

"Too bad he didn't start his company here," I said.

"Yeah? I'll put my box in the office. We can discuss details later."

The shop door opened, and Glady came in as I called after Burt, "Noah could've made T-shirts for the Mrs. Bundy Fan Club."

Glady stopped in the open door and gave me a beady-eyed look she must have picked up from hanging around with Mrs. Bundy. Her fists went to her hips, her elbows sticking out like wings. "Why didn't you tell me about your fan club?" She pivoted when Burt came out of the office and turned her two-fisted fury on him. "You told me you were going to the library."

"Did not. I told you I need to run to the library. I still do. Just not this afternoon. Calm down, Glad. Just because I joined the club before you doesn't mean you can't."

"Subterfuge," she sputtered. "You're a miscreant making misleading statements."

"Joining the club was an afterthought," I told her. "Burt really came to see if I'd like to sell his ships in bottles."

Before our eyes, Glady un-riled herself. "Well. That's good." She came in without closing the door. "It's about time, you old fool. I hope you said yes, Maureen."

"Of course I did."

"Allen didn't," Burt said.

"Because you showed him your first attempts," Glady said. "They looked like shipwrecks in bottles."

"You're too kind, Glad. He said they looked like flotsam in bottles."

"You never told me that," Glady said.

"Because it hurt and I decided I'd never show him another. I was just getting around to thinking about showing him some of my new ones but, then, well. Let that be a lesson to you, Maureen. Don't put things off. People drop dead."

The shop got so quiet you could have heard a dead body drop.

"Sorry, Maureen." He shifted on his feet uneasily.

"It's okay, Burt. It's good advice. It's a fact of life. Grief is, too, and I don't need people tiptoeing around me."

"Knock-knock," said a nasally rasp at the still-open door behind Glady.

She bristled, no doubt recognizing the voice of Doctor Irving Allred behind her. She probably would have whirled to face him, like a threatened cat, if her knees had nine lives. She turned more slowly but too late. Allred slid around behind her into the shop.

"Afternoon, friends," Allred said. He grinned at each of us in turn. Because of his hunched shoulders and beaky nose, I usually thought of him as one of the smaller, stockier herons seen in marshy areas. Today, his sharp nose and grinning teeth had me wondering if I'd also see a hairless tail twitching behind him. He was a sly, conniving possum if ever there was one, and if Mrs. Bundy had a nest of eggs, I'd tell her to keep an eye on them.

Glady took advantage of the fact she now faced the door. "*So* sorry I can't stay and chat, Irving," she said over one shoulder, and, "See you later, Maureen," over the other, and skedaddled.

"A shame," Allred said to the door Glady had just banged shut. "I see so little of Gladys these days."

"Calling her Gladys won't help." Burt began sidling toward the door. I toyed with the idea of joining him but didn't want to leave ghost-snooper Allred alone in the shop.

"A nineteen fifty-three Kaiser Manhattan is a rare bird," Allred said apropos of nothing.

Burt reacted like a dog hearing the word *squirrel*. "You've seen that beauty?"

"Indeed I have," Allred drawled. "A green and white apparition of elegance. Its splendor is only eclipsed by his nineteen fifty-four Kaiser Darrin convertible."

"No," Burt said. As if hearing Allred in a dream, he slowly shook his head. "No. I don't believe it. You can't tell me Sullivan owns a Manhattan *and* a Darrin. Is the Darrin here, too? On the island?"

"Not this trip," Allred said. "But I've seen it."

"How does one man . . . ?" Burt hadn't stopped shaking his head. "Only four hundred and thirty-five Darrins and six prototypes were ever built."

"Their beauty is eclipsed only by Lenrose," Allred said. "His wife and the love of his life."

I'd retreated behind the sales desk to escape the flood of automotive lust, but my ears pricked at his mention of Lenrose. "You know Lenrose?"

Allred's answer was a noncommittal shrug and a smile.

"I saw a rust-spotted Kaiser for sale in an online forum," Burt said, almost breathless. "I can't remember if it was a Manhattan or a Darrin—"

"Manhattan, most likely," Allred said helpfully.

"Most likely, and *minus* its top and most of each seat, *and* the engine, it was listed for thirty-nine thousand, nine hundred ninety-nine dollars."

"Sullivan's are apparently in tip-top shape. All parts present and in working order," Allred said. "And you can say the same for the lovely Lenrose." The possum grin appeared again. He tipped an imaginary hat and left.

"What came over me?" Burt shook himself. "Maureen!" He fairly stumbled toward me. "Promise you won't ever tell Glady what you just witnessed."

"What did I witness?"

"Me enjoying a conversation with Irv. I won't hold you to it, though, because she'd never believe you anyway. I can hardly believe it myself. In fact I was just beginning to feel queasy about it when Irv gave his slobbering opinion of Lenrose."

"That brought you to your senses?" I asked.

"Like a slap in the face, and all was right with the world again." Burt looked at me. "But not with your world? You look troubled."

"What did Allred want? Why did he come here?"

"Because it's a shop?" Burt said. "Because Glady left the door wide open and he buzzed in like the pest he is?"

"Maybe. He didn't look around, though. Didn't act like one of his murder tourists. He mentioned the car and—"

"Two cars," Burt said. "Two *extraordinary* cars."

"Snap out of it, Burt. Allred mentioned the cars and he slobbered about Lenrose. Think about it. He dropped a couple of baited hooks into the water to see what's biting."

"Oh," he said. "And we bit." He scratched the new beard. "But, knowing Allred, do we really want to know what that means?"

Chapter 21

I decided to ponder Allred's weird visit to the Moon Shell later. It might have been about nothing, or it might have been about something that no one who wasn't Doctor Irving Allred would want to explore. Exploring *extramundane*, the word Emrys had tossed out to describe himself, sounded more interesting and probably better for my mental health. Did it have something to do with being extraordinary? I tapped my way to *Merriam-Webster* online and discovered it was better than that. *Extramundane* referred to something in, or relating to, a region beyond our material world or universe.

"Cool," I said to Mrs. Bundy. "Like a ghost."

"If Mrs. Bundy ever had a ghost, it is long gone." Emrys appeared nose to beak with the seagull. "Seagulls are not as intelligent as crows."

"Do birds have ghosts?"

"Not that I've ever noticed. Can you imagine how crowded the air around us would be if all the birds and bugs that ever were still swarmed around us as ghosts?"

The shop door opened, and a tall, broad, and tanned man came in, followed soon after by a woman. She reminded me of cotton candy with white-blond hair spun into a fifties-style pile on top of her head.

"Hi. Welcome to the Moon Shell," I said to both, not sure if they were together.

"Good afternoon." The man came straight to the sales desk and held out his hand for a shake. "I'm an old friend of Allen Withrow's. The name's Victor Sullivan."

"Oh!" I shook his hand. "I'm sorry I wasn't here the first time you came in. I'm Maureen Nash."

The woman shuffled sideways from behind Victor, her face somewhat blank as she emerged. Then a smile started in her eyes and at the corners of her mouth and slowly spread, as though reappearing after being eclipsed by Victor's broad back. "Hello." She fluttered her fingers at me.

"There you are, honey." Victor put his arm around her. "My wife, Lenrose."

And just like that, I didn't need to worry about breaking the news to Emrys that Lenrose was alive. "It's nice to meet you, Lenrose." I glanced quickly at Emrys, to see his reaction, but didn't see one. He looked as blank as she had before she smiled. And then I didn't see him at all. In a blink, gone again.

"I've met your fig friends," I said to Lenrose.

She continued smiling but raised her eyebrows.

"I had lunch with Kathleen, Roberta, and Paula," I said. "I've known Kathleen for close to thirty years."

"Imagine that." Lenrose tapped Victor's shoulder and whispered loudly, "Do I know the people she's talking about?"

"She's talking about your online fig friends, darling."

"That's all right, then," she said. "Why don't I wait outside?"

"Sit in one of the chairs on the porch or in the car," Victor said. "I won't be long."

Lenrose turned at the door. "Shelly?"

"Yes, Sug?"

"Do I like figs?"

"You love them."

Victor watched until the door closed behind her. I saw the

pain in his eyes when he turned back to me, and I couldn't help asking, "Will she be okay out there by herself?"

"She will. She's actually doing better since we've been here."

"She called you Shelly."

He laughed. "My nickname was always Sully, for Sullivan, but I love shells, so it's morphed into Shelly."

"Makes perfect sense," I said. "I'm glad to hear that Ocracoke is doing good things for Lenrose."

"We love it here. It's where she fell in love with figs and I fell in love with shells. I blame Allen for that. He and I became friends, exchanging many emails over the years and discussing the business of shells. He sold me some wonderful specimens—quite a few he never displayed here in the shop." He shook his head. "I have no illusions about Lenrose's health. I'm losing her by bits and pieces. And then I came in here expecting to see my old friend, to spend some time talking shells and have a few good meals together, and instead I found out I lost him in one terrible blow. I don't know which way of losing is worse or crueler. I truly don't." He drew in a deep breath and let it out slowly through his nose, looking past me, eyes unfocused.

The crows started making a fuss somewhere nearby. Their racket seemed to rouse Shelly.

"I never did understand how Allen could like the noise of crows." He slewed around and eyed Mrs. Bundy. "Or gulls. I wrote to him in August to let him know when I'd be here, and when I saw that thing hanging there I figured he hung it just to get at me. Am I right?"

"Glady put it up after Allen died. Sorry to disappoint you." I was touched to see that he really did seem to be disappointed. "Was Allen expecting you for any specific reason? Anything that I can help you with? I mean, other than taking down the dreaded seagull?"

He shook his head. Then he did a slow three-hundred-sixty-degree turn, taking in the shells, the shop, the life of his old friend. "End of an era," he said softly. "A great era." When he faced me again, his voice was all business. "How long will the store remain open now that Allen's gone? I assume it's open now as a way to reduce the inventory. Do you know if arrangements have been made for disposing of the inventory that doesn't sell?"

"I—"

He flicked an open hand, up then down—a signal I shouldn't interrupt with answers? He must have thought so, but I tend to have a knee-jerk reaction to being hushed by people who seem to assume they're in charge of any space they enter: I keep talking. He kept talking, too, with the result that neither of us heard each other. I won the competition, though, because he stopped talking first.

Another knee-jerk reaction I suffer from is immediately feeling bad for being annoying. "I interrupted," I said. "I'm sorry. You were saying?"

If I'd irritated him, he covered it quickly with a limited smile. "I was saying that I occasionally helped Allen source inventory for the business."

My ears perked at that information, and I cursed my knee-jerk motormouth. "I've been wondering where he bought stock. I haven't found his records yet."

"I'm sure whoever liquidates the business will be able to find the records," he said. "They'll be needed for return purposes to whatever wholesalers Allen used. The sources I mentioned, however, were private collections, and the shells in question would be rather high end. The reason I bring it up is that I might be interested in negotiating terms for buying those pieces myself. To be honest, it would mean a great deal to me to have something to remember Allen by. Here's my card. Will you pass it, along with my offer, to the powers that be?"

"Gosh, I sure will." There, no knee-jerk jerkiness from me that time. Just a parody of a sweet-tea-infused Southern missy. Shelly didn't know me, so the act went right over his tanned forehead and silver widow's peak, thank goodness. If I didn't know better, though, I'd say it put a smile on Mrs. Bundy's beak.

Shelly's eyes strayed to the locked case with the moon shell and the other beauties that weren't for sale. He went to it, and I followed.

"Are these some of the shells you found for Allen?" I asked. Just because he was condescending—condescending and dismissive—didn't mean he hadn't found great shells for Allen or been a good customer. "People love looking at them."

"So do I," Shelly said. His smile had relaxed. "A few of these probably are ones I helped him get. Or some that I gave to him." He bent to peer at two nearly identical eight-inch chambered nautili on the lower shelf. Jacques, the birthday boy, had bought the third, larger nautilus. Allen had put a copy of *The Chambered Nautilus*, a poem by Oliver Wendell Holmes Sr., on an easel between the twins. Most people didn't bother to bend or squat down long enough to read a poem of thirty-five lines, but it was a nice touch.

"Recognizing a single shell without seeing it from all angles probably isn't easy," I said.

"You're basically right," he said. "With some shells it's easier to distinguish between individuals than others, though, and some types of shells make it easier, too." He straightened. "It was a pleasure meeting you, Maureen. I'm sure you'll see me again. Don't forget to pass along my card and message, will you?"

"Consider it done."

I followed Shelly out to the porch to get a look at the car that had Burt and Allred going gaga. Okay—I could see why. Sunlight glinted off every sleek surface. The lines and two-tone paint immediately made me think of the saddle shoes and bobby socks I'd seen in fifties-era movies. Lenrose, with her updo, sunglasses, and her arm propped in the open window, looked exactly right sitting in the front passenger seat. I couldn't imagine going to the trouble of fixing my hair the way she did. Couldn't imagine how many pins or how much hairspray it must take to maintain. The bouffant style looked as natural to Lenrose, though, as she did to the car. She smiled and waved goodbye when they drove off.

Back inside, I found Emrys sitting behind the desk in the office running his hand over the journal.

"What do you feel when you touch it?" I asked.

"Nothing. No, that is false. I feel a memory."

"I bought that for you," I said. "And the pen."

He looked at me and then stroked the journal again. He picked up the pen and stared at the galaxy captured in it. "What good is owning to a ghost?" he asked gruffly. "I haven't owned anything in a century or two."

"Or three."

"As you say. What would I write in it?"

"Anything you want."

"I wouldn't want to spoil it with drivel."

"Fear of the blank page is common," I said. "There are probably twice as many, make that three or four times as many, empty journals in desk drawers than there are filled ones. But you can't spoil a journal any more than you can spoil a ball of yarn or a piece of leather in a cobbler's shop."

"My father might not agree with you about the leather. His words would have scalded your ears if you'd heard him upbraid my brother John over his clumsy attempts at learning the trade." He stroked the journal again then said, "That woman who was here—I followed her outside."

"Lenrose," I said gently. "You followed Lenrose."

"She sat in one of the chairs on the porch. I sat in the other." He picked up the pen and twirled it around his fingers.

"When did you learn to do that?" I mimed the twirling.

When he looked at his hand, his fingers fumbled. The pen dropped. "That woman is not Lenrose."

Chapter 22

"She really seems to be Lenrose, Emrys."

"*Seems* is far from proof," he said. "The crows do not know her. Did you hear them a short while ago?"

"I did."

"They're the reason she left the porch to sit in the car," he said. "The crows were talking about her. Talking against her."

I watched him pick up the pen and try twirling it again. The crows had been talking about *something*, but rather than start another argument, I let it drop. The pen dropped, too.

"Do you remember Allen and Shelly talking business?" I asked.

"As we've established, I'm not terribly business-minded."

"I don't know that I am, either." I told him about my conversation with Shelly, ending with, "I might have made a mistake by telling him that I haven't found Allen's records."

"Why?"

"That's when Shelly said he'd found sources for shells for Allen. Because he thinks the shop is closing, he wants first crack at buying those shells."

"That sounds fair," Emrys said.

"He might also want the shells he gave Allen. But what if he didn't really find shells for Allen or give him any? He knows I don't have Allen's records. So, what if he goes home and creates false records?"

"Is the world so full of pirates?"

"Good point," I said. "I'll try to keep a lid on my paranoia and what-ifs. But . . . what if Allen told Shelly about the stuff in the attic, and now Shelly wants to get his hands on some of it?" I couldn't help glancing toward the ceiling and then remembered I'd seen customers do that. Specifically Aw Shucks and Beak Booper. "What I'm saying is you were right last night. We need to be careful with the treasure."

"I felt sure you would eventually come to your senses." He cocked an eyebrow. "I would also like you to believe me when I say that woman is not Lenrose. But you look away and cannot meet my eye."

"Is this better?" I sat in the spindle-back chair across from him and looked him square in the eyes. "I still find it hard to believe she isn't Lenrose. It's hard to refute the proof of her husband thinking she is." I paused. "On the other hand, I believe I'm sitting here talking to a ghost, so the line has definitely shifted for what I can and can't believe."

"Imagine how I felt when I finally had to believe that I *am* a ghost."

"You're carrying it off well," I said.

"You're very kind."

"Tonight I'll look through Allen's laptop for correspondence with Shelly. Unless you'd like to?"

"I am adept at finding obituaries in *The New York Times,* but that is apparently my limit."

"Have you been looking for something?"

"Fruitlessly."

"I'm pretty good at finding things online. Burt's probably better. What were you looking for? Maybe we can help."

"The endless quest—evidence that Allen followed through on his promise to find a way for me to rest in peace. But as

Mister Jonathan Swift so ably put it, 'promises and pie-crust are made to be broken.' Mister Swift, if you did not know, is also long dead. However, he is properly buried. The more I know about Allen, the more I know that I did not know him."

"The laptop might have a history of Allen's online searches," I said, "and if he found something, he might have saved it to a file. Do you know about files?"

"The files with which I'm familiar would break a laptop as easily they would break Mister Swift's piecrust."

The shop door opened, and people with happy voices came in.

"Remind me to tell you about another kind of file," I whispered.

"I'm sure I'll find it delightful."

The people with the happy voices were the last customers of the day, and they spent an amount that made me happy. As I settled the cash register after locking the door behind them, someone knocked. It was Rob Tate.

"Sorry to barge in after closing again," he said.

"It's all right. What can I do for you? Take your picture for the Mrs. Bundy Fan Club?"

"The what?"

"Just a silly thing we're doing. A fan club for the seagull."

"Oh. Sure. Good idea." He looked more exhausted than he had on Monday and sounded as brittle as a sand dollar. "I came to let you to know that I don't believe you wrote the note."

"That's a relief. Thank you."

"Thank Glady. She called and said she'd hound me until my dying day and long after if I didn't see that you couldn't have written it." His eyes briefly sparkled. "But so you don't think I'm that easily pushed around, I also spoke to someone who saw you get off the ferry."

"May I ask who?"

"Irv Allred."

"Darn. I thought I'd slipped past him. Not that I make a habit of trying to slip past people, but Doctor Allred—"

"Understood."

I asked Tate if he'd heard of the podcast about Allen's murder. He hadn't, but that news made him briefly pinch the bridge of his nose. Hearing that it had been taken down revived him.

"I'll let you get on with your evening," he said.

"May I ask a question before you go?"

"Sure." Did his hand look anxious to pinch the bridge of his nose again?

"Do you think there's any possibility the unidentified body *is* Lenrose Sullivan?"

"No. And here's what I told Glady when she asked the same question. Move on from that idea. There is nothing for you to see there. There is nothing for you to get involved in." This time he went for scrubbing his face, bringing a palm from his eyebrows to his chin. Maybe that did something for him, because he added, "Much as I appreciate your interest and willingness to help," and then plodded wearily out the door.

Emrys strode in from the office like the swashbuckler he claimed he never really was. "Captain Tate's 'no' rang out like a slammed door," he said. "The bard would say that Tate 'has not so much brain as ear-wax.' I suggest that you open our front door and slam it with enough force to boil that earwax."

"I'd rather not jar the door."

"Wise, but such a pity."

"Emrys, have you ever heard of Opposite Day?"

"I have heard of Saint Opportuna's Day, though I doubt there is any relation between it and yours. I also have no idea why Opportuna sticks in my head, for I am neither Roman nor religious. Nor do I know why she came into my head just now. Perhaps because she is known for leading others by positive example, unlike my brothers who did the opposite."

"Opposite Day is when you do the opposite of what someone asks you to do or you say the opposite of what you mean."

"Is this legal?"

"It's a kids' game, often played by pesky kids, and it doesn't often last much longer than it takes for kids to laugh themselves silly or for one kid to start crying."

"My brothers would have loved it," he said. "Why are we interested in this torment?"

"Because you and I are on the same team, and we're not out to make Tate cry. But he said, 'There's nothing to see here,' and, 'There's nothing to get involved in.' I believe the opposite is true. The unidentified woman has a name."

"Lenrose," Emrys said.

"I'm willing to believe that might be true, but if it is, then it raises questions. A big one is this—who's the woman pretending to be Lenrose? Tate isn't getting involved in that because he sees nothing there."

"Confusion could well run rampant with this Opposite Day game," he said, "but I'll give it a try."

"Good."

"I should tell you, by the way, that under no uncertain terms should you open my journal and read it."

"That's completely understandable. I wouldn't think of it without your permission."

"You have already forgotten," he said with a roll of his eyes, as gray and ghostly as the rest of him. "It's *Opposite* Day. In truth, I would be honored for you to read the little I've put down so far. Not my own words but several quotations that I like. My way of priming the pump for thoughts to come."

"Cool. You're sure you don't mind?"

With a bow, he gestured for me to go ahead of him into the office. He also did his ghost thing and appeared in the ergonomic chair behind the desk before I'd taken two steps. I sat in the spindle-back chair, which I actually liked quite a lot, and suggested Emrys read the quotations aloud. His cheeks turned grayer in a blush.

"'All eyes and no sight,' William Shakespeare." He looked up. "That's from *Troilus and Cressida*. This next is from Arthur Ashe."

"The tennis player?"

"Please, no interruptions. Ashe said, 'Start where you are. Use what you have. Do what you can.' Then there is this from Walt Whitman. I believe he is a poet. He said, 'Re-examine all you have been told at school or church or in any book, dismiss whatever insults your soul.' I cut Whitman off there because he tends to go on at length. I abbreviated the last quote as well. This is another William—William Faulkner—who said, '. . . the tools I need for my work are paper, tobacco, food, and a little whiskey.'" Emrys closed the journal and sat back. "There are only those four, but it is a beginning."

"Interesting choices. How do you know the Whitman, Faulkner, and Ashe quotes?"

"Allen knew that I enjoy quotations, but he was not 'into Shakespeare,' as he put it. Occasionally, when he would indulge in more than a bottle or two of beer, he entertained himself by 'trawling the net' for the types of quotations he preferred so that he might 'broaden my horizons.'"

"Did he have good taste in quotations?" I asked.

"I will defer to Mister Shakespeare. In *Love's Labour's Lost*, he says, 'Beauty is bought by judgement of the eye.' Allen's taste was neither all good nor all bad. Do you know why I chose these four quotations to prime the pump?"

"The first three offered advice. Faulkner's sounded more like an unhealthy prescription."

"And where I'm concerned, a useless prescription. Except the need for paper." He picked up the pen, this time twirling it without dropping it. "Paper and pen will be useful in our investigation. So will the other three quotations, because each one offers a piece of insight or advice useful to the astute detective."

"Do they?"

"Absolutely," he said. "I'll write them out on a separate sheet of paper for you. That way you'll have them to study and refer to in times of quandary."

"Nifty. I wonder if those four guys ever dreamed they'd end up in an elite advisory quartet for a group of amateur detectives."

"We'll never know. Like Jonathan Swift, they're all dead and properly buried."

"Unlike you."

"And poor Lenrose."

A problem arose with the journal. Emrys couldn't carry it up to the apartment. He could push it across the desk. He could open it and turn pages. But he could only lift it an inch or so before it fell back onto the desk. I offered to take it upstairs for him if he wanted to join me for the evening. He declined. He also declined to join me without it. While filling a small bowl with crunchy fish stuff for Bonny, and fixing and eating a grilled cheese and fig jam sandwich, I heard a series of thumps from downstairs. The sort of thumps made by something not terribly large or hard dropping to a wooden surface. Over and over. What sounded like a muffled oath followed each thump.

After doing the dishes, I took Allen's laptop to the recliner, opened the computer, and scrolled through his emails. Thousands and thousands of emails. Had the man never hit *delete*? Bonny asked for her turn as my laptop, so I moved the computer to the coffee table and tried every variation of Shelly's nickname, his original nickname, first name, and last name in the email folders and archive. I tried Lenrose and every combination of Shelly and Lenrose. I did keyword searches in the inbox, sent folder, trash, spam, and archive. Nothing.

I sat back, muffling a few oaths of my own. That out of my system, I realized the oaths and thumps from downstairs had stopped. Then a jaunty tune floated up the stairs, toward me, followed by Emrys.

"Good evening, Mistress Nash." He made an exaggerated show of patting his coat pockets and discovering something tucked inside one. His hand disappeared into the pocket and reappeared with the journal. He dropped the journal on the coffee table. With a smug flip of his coattails, he sat on the settee. An antique sitting on an antique. Neither one living or breathing. "Can you believe that, in all my years in this condition from which I suffer, I've never tried putting anything into my pockets? What an interesting phenomenon. Now, what is this about laptops and files that you're so anxious to tell me?"

"Files!" I bounced the heel of my hand off my forehead and bent over the laptop again. Bonny, still in my lap, helped by putting her paw on my arm. "Files are places to keep information in a laptop," I told Emrys. "Think of the laptop as a ghost's pocket—actually as pockets within pockets within pockets."

"Or a filing cabinet?"

"Well, yes, but filing cabinets are so mundane. Computers and a ghost with pockets are not."

I hadn't spent a lot of time digging around in the laptop. Just enough to know there were no folders or files conveniently labeled *Business Records*, *Wholesalers*, *Shell Dealers*, or the like. And now I didn't find *Shelly*, *Sullivan*, *Sully*, or *Victor*. But I did find *Victory*. Goosebumps rose on my arm as Emrys shimmered over to look at the computer screen.

"Do you see this list?" I ran my finger down the screen. "It's a list of folders in the computer."

"In?"

"When my son Kelly comes for a visit, we'll get him to explain. For now, think of the laptop computer as a ghost's pocket of infinite capacity."

"When will he be here?"

"I'll ask next time I talk to him." I gave Emrys a basic explanation of folders and files and how to open them, and he nodded along. "So, let's see what's in this folder."

I opened *Victory*. Allen was much craftier about hiding the entrance to the attic than he was in hiding his correspondence with Victor, aka Shelly. The folder held their emails and another folder labeled *Victory Transactions*. I opened that first. It held roughly two dozen photographs. The name of each was a single word followed by three numbers separated by periods. I opened the first photograph, labeled "Juno 7.28.19," and saw a cream-colored, brown-spotted seashell lying next to a ruler. The shell was a six-inch Juno's Volute. Beautiful and, while not rare, unusually large. I clicked through the rest of the pictures. Each showed a single item with a ruler. Most were pictures of shells. Two showed ornate glass jars filled with shells, similar to the two jars in the safe downstairs. Four showed antique books about shells.

"Are we looking at a portion of our treasure?" Emrys asked.

"Maybe."

"The exchange of goods for money," Emrys said. "Transactions. Did Allen buy these from Shelly or vice versa?"

"Or a bit of both? The numbers are probably dates of the transactions." I closed that folder and scanned the list of emails. "Here's an email named 'Juno 7.28.19_ AW.'"

I clicked it open. In a terse note dated July 28, 2019, Allen told Shelly, whom he called Victor, that a six-inch Juno's Volute, *Scaphella junonia johnstoneae*, was still available for $395. I opened two more emails with AW in the name and three with VS. Neither man was chatty, although they usually threw in a line about the weather (Allen) or a recent or imminent visit (Shelly). Each email mentioned a shell or shells and hefty prices.

"These don't look like receipts or invoices," I said. "There's no mention of payments made or received. Nothing about tax or shipping and handling."

"You haven't read all of them," Emry pointed out.

"We've opened a sampling of them, and they seem to corroborate Shelly's story. Up to a point. What worries me is the pictures that look like the stuff in the attic. They make me wonder if Allen was selling it off bit by bit." I checked the time. "It's been a long day, and I want to call the boys. If you'd like to, you can read the rest of the emails."

"I shall love to, and if there's any hint of dishonorable behavior to be found, I shall be the one to sniff it out." He chortled, rubbed his hands, and went to work.

I called Kelly first. As usually happened, the call went to voicemail, so I left a cheery message about settling in. O'Connor answered on the third ring.

"Mom! You sound better. Wait, that didn't come out right. I hear an encouraging difference in your voice. You don't sound tired and worried. What's going on?"

"Emrys is back and—"

"Fantastic!"

"And Kathleen Thomas is here on vacation."

"That's great. Tell her hi for me. And? What else?" he asked. "I hear . . . not exactly excitement in your voice, but something."

"You have a good ear, Con. Excitement isn't the right word, but things *are* going on here." I filled him in on the murder, about Kathleen and her friends finding the body, and how I found Emrys at the site.

"Yeow. Is Emrys there now? Can you put him on the phone?"

"We can try. I'll put you on speaker. Hang on." I tapped the speaker icon and then interrupted Emrys. "O'Connor wants to talk to you."

"Will he be able to hear me?" Emrys asked.

"I hear you loud and clear," O'Connor said. "I have a favor to ask, Emrys. Mom told me about this murder, and I know how you guys got involved with the last one. Will you try to talk her out of doing anything dangerous this time?"

"I will do my best," Emrys said. "However, I believe community involvement is good for the soul, and souls are a subject about which I am especially keen. I must say, speaking to you like this is rather like communicating with an unseen spirit."

"It's cool, isn't it?"

"It isn't just cool," Emrys said. "It's extramundane."

After hanging up with O'Connor, I sent texts to Glady and Burt inviting them to a breakfast meeting in the morning.

Discussion item: How we prove the unidentified body is Lenrose Sullivan.

Glady sent a thumbs-up emoji. Burt sent two emojis—the thumbs-up and a muffin.

Chapter 23

"First things first," Glady said the next morning after beating Burt to the recliner. "Maureen, have you started—"

"Sorry, old girl," Burt interrupted. "Beat you to it. The first things were Maureen's excellent coffee and my estimable cinnamon apple muffins." He leaned toward her from the settee and ate half a muffin in one bite.

Glady didn't rise to the bait. She did, however, take a second muffin. "Maureen, you asked about my writing, but I haven't asked you. Have you started working on your accidental-pirate picture book?"

"I have a title."

Emrys, sitting at the opposite end of the settee from Burt, swiveled toward me. "Is this true?"

"I haven't had time to put much thought into the story yet."

"A title is a fine place to start," Glady said. "Are you a jinx believer, or would you like to share the title?"

"Hang on." I patted my pockets. No small notebook. "Be right back." I trotted to the bedroom and grabbed the notebook from the bedside chest. "Your question miraculously made a new title jump into my head," I called back into the living room. I scribbled the new title and rejoined them. "The old title was *Lightning Whelks and Lingering Spirits*."

"Atmospheric," Burt said.

Emrys and Glady nodded.

"Also true to life," Emrys said. "What's the new title?"

"The new one is *Alexander Meerkat, Accidental Pirate.*" I watched for their reactions.

"I like the first," Glady said, "but I love the second. More exciting. More kid appeal. Save the other for a ghost story."

Burt agreed by toasting me with his coffee.

"I have to disagree," Emrys said. "Why belittle this Alexander by calling him a mere cat? From my experience, cats don't see themselves as mere anything. More likely they believe they are the lords and ladies of the realm."

"Problem." Burt stared at his phone. "Meerkats weren't discovered until seventeen seventy-six. The Golden Age of Piracy was over by seventeen thirty."

"Not a problem," Glady said. "Beside the fact the book is fiction, meerkats existed long before white men 'discovered' them. If you're going to fuss about their discovery date, you might as well fuss because they don't know how to sail and don't have opposable thumbs to hold cutlasses."

"Touché," said Burt.

"Discovered," Emrys murmured. "I look forward to discussing this later."

"One more off-topic question, if you don't mind," I said. "Have you had a chance to come up with a written lease for the building yet?"

"Of course we don't mind, and we have plenty of time to talk about the lease," Glady said. "Just not right now."

"Agreed," Burt said. "We need to get down to the real business. Why do you think we need to prove the unidentified woman is Lenrose? More to the point—"

"Why do you think she *is* Lenrose?" Glady asked.

Burt muscled his way back into the scrum, asking, "And how do you think we can prove it?"

"The note," I said. "The person who left it doesn't just think she's Lenrose. This person knows she is."

"Excellent," Glady said. "Exactly what we thought. Now, how do you plan to find this person?"

The night I met these two, they'd peppered me with questions like this and acted just as skeptical and contrary. To clear my mind? Focus my thinking? If that was their goal, they needed a new schtick. This just made me want to arch my back like Bonny. Maybe spit. But I didn't. I borrowed their technique of not answering questions.

"The Sullivans stopped by the shop yesterday afternoon," I said.

"Old news," Burt said. "Glady saw the car."

"And you didn't come over to drool over it or ask if you could sit in it?"

"I was in the middle of stirring pudding," he said.

"Chocolate pudding," Glady added. "It would have been a tragedy to leave it. As luck would have it, the pudding was spectacular, and we scarfed up every bit."

"Not luck." Burt's nose went in the air. "Total skill. And we weren't supposed to eat it, but we got carried away. I made it to fill éclairs."

"As luck would have it," Glady said, "you have the recipe and can make it again. What's your assessment of the Sullivans, Maureen?"

"Victor, who goes by the nickname Shelly, is used to being in charge," I said. "He's the kind of person who asks questions and then holds up his hand to stop you from answering. Then, when he lets you answer, he looks disappointed in your brainpower."

"All that gleaned from a short visit to a small shell shop?" Burt asked.

Glady held up her hand to Burt. "Trust us, Burt, it doesn't

take any time at all to recognize that type. What else, Maureen?"

I hid a smile. Burt hid his afront in another cup of coffee. "Shelly seemed to think he was a customer with benefits due to his friendship with Allen. He and his wife have been visiting Ocracoke for years. He said he helped Allen get hold of high-end shells that Allen didn't display for the hoi polloi."

"He said that?" Glady asked.

"No, but he wanted me to get that impression. He said he might be interested in negotiating terms for buying those pieces back. That it would mean a great deal to him to have something to remember Allen by. He gave me his card and asked me to pass it along to the powers that be."

"You didn't tell him you're the power?" Burt asked.

"He assumed I wasn't and didn't give me the chance to say otherwise."

"You didn't like him," Glady said.

"I'm keeping an open mind."

"You do that," she said. "You're the power. I'll dislike him for you."

"As the power, you can send him packing if you want," Burt said. "Devil's advocate, though, Maureen. You said they've been coming here for years and he's a friend of Allen's, right? Then—"

"Then why wouldn't Allen have taken one look at this other woman and known she wasn't Lenrose?" Glady asked. "They both came in the shop the day I was here."

"She's got you there, Maureen." Burt smiled at Glady and passed her a muffin.

"Lenrose left the shop pretty soon after they came in yesterday," I said. "Maybe she didn't ever spend as much time in the shop or with Allen. She might not have come in at all on some trips."

"She stayed as long as he did when I saw them," Glady said.

"Maybe, despite acting shocked when you told them that Allen's dead, she already knew. It's not like it wasn't in the papers." But I couldn't help wondering if Kathleen and her friends were right that this woman was their online friend Lenrose. Why wouldn't she be? I looked at Emrys.

He looked back at me and crossed his arms. "That woman is not Lenrose."

I sighed. "I know," I said to Glady and Burt. "It's a stretch but—"

"But there's nothing wrong with a good stretch," Glady said. "Isn't that right, Burt?"

"That's what Mama always said," he agreed.

"Okay." I glanced at Emrys. Arms still crossed. "Here's something else." I told them about the Fig Ladies, their part in finding the body, that Kathleen and I were old friends, and that I'd had lunch with them. "They showed me the inlet where they found the body. They've decided to call themselves the Fig Ladies because all the best teams of detectives have names."

"What?" Burt said. "A rival trio?"

"Or reinforcements if we work together," I said.

"You obviously haven't heard the old saw about too many sleuths being a crock," Glady said. "Detecting is *our* game."

"It isn't really a game, though," I said.

"Don't play the semantics game with me," Glady countered. "There's another problem with your cockamamie idea. I've thought of a way you could have done it."

"And by *it* you mean . . ."

"Written and delivered the note. And killed Lenrose, for that matter."

"Tate told me yesterday that you convinced him I had nothing to do with it."

"This is news to me," Burt said. "Not that Glady convinced Tate, but that she led him astray."

I started to protest.

He shushed me. "You have to admit, Maureen, you are full of good plans and ideas."

"Exactly," Glady pounced. "Maureen, you could have arrived on the island the same way you did after the hurricane—brought by a boat or boats unknown. You could have whacked Lenrose and departed the same way, but not before you wrote the note, slipped into the Moon Shell in the dark of night, and left it on the desk for me to find."

"Why would I kill Lenrose and then identify her?"

"Whacker's remorse," Burt said.

"Guys, you're making me feel sick. If I agree I could have done all that, but assure you I didn't, can we move on?"

Glady and Burt looked at each other, shrugged, and nodded.

"I agree that coordinating among six people might be hard," I said.

"Correction," Emrys said. "Seven."

I briefly closed my eyes. "But hard or not, there's a woman on the island passing herself off as Lenrose and—"

"If she isn't Lenrose," Glady said, "is *he* Lenrose's husband?"

"Good one, Glad," said Burt.

"It is," I said. "That's why the Fig Ladies should be helpful." I told them about Lenrose's supposed dementia and why the women had come to Ocracoke.

"Let me get this straight," Glady said. "They know Lenrose, and they found the body, but they didn't identify her for Rob Tate?"

"They might not have seen her face," Burt said.

"But don't you think it sounds fishy?" Glady asked.

"They only knew Lenrose online. None of them had met in person before this trip," I said. "But they've chatted back and forth on Facebook for years."

"Facebook implies they know her face," Burt said.

"Nothing fishy," Emrys said. "Crabs. The crabs in the inlet were . . . hungry. To be completely accurate, the crabs found Lenrose before the crows."

Feeling even sicker, I asked Glady and Burt if there were crabs in the tidal inlets. Glady didn't answer, but she looked at the muffin in her hand and put it back on her plate.

"Well," Burt said. "That's—" He got up abruptly. "We'll leave it to you then, Maureen, to break the seafood news to your Fig Ladies."

"Burt Weaver." Glady stamped her foot. "Enough."

After they left, I told Emrys I was inviting the Fig Ladies for lunch. "Lunch with an ulterior motive. We'll see how their investigation is going and let them know our suspicions."

"Judging by how green Glady and Burt turned," Emrys said, "perhaps you should wait until after lunch to tell the Fig Ladies about the hungry crabs."

Chapter 24

The storeroom had plenty of room to set up a folding table for lunch—after rearranging Allen's boxes of who know what. I had plenty of time before opening the shop, though, so I set to work. I peeked in a few of the boxes and found the kind of stuff that Jeff used to keep in our basement (that were still in our basement) in case he needed it. I didn't judge. I had boxes like that, too.

"Watching you work so hard moving boxes reminds me of moving all those chests from the *Nuestra Señora de Guadalupe*," Emrys said. He'd perched himself on the top chair in a stack or six of them in the corner. Seeing him there reminded me of something but I couldn't think what. There were two more stacks beside his. I'd put three of the chairs on the porch the other day but that still left an amazing number.

"Why did Allen have so many chairs?"

"He lined them up along the street so people could watch the Pirate Jamboree golf-cart parade in comfort," he said. "It was really very good of you to arrange for the Fig Ladies to come here so that I can get to know them. It's a shame that I can't join you in your sleuthing around town. I'd be greatly obliged, though, if you conduct as much of the investigation here as possible."

The table was a cumbersome thing to move and unfold by myself. It was dusty, too. I stopped wiping it to wipe my forehead and respond to Emrys. "You do leave the shop, though."

"I do. I used to leave more frequently. Of late, I've left only when urgency requires it."

"You go to the library."

"The library is a pleasant distance, and I go out of habit," he said.

"That reminds me. When I was here last month, I said I'd take some Nero Wolfe books out of the library for you. I still need to do that."

"He's the detective who never leaves home?"

"He does on rare occasions."

"The kind of man I am. I'm sure I'll like the books."

"But you could try sleuthing around town."

"I don't think so," he said. "I'd rather not wander about."

"Why not?"

"See if you feel like wandering when you've been dead three hundred years."

"Okay, I have a question then." I dusted chairs and put them around the table while I thought how to phrase it. "Have you noticed a change in how you feel over the years? Living people tend to be less active as they age. They slow down. Do you think your energy—whatever energy you consist of—has weakened over time?"

"In some cases I've gotten stronger." He took his pen from one of his pockets. "Look at me twirling my pen like a champ. But gadding about is different. I'm more comfortable with my focus on the shell and the shop, and the obituaries at the library. I don't know what will happen if my focus becomes too scattered."

"You're afraid—"

"If you want to put it that way," he said with a sniff.

"I didn't mean to insult you. I hadn't finished my thought—

my *clumsy* thought. Are you worried that you might . . . disappear? That you might cease to exist if you lose your focus?" I saw it in his eyes. He *was* afraid.

"If I were to disappear—" He spoke so quietly that I moved closer. "If I . . . cease, where would I go? Would it be to Heaven? Do I dare take that chance?"

He didn't disappear, but he slipped from the stack of chairs and shimmered through the door to the display case with his shell. And I was left wondering how to reassure a ghost who was afraid of dying.

Glady came in through the shop's front door at the same time the Fig Ladies came in through the back. I'd told Katheen she should have an easy time driving her chair in that way. The ladies had kindly stopped along the way to pick up the sandwiches, chips, and drinks I'd ordered from the Ocracoke Variety Store. Glady jumped at the chance to cover the shop when I told her who was coming to lunch. I felt confident she'd find reasons to visit the storeroom while the Fig Ladies were there. My bet was on Burt making an appearance, too.

"We want a quick tour of the shop before lunch," Paula said. "If I don't find enough good shells on the beach, I'll come back and buy some, and no one will know the difference."

"They will if you don't buy the right kind." Roberta picked up a starfish. "Not this one."

"The North Carolina shells are labeled and displayed next to each other," I said. "Under the window straight ahead of you."

Roberta glanced around the shop, her eyes dancing past the starfish she'd replaced and all the other shells. "This is like having a new house to decorate."

"Roberta's a perpetual paint-slinger," Kathleen said. "How many times have you repainted your living room in the past ten years?"

"More times than I've been married."

Glady caught my eye and tapped her wrist. I nodded.

"Ladies, I'd like you to meet Glady." Bonny, not to be left out, leapt onto the sales desk. "And this is Bonny. Glady and Bonny, these are the Fig Ladies, Kathleen, Roberta, and Paula. Glady kindly gave up her lunch hour for us, so—"

"So, let's eat," Paula said. "Nice to meet you, Glady." She led the way back to the storeroom. I stayed behind to let Glady know there was a sandwich for her, too, if she wanted one. "There's egg salad and chicken salad. Come help yourself. Take one for Burt, too."

"Already did." She lifted two plates from behind the sales desk.

Emrys saluted me from the top of the taller stack of chairs when I joined the Fig Ladies. They each had a sandwich, and Roberta was pouring drinks. I grabbed an egg salad and sat across from Kathleen.

"I'm so happy for you," Kathleen said. "The shop is shell heaven."

Emrys chuckled.

"Someone in the Ocracoke Variety Store said there's a great big shell here, with carving on it, and I forgot to look for it," Paula said. "And it's called the murder shell? Why would you call it that?"

"The *what*?" Emrys leapt from the chair stack to stand at the end of the table, fists on his hips.

"I don't and it's not," I said.

"Whoo-oo-oo." Roberta shivered her hands like she was scared. "The murder shell."

"Let's not call it that," I said. "It's disrespectful to the artist and demeaning to the piece of art. The shop gets its name from the shell. It's called the moon shell. You can see it before you leave, but while we eat, I'd like to hear how your investigation is going."

Emrys bowed and returned to the stacked chairs.

The door between the storeroom and the shop opened. Glady stuck her head in, and the rest of her followed. "Sorry to interrupt. Don't mind me." She tiptoed over to the stockpile of paper bags. And puttered.

"We've talked to people living or renting along our road," Kathleen said. "We planned to be cagey and casual about it, but the body is all anyone wanted to talk about."

"What did they learn?" Emrys asked.

"We learned zip," Paula said, startling Emrys. "No one noticed, saw, or heard anything unusual in the days before we found her. Do you know how hard it is to investigate a crime when you start with so few facts?"

The bell over the shop door jingled. Glady cocked her head. Burt's voice came to us, greeting the customers. Glady took a two-inch stack of the smallest bags.

"The smell," Roberta said. "They noticed that. And we might not have many facts, but we have a theory."

At the word *theory*, Glady replaced the stack of bags she'd taken, chose the next larger size, and took a stack of those. On her way out, she left the door ajar.

"We have a theory and the skills," Paula said. "We all read mysteries and domestic suspense, and I read true crime. That has to count for something."

"But they don't—" Roberta tried to cut in only to be rolled over by Kathleen.

"You listen to podcasts, too, Paula," Kathleen said. "All that info about tracking down bad guys is working in the background up there in your head while you go about your day."

"I can't take this. Waving the white flag here." Roberta twirled her napkin over her head. "The mysteries you two read and the podcasts don't amount to a hill of—who's this?"

Burt bumped the door farther open with his shoulder. "Afternoon. Sorry to intrude. Were you about to say a hill of figs?" He twinkled his eyes at Roberta.

"Ladies, this is Burt, Glady's brother." I introduced the women to Burt. "Anything I can do for you?"

"Nah." He held up a familiar stack of bags. "Glady didn't need these. I'll just put them back. A pleasure to meet you, ladies."

"I would like to hear their theory," Emrys said. "You should bring your meeting to order."

"What matters," Roberta was saying, "is that we don't just look at this case, we need to actually see it."

"Really?" Paula said. "You pooh-pooh books and podcasts and then trot that out? You got *don't look, see* from the Internet."

Kathleen looked across the table at me. Suppressing a laugh she said, "I see someone itching to get a word in."

"By all means," Roberta said. "You have your say, Maureen. I'll have another sandwich."

"I will, too, if you don't mind," Burt said. He took the last egg salad and moseyed back to the shop, leaving the door open farther than Glady had.

"I'd like to hear your theory first," I said.

"It isn't earth shaking, but we like its simplicity," Kathleen said.

"Because in the end, so many crimes have a simple solution," Paula said.

"Which people fail to *see* because all they do is *look*. And fail to listen." Roberta said that to her sandwich.

"We think the police haven't identified the woman because no one knows she's missing," Kathleen said.

"A most excellent theory," Emrys said, "because it's true."

"It is." We nodded at each other.

"What is?" Kathleen asked.

"Sorry. Thinking aloud," I said. "Your theory dovetails nicely with ours."

"After more thought," Emrys said, "I believe their theory is more of a hypothesis than ours."

"Who is part of this 'ours'?" Paula asked.

Ah, I hadn't told them about our rival trio. "Hang on." I got up and closed the door. "I'll explain that, but let me tell you the theory. We think we know who's missing and why no one has identified her. 'We' is Glady, Burt, and me. We helped solve the last murder on the island, so we're—"

"Pumping us for what we've found out so you'll get all the credit," Paula said.

"No." I sat forward. "No, we don't care about getting credit. We didn't claim any last time. We think it would be good for the six of us to work together."

"Let me get this straight," Roberta said. "You've been on the island for how many days?"

"Two whole days and part—"

"And you've known about the body for how long, and you know more than the police?" Roberta said all that in a rush and then took a quick breath. I started to open my mouth, but she rushed on. "Have you told the police?"

"Yes. They don't believe us."

"I admire your calm while they yawp their disbelief," Emrys said. "I also admire their passion. Harness calm and passion, and our company of detectives will be invincible."

My admirable calm let me ignore his hyperbole. I checked the time. Not much left. "The police don't believe us because they don't believe this woman is missing. We're fairly certain we know who she—"

"Completely certain," Emrys said.

"Correction. We're almost completely certain we know who she is."

"You're hedging," Kathleen said, "but I recognize that look on your face. You're more than *almost* completely certain."

"We are. I'll tell you her name. It might be hard to hear, but if you can hold off on questions, I'll explain what we know, and what questions we still have."

Kathleen and Paula agreed. Roberta shrugged a *whatever.*

"We think she's your friend Lenrose. A person, a witness of sorts, wrote a note—"

That was as far as I got. They'd gone completely silent, maybe hadn't breathed after I said Lenrose's name. Then they couldn't help themselves, and I couldn't blame them. I rested my chin on my clasped hands, staring at the table, until they wound down.

"The police know about the note?" Kathleen asked.

"They have it." I told them how Glady found it, that Captain Tate came to get it. Our evidence was really shockingly thin. "When you found her, you didn't see the woman's face, did you?"

Paula had tears in her eyes. "She was face down."

"This is a lot to think about," Kathleen said.

"It's a lot of bull." Roberta got up and started snatching up the used paper plates and napkins. "Where's the trash?" When I told her I'd clean up, she grabbed her purse and stormed out the back door. Paula followed her.

"I'm sorry, Kathleen."

"It's just a lot," Kathleen said again. "I'll text you later. Maybe tomorrow."

"The Fig Ladies weren't ready for such a weighty revelation," Emrys said. "I like them, though. I realize, now, that I met them at the inlet. They did not meet me, of course. They were respectful of Lenrose when they found her body."

I sat for another minute or two and then cleaned up and went back to work. Glady and Burt were alone in the shop, their eyebrows asking questions before they opened their mouths.

"Postmortem on that 'meeting,'" Glady said, putting air quotes around *meeting.* "They aren't serious detectives. They like the idea of it but aren't ready to do the necessary work. If they were, they would have made more progress."

"It's giving them something to bond over," I said. "Something to think about instead of their poor friend who's beginning to forget them. And then I told them she's dead. Real nice."

"Don't beat yourself up over it," Burt said.

"Burt's right. Not worth it," Glady said. "Worry more about the undercurrents."

"What undercurrents?" I asked.

"Unsure. I felt them when they were in the shop," she said. "That's why I came into the storeroom. To get a better read on them. And why I sent Burt in."

"To be blunt," Burt said, "we're suspicious of your Fig Ladies' motives."

"Is that the same as being suspicious of the ladies themselves?" I asked.

"It's best we don't get too philosophical," he said.

"Friction. That's what I felt," Glady said. "The friction between a match and a matchbox. Let's hope it doesn't lead to this." She struck an invisible match. "Whoosh."

Chapter 25

Thank goodness Coquina Ochoa, in a turquoise tutu, whooshed into the shop that afternoon. From the starfish dancing on her headband to her pink sequined sneakers, she sparkled—her eyes most of all. Thoughts of malevolent undercurrents, which had been dragging me down, evaporated as Coquina pranced around me.

"We're here for our job interview," she said. "How much will you pay us?"

Yanira, a grown-up though less sparkly and twirly version of her daughter, came in behind her. "Niña, have you forgotten?"

"No, Mami, I was waiting for you so you could hear how polite I am." Coquina came to a standstill in front of me and clasped her hands at her waist. "Welcome back. I'm very happy to see you again. Hey, Maureen, did you see my shoes?"

I crouched for a better look. "They're so cool. Can I touch the sequins?"

"Sure."

I stroked the toe of her right shoe. "Super cool. Did you know I have a pink life jacket?"

"With sequins?"

"No."

"Because, if it did, I would be overjoyed." She grinned. "Do you know what trapezoids and rhomboids are?"

"Shapes?"

"And they're *oid* words just like *overjoyed*. Where's Bonny?"

"At lunchtime, she tried to get a bite of Glady's sandwich, which was cuboid in shape. Now she might be taking a nap in the office."

"Let Bonny have her nap," Yanira said. "She already works here. You and I are having a job interview to see if we will, too."

"I really only have two questions for you, Yanira, and one for you, Coquina."

"Me first!" With a quick look at her mother, Coquina added more calmly, "Please, Miss Maureen."

"Coquina, I know that you like shells, and you like this store, but will you jump at the chance to work here?"

"Cuboid!" Coquina shouted and jumped straight up in the air.

"Very persuasive. Thank you. Yanira, your questions are straightforward, too. Are you comfortable using an electronic cash register, and what kind of hours would you like to work?"

"If cuboid now means yes, then to answer your first question, cuboid," Yanira said with a laugh. "If I can keep school-year hours to two weekday afternoons and one weekend day, and still be helpful to you, that would be great. For summer, I'd like as many as you can give me."

"Sounds like a deal to me," I said. "Yanira, Coquina, consider yourselves em*ployed*." At that, Coquina whooped and then whooshed outside to celebrate.

"Don't worry about that one," Yanira said. "She'll use her school manners when she's here, or she won't stay employed for long. Thank you, though, for letting me bring her. I'm having a hard time letting her out of my sight since last month. Since your quick thinking."

I shook my head. "If I'd been quicker I would have sent Coquina back to Glady's as soon as she showed up." Glady and

Burt had been watching Coquina the afternoon a killer came calling at the Moon Shell.

"All's shell that ends shell," Emrys said, shimmering into view in the office doorway. "Am I to believe the shrill child will spend more time here than ever before?"

"Would you like us to come Saturday so I can shadow you?" Yanira asked.

"Yes," I said with a smile for both. "I can hardly wait."

Coquina swirled back in with two women in tow. "We have customers, Maureen." She turned to the bemused customers and, with her hands again clasped at her waist, asked, "Are you looking for pretty shells, North Carolina shells, ovoid shells, or pointy shells?"

"Niña," Yanira called gently, "also ask if they prefer browsing on their own."

Solemnly asked, the customers assured Coquina they'd like the guided tour. Emrys paced behind like a spectral schoolmaster; even he was impressed by Coquina's calm and accurate descriptions of the shells she pointed out. As one of the pair paid for the shells they'd chosen, the other sidled over to Yanira.

"Can she accept a tip for her excellent guidance?"

"You're very kind," Yanira said, "but no."

"A compliment then?" At Yanira's nod, the woman said, "Coquina, you are a star, and you will go far."

"Thank you," Coquina said. "But I'm a star*fish*."

As Yanira and I settled on a time for Saturday, and the starfish discovered Bonny napping on the office chair, Shelly arrived. I tensed and then relaxed. His smile actually looked like a smile instead of the condescending thing he'd allowed himself the day before.

"Afternoon, Maureen," he said. "Beautiful day, isn't it?"

Coquina appeared in the office door, her face lit with curiosity and then with recognition. "Hi, Shelly." She ran over to him. "Do you remember me? I gave you your nickname."

The actual smile faded, and Shelly started coughing. "Sorry," he rasped. "Swallowed something."

"Would you like water?" Coquina asked.

"No." He pulled his phone out, looked at it, and shook his head. "I'd better handle this," he said and left.

"You met him here, Coquina?" I asked

"He came to visit Mr. Allen sometimes. Mr. Allen called him Sully, but I changed it to Shelly because all he talks about is shells."

"Did you meet Shelly's wife, too?" I asked.

"I don't think so." She sighed dramatically. "It's too bad he still doesn't like children."

"It's too bad he only pretended to get an important text," Emrys said.

I got an important text that evening from Kathleen. Important because, in the way of blowing mistakes out of proportion, I'd been afraid I wouldn't get to see her or talk to her again before she left the island. Also important because she said the Fig Ladies had a few things to tell us and wanted to meet with Glady, Burt, and me. Rather than text that to Glady and Burt, I went across the street and knocked on their door. I wanted to tell them when I could hear what they had to say and see if their faces agreed with it.

"It's a pleasant evening. We'll step out on the porch," Glady said, pulling her sweater around her and shivering in the gusting wind that threatened to spit rain any minute. "Burt's making his usual mess inside."

"Ships in bottles?" I asked.

"Possibly," he said.

"Kathleen says the Fig Ladies have a few things to tell us and they'd like to meet with us. What do you think? Reasonable? Safe? Invite them for breakfast at the Moon Shell tomorrow? Skip it and go our own way?"

"Your mind's a ping-pong ball this evening, Maureen," Burt said.

"It feels like it. Here's another ping. Shelly came into the shop this afternoon while Yanira and Coquina were there." I told them about Shelly's reaction to Coquina's cheery greeting. "Lenrose wasn't with him. Coquina says she doesn't remember ever meeting her."

"That little button doesn't miss much," Glady said. "Not that she's in the shop twenty-four–seven. What do you think about meeting with the Figs, Burt?"

"Keep your enemies close?" Burt's answer came with a bit of a smile, but his eyebrows quirked in question.

"I'm not sure we should think of them as enemies," I said.

"You're right, Maureen," said Glady. "Go ahead and invite them for breakfast. The few things they've thought of might help us out." Her smile was a tad bigger.

"Good. I'll text Kathleen."

"And how about this?" Glady threw in. "You smile. I'll bring the bat."

In the morning, Glady actually brought the bat.

Chapter 26

The first joint meeting of the detecting trios started out not with the crack of a bat but with a simper. Glady did bring the bat, but she leaned it against the wall where (I hoped) it would go unnoticed and stay. It was within easy reach of where she planned to sit, though. She staked her claim at the head of the table by draping her sweater on the chair. Burt shucked out of the flannel shirt he'd worn over his usual T-shirt and used it to claim the foot of the table. They'd arrived early, which meant the Fig Ladies missed Glady's practice swings with the bat. Glady brought the simper, too, and kept it plastered to her face throughout the meeting, as lethal or more so than the bat. Burt brought muffins.

"I hustled this morning," he said. "To get the muffins in and out of the oven in time to hustle Glady across the street. We wanted to be here before the Figgity-do-dahs."

"Gives us the home-turf advantage," Glady said.

Their attitudes weren't making me feel optimistic for the meeting's outcome. Burt's muffins tended to soothe my wild nerves, though. "What kind of muffins this morning, Burt?"

"Just a simple recipe I tossed together so I could double it and have enough for everyone. Maybe send some home with our guests, too. A little peace offering after you upset them so yesterday. Are the Fig-diddly-squats bringing juice?"

"Yep, and I've got the coffee." Why Allen had two insulated carafes in the kitchen upstairs, I didn't know, but maybe he'd had interesting meetings in the storeroom, too. "Burt, how about we lay off fiddling around with their name? At least while they're here."

"Did you say figgling around?" Glady asked.

"Please?"

They agreed, though when the ladies knocked on the back door, and Burt went to let them in, I was pretty sure I heard him softly singing, "Fee, fi, figgly-i-o."

Emrys shimmered into view on top of the stack of chairs, and I suddenly realized what he looked like up there. A lifeguard—in fancy dress.

Paula had also been up early baking. "Just to be sure there are plenty of muffins to go around." She set a plastic container on the table. "Nothing fancy. Just muffins with a half cup of fig preserves in the batter to honor being here in Ocracoke." She took the lid off, revealing muffins as pale as I am by the end of winter.

"They look scrumptious," Glady simpered. "Who knew a half cup would be enough to give the real flavor of figs."

Burt opened his box, half again as large as Paula's. "Rye, apple, fig muffins with cheddar."

We all leaned forward and inhaled. Burt's muffins sounded, looked, and smelled divine.

Glady looked from the pale muffins to their gorgeous brown counterparts and back again. She and her simper seemed to be enjoying the prospect of dueling muffins. "Take your seats, everyone," she said. "And let's get going, shall we?"

I took the chair next to Kathleen. While the others dragged their chairs out, sat, and then scraped them forward, I leaned over to her and whispered, "Wish us luck. Here goes nothing."

We passed the muffins, poured coffee and juice, and I watched Roberta watching Glady. As soon as Glady took a bite of pale muffin, Roberta pounced.

"We're happy you agreed to meet with us this morning. We'd like to start by introducing ourselves properly so that you understand us better."

Glady swallowed wrong and coughed through Roberta repeating their names. By the time Glady recovered, Roberta had summarized their careers (Paula: data manager for a supportive housing organization, Roberta: retired English professor, Kathleen: former bookseller) and turned the floor over to Kathleen.

"We'd like you to know our strengths," Kathleen said. "Paula, with her data-oriented mind, is the Fig Ladies' recorder. Roberta is our eagle-eye. She's the one who first noticed that Lenrose's messages had changed."

"Which one are you, Kathleen?" I asked.

"I'm the Foremost Fig because I've grown figs the longest."

"She's the levelheaded one," Paula said. "Good in dire situations such as, oh, say, finding dead bodies."

"Or the most harebrained," Kathleen said, "because who goes looking for dead bodies?"

Glady (simper redoubled), Burt, Emrys, and I raised our hands.

"Fablious," Kathleen said. "We're in good company."

"We talked over your theory about Lenrose," Paula said. "And we have a major question. If the woman isn't Lenrose, is the man with her Victor?"

"I like that question," Glady said. "The matter-of-fact way you asked it implies you're open to the idea of a fake Lenrose. We can answer it, too. Maureen?"

"He *is* Victor Sullivan. He goes by the nickname Shelly, by the way. A witness recognized him when he came into the shop yesterday afternoon."

"Credible?" Roberta asked.

"Unimpeachable," I said. "She knew him immediately. She's the one who gave him the nickname."

"We know that raises more questions," Burt said. "We don't have the answers to them."

"Yet," Glady said. "Now the ball is yours. What few things did you come to tell us?" She sounded mobbish to my ears, but she took another pale muffin and didn't look at the bat.

"We've come up with a few reasons why we *might* believe we haven't been talking to the real Lenrose," Roberta said. "There are little things that don't add up."

Burt nodded. "They wouldn't be able to carry it off if big things didn't add up."

"Right," Kathleen said. "One thing is that we know they've been to Ocracoke before, but Lenrose always wanted to be here for the Fig Festival, and that never worked out. But last night we remembered that when we saw them at the beach—what day was that?"

"Wednesday morning," Paula said.

"She told us she loved the Fig Festival," Kathleen said.

"We don't think that's the kind of thing Lenrose would be confused about," Roberta said.

"It's possible, though, isn't it?" I asked. "If she has good days and bad?"

"Sure," Kathleen said. "Or she could have meant that she loves the *idea* of the festival."

"That's one thing you've told us," Glady said. "What else have you got?"

"The wrong shoes," Roberta said. "I need more coffee." She held her coffee cup out. Paula refilled it and Roberta continued. "The current Lenrose wears sandals with heels. The Lenrose we know would never."

"You only know her online," I said. "How can you be sure?"

"We like to say we're all figs all the time, but we do talk about other things," Roberta said.

"For instance," Paula said, "I took a trip to Portugal a year and a half ago. When I posted pictures of the fig farm we visited outside of Lisbon, Lenrose zeroed in on the fact I was wearing flip-flops, and the woman next to me wore little white tennies."

"Oh my God, yes," Roberta said. "She would not stop talking about 'appropriate footwear.'"

"Her feet bothered her," Kathleen explained. "She said she'd never take a three-hour tour of anywhere without wearing sturdy walking shoes."

"These are excellent pieces of information," Burt said. "Not definitive but—"

"But it's the little pieces that add up," Paula said.

"A question for you then," Glady said. "And I'm sorry to bring this up. I'm sure finding the body was a terrible experience. The vines shrouding her, how do you know they were honeysuckle?"

"Once upon a time I earned my Master Gardener certificate," Kathleen said. "I recognized it as a type of honeysuckle."

"I see what you're getting at, Glad," Burt said. "Where did the honeysuckle come from?"

"Not right there in the woods?" Roberta asked.

He shook his head. "More likely from a yard."

"Tate or the deputies must have thought of this and looked for areas of recently cut honeysuckle," I said. "I wonder what they've found."

"If someone cleared it out of their yard, where would they put it?" Kathleen asked. "Compost bin? Burn pile? And how easy would it be for someone else to come along and take it away?"

"Anyone cutting it or taking it with the intent of shrouding a body probably wasn't doing it openly," Roberta said.

"Here's another question and then a worry," I said. "Did

Shelly kill Lenrose, or did Fake Lenrose do it? Or the two of them together? Or did one kill her and the other hide the body? The worry is this—we need to figure this out fast. If Shelly and Fake Lenrose are guilty, they could leave the island any time and disappear."

"Why haven't they left already?" Paula asked. "In fact, that leads us to one more thing to tell you." She looked at Roberta and Kathleen, who nodded at her. "We propose that we find out where they're staying, and then we go there to look for clues."

"Inside," Roberta clarified.

I'd just swigged the last of my coffee and almost spit it across the table. While I sat goggled-eyed, Glady and Burt agreed it was a great idea.

"No, it isn't," I said. "Do you even hear what you're agreeing to?"

"Pay no attention to her," Glady assured the Fig Ladies. "Maureen has her head too screwed on for her own good sometimes. I make a motion to explore this avenue of investigation. Do I hear a second?"

Paula and Emrys seconded.

"All in favor?" Roberta asked.

The motion carried six to one, after which Kathleen said, "Good meeting. Very productive. I'd like to make one more proposal—if we're jamming our sleuthing trios together, then why don't we call our new team the Fig Jams?"

Glady made a motion to accept the new name. Burt seconded the motion, and everyone who wasn't still sitting there in shock wondering how she would keep her friends from getting into serious trouble—or worse—voted in favor.

Six people cleaning up after the meeting made short work despite the one in a daze. When the Fig Lady half of the Fig Jams took its leave, Glady and Burt argued over who decided first that the Fig Ladies were all right. Burt insisted he had, because he and Paula bonded over muffin recipes. Glady said she had as soon as she realized the friction she'd sensed the day before arose from their worries about Lenrose.

"But never fear," she said, eyes gleaming, "I'll see what I can do to ease their minds."

Chapter 27

" 'By the pricking of my thumbs,' " Emrys intoned as he drifted back through the closed front door, " 'something wicked this way comes.' "

I had customers and couldn't ask him what *MacBeth* had to do with the ruckus of crows he'd drifted out onto the porch to investigate. Unless he was talking about himself? Probably not. He had a more than healthy opinion of himself.

Emrys leaned suavely against the glass case. "To be less cryptic, someone we assume is wicked has parked his great, shiny car in front of the shop."

Oh? I looked up from wrapping sand dollars as the door opened and Shelly walked in. Three days in a row. What an honor. So far an empty honor, as he hadn't spent a penny. The customers before me *were* spending a pretty penny, so I returned my attention to them.

Shelly browsed, along with a few other customers, acting more interested in general run-of-the-mill shells than seemed necessary. If there'd been a "Browser with the Most Staying Power Award," he'd have won it hands down. He'd made his way around the room to the glass case and was gazing in at the cameo shell when the door closed behind a group of satisfied, shell-laden customers. At least for the moment, we were alone. Except for Emrys.

Shelly must have been keeping track of the other customers, too. Without looking away from the shell, he said, "You didn't tell me that you now own the Moon Shell."

"I'm still getting used to the idea," I said.

He made a noise I chose to hear as noncommittal. I didn't know him well enough to slot it into the disbelief column. He moved around the corner of the case and bent to look at the cameo from that angle. Emrys, on the opposite side, bent to look at Shelly.

"A vein near his left eye twitches," Emrys said. "Both eyes are as predatory as Mrs. Bundy's."

Shelly snapped his fingers. "I knew there was something different about the moon shell." He straightened and looked at me. "Why is the velvet missing?"

"An accident of sorts. It didn't survive getting soaked in Pamlico Sound. The silk is pretty too, though, don't you think?"

"Soaked in the *sound*? My wife gave that velvet to Allen. It was a remnant from the last quilt she was able to finish. What kind of accident? It sounds unbelievably careless."

Emrys stepped closer to Shelly. "The twitch has more life than I do."

At least I hadn't said the silk was an improvement over the too-showy velvet. "It was an unfortunate accident associated with Allen's death. I'm so sorry."

Shelly closed his eyes.

Emrys, still very much in Shelly's face, studied those closed eyes. "I would feel more sympathy if I knew the source of his distress. Is it Allen's death? The lost velvet of midnight blue? The wife no longer plagued by this mortal coil? Or is it, perhaps, the wife impatient in the car outside?"

"Is Lenrose outside in the car?" I asked.

"Indeed," Emrys said.

With a ragged sigh, Shelly opened his eyes. "She is. She feels safe there. Not that she doesn't love being here on the island.

But the car is familiar. She probably doesn't remember giving Allen the velvet. She never mentions quilting anymore. We're moving soon after we leave Ocracoke. I'll look through her fabric stash before I donate it to the senior center. If I find any more of the velvet, I'll send it to you."

"You're very kind, but don't do it if it's too painful." I wanted to be brusque and unfeeling but couldn't. An obvious failing when dealing with a killer. But either he'd lost his wife—okay, cruelly murdered her—or he was losing her to the cruelty of dementia. Either way, she was gone and at some point he'd loved her. Couldn't a half-baked sleuth show at least a sliver of empathy for the bad guy's grief? Sleuth life—very confusing.

I snapped from empathy mode to heightened wariness mode when he came to the sales desk holding out his phone.

"I'd like to show you a few pictures."

"Sure. Why don't you scroll through them so I don't smudge your screen?" I rubbed my fingertips with my thumbs. "Olive oil lotion is not your screen's friend." Possibly true, but as I'd never used olive oil lotion, I couldn't vouch for it. And I sure didn't want my fingerprints on his phone.

Shelly didn't bat an eye, so maybe I was now flirting with paranoia mode. He held the phone so we could both see it and scrolled through several photos of elaborate and froufrou antique shell art. The kind most people only see in coffee-table books or online. Or in the Moon Shell's office safe and attic.

"Beautiful stuff," I said.

"Did you know Allen?"

"No."

"A shame. I'm sure you wish you had." Another sigh, this one not ragged and not especially convincing. "Allen promised to show me the pieces in these photographs, or pieces like them, when I stopped by this trip. The business is all new to you, but I wonder if you know the inventory well enough to say whether the pieces are still here?"

"The business is new to me but I'm a quick study. Believe me, if anything like those pieces was in the inventory, I'd be overjoyed."

Shelly's eyebrows rose and then fell in quick doubt, and his eyes, in cahoots, strayed toward the door to the upstairs apartment. As quickly, he changed the subject.

"I've always known how much Lenrose loves figs, but I had no idea her online group was such a major part of her life. These friends of hers—they call themselves the Fig Ladies?"

"That's what I've heard."

"They seem to think she's been wrapped up in their online group. I have to wonder about them, though. They came all the way here on a whim to see Lenrose? For what purpose?" He shook his head. "It's hard enough losing my wife little by little. Now here they are like three crows watching and waiting. Well." He looked around as though remembering where he was. "I do wonder about these women. Maybe you should wonder, too."

Emrys paced back and forth after Shelly left. "He likened the Fig Ladies to crows in a most uncomplimentary way. He mentions his wife as though he holds her dear. He makes inuendoes and, I daresay, he lies about Allen's promises. But even if he's a villain and he killed Lenrose, at least he knows what became of her and where he left her body. Or if we're wrong about his guilt? Then one day, if he's unlucky enough to lose her to a natural death, I would still count him as lucky to know how her life came to an end and where she's buried."

"And you don't know either about your wife."

"No."

"Emrys, my trip here from Tennessee took two days. I stopped overnight in Edenton."

He stood still but didn't look at me.

"In the morning, before I got back on the road, I went to Saint Paul's Episcopal Church. As far as I could tell, it's the oldest church in Edenton."

"Angharad—did I tell you my wife's name?"

I shook my head.

"Angharad, and I attended Saint Paul's."

"The churchyard is quiet and peaceful. It feels protected, like a place outside of time. It has massive magnolias. Lots of deep green moss, and brick pathways, and the smell of bay laurel is everywhere. Emrys, I looked for Angharad's grave."

Shelly's ragged sigh had nothing on the ragged breath of the bereaved ghost in front of me. With another, and a shudder, he was gone.

Glady arrived with the next wave of customers. She chatted with some and showed others her favorite shells, then came to lean an elbow on the desk after they'd paid and left.

"I saw Shelly and the Fake Lenrose here a while ago and came over to make sure you're all right. It seems the neighborly thing to do in times of murder and mayhem."

"He left half an hour ago. I might've exsanguinated."

"Couldn't be helped. It was my turn to make lunch. What did he want?"

I hit the highlights and then told her how Shelly's reaction to the velvet had confused me. "If he killed his wife, would he be so emotional about a scrap of her quilt fabric?"

She thought about that. "Maybe if it was a mercy killing. I could see that."

"But who, in his great mercy, drops his beloved's body in a tidal creek and then tootles around an island paradise with that beloved's lookalike?"

"I think," she said, "that his remark about not knowing the fig group meant so much to her is an admission, and the Fig

Ladies have him worried. He had a plan, and it didn't include them. And we know what that plan is—remove Lenrose and replace her."

"We need to be careful."

"Agreed." Glady nodded. "Like you said this morning, we can't let Shelly and Fake Lenrose leave the island and escape justice."

"I meant we need to be careful while we sleuth so no one else gets removed."

Chapter 28

My bike and I took a jaunt after closing up shop that Friday. Except for the here-again, gone-again pirate ghost, and the murderer sniffing around the treasure buried in my attic, it had been a decent first week in residence. Now I rode to the library, applied for a card, and checked out three Nero Wolfe books for Emrys. After that, the bike, the books, and I took a meandering ride to the shorefront property. I'd graduated from calling it Allen's shorefront property, and maybe someday I'd automatically call it mine. It was still too weird owning a stretch of Pamlico Sound beach to go that far. Though not as weird as borrowing library books for a ghost.

O'Connor had camped on the property when he'd visited the month before. He'd discovered freshly dug holes left by someone looking for actual buried treasure. I lowered the kickstand and hiked to where he'd pitched his tent. I didn't expect new holes and didn't find any. Good.

The narrow beach, with its lapping water and fringe of seaweed along the tide line, felt like the edge of uncharted territory. If I walked that tightrope of sand, one foot balancing in front of the other, what adventures would I meet? Would I fall? But I'd skipped lunch, so adventures had to wait. I plucked a lettered olive shell from the water and turned the bike toward home. Halfway there, I saw Shelly's green and white Kaiser Manhattan, and a different kind of adventure presented itself.

The village speed limit topped out at twenty-five miles per hour. Add to that Friday evening golf-cart traffic as people headed out on the town, or to find the best spot to see the sunset, or to gawk in general—many of them steering erratically as they pointed out the sights to their passengers—and, suffice it to say, the Manhattan moved at a mollusk's pace. So did I, staying well back as good tailers do. It wasn't hard. The Manhattan stuck out like a great white (and green) shark amid a school of clown fish.

We rolled steadily toward Irvin Garrish, the highway into town. Also toward Howard's Pub, which would be a great place to grab supper after such a busy day. Because I wasn't *really* following Shelly and Lenrose, was I? Why would I do a conniving thing like that?

Shelly and Lenrose turned in at the Shell Inn. I braked at the entrance and watched them pull in behind the building. Then I pedaled to the building's back corner and casually looked around that corner in time to see Lenrose use a key card to enter the inn's back door. I debated what to do with that information—and won the debate handily. I sent a quick text to the Fig Jams.

Golf carts lined up outside Howard's Pub like horses tied in front of a cowboy saloon. I locked my bike in case of bike rustlers and moseyed on in. It wasn't really a cowboy bar. Fried fish, the clink of beer bottles, and an exuberance of neon beer signs and old license plates tacked to every upright surface reigned supreme. Aw Shucks and Beak Booper, resplendent in their Hawaiian shirts, splayed themselves at a table near the door. They saw me and waved wildly, Beak Booper with a fry in his hand that broke and flew free. I ignored them. I was about to turn tail and leave when someone else waved at me—Captain Tate.

"Gotta love the Friday night energy," he said. "Are you coming or going?"

"That's something I often don't know. But I think..." I glanced around. "I'll come back on a lower energy night."

"If you like fried fish sandwiches, come on back to the station. Matt's there, and I just picked up enough for four."

"Fries?"

"And hush puppies," he said.

"I'm in."

When I walked into the station with Tate, Matt grinned and dropped a folder on the floor. He retrieved it and I unpacked the food bags. Tate brought two more chairs to the desk. The three of us chitchatted idly as we dug into the sandwiches made with delicious local fish fried to crisp perfection on the outside, piping hot, mild, and tender on the inside. Matt admitted he'd only ever driven past the Moon Shell. I told him he should drop by and I'd give him a tour.

"You need to see the carved shell," Tate said. "The shell's like this." He put his sandwich down and held his hands apart. "And I've never seen anything like the carving."

"I'd like to take up wood carving," Matt said.

Tate gave Matt's cast an exaggerated look. "Is that wise?"

Matt laughed and took the last of the hush puppies.

"I'm glad I ran into you," Tate said to me. "We've had no luck identifying our Jane Doe, and I just released more information to the public. Maybe some of the details we've held back will help give her a name." He wiped his hands and took a piece of paper from an "in" basket on the corner of the desk. "Would you like to hear them?"

"Please."

"She was wearing a necklace but no other jewelry. She wore a yellow scoop-necked T-shirt with embroidered flowers, pastel orange capris, and white tennis shoes. She had no unusual moles or obvious scars. The biggest identifier is the fact she had no teeth. They'd been pulled but not recently. No dentures have been found. That also means no dental records."

White tennis shoes. According to the Fig Ladies, that didn't sound like Lenrose. They'd said nothing about dentures. But would they necessarily know? "What does the necklace look like?"

"Blingy," Matt said. "A gold circle set with imitation jewels. The kind of thing my memaw loves."

Tate was watching my face. "What are you thinking?"

"That with those details, someone ought to recognize her. How far did you search for the dentures?"

"They weren't in the inlet or anywhere near either side of the inlet. We checked all along the access road on the other side of the inlet, too."

I'd seen the narrow path across the inlet but hadn't realized there was an access road. "Will you release pictures of the necklace and clothes?"

"Yes."

"At the risk of sounding like an amateur sleuth, will you send the release and pictures to me, too?"

"Amateur sleuths get the job done," Matt said. At a look from Tate, he added, "In the books, anyway. I've had a lot of time to read lately."

"Just remember to keep it clear in your head the difference between fact and fiction," Tate said.

Matt leaned toward me and whispered, "Fiction's more fun."

Bonny smelled fish on my breath when I got home. Lucky for her, I'd brought a tidbit for her. She licked her lips with appreciative gusto, and I called the boys. Kelly answered almost immediately, as though he'd been wondering when I'd call.

"Hi, Mom. Solved any murders lately?"

"Hmm, not lately. Not yet. Next time there's a body, would you like me to call and leave that fun information in a voicemail?"

"We're both aces at sarcasm, aren't we? Sorry, Mom. O'Connor told me, and then Carter Thomas called me. But you'll notice that I didn't call you to ask what the hel—what the heck is going on because I didn't want you to worry about me being worried."

"Around here we ask what the *shell* is going on. And believe me, if I knew, I'd tell you. What did Carter say?"

"That he'd heard from his mom, and she had a wild story about Ocracoke and a dead body, but, given the kinds of escapades you and she got up to, he wasn't sure he believed it."

"The mundane becomes extramundane in the retelling," I said.

"And you and Kathleen are great at the retellings. *Are* you trying to solve the murder?"

"Kathleen's here with a couple of friends. They have a personal stake in finding out what happened."

"And you?"

"I have more of a personal stake in keeping the others out of trouble."

"Which side is Emrys on?" Kelly asked "The gumshoes or the guard dog? Oh, wait. The answer's obvious. He's on the ghost side."

I laughed. "He'd love answering questions like that himself. Any idea when you might come for a visit?"

"Sometime before Christmas?"

"That would be great."

"Good. Talk to you later, Mom."

My call to O'Connor went to voicemail. I left a message.

Footsteps woke me in the middle of the night. Footsteps downstairs in the shop.

Chapter 29

Stealthy footsteps . . . of two people? Shelly and Lenrose? I groped on the bedside table for my phone. Found it. Fumbled it. And Emrys popped in—his face right in front of my nose. I yipped.

"Two varlets below decks," he growled. "They crept in through the window in the storeroom. They look the very definition of 'beetle-headed, flap-ear'd knave,' and drunken to boot. Shall I repel them?"

"Can you?"

"I shall do my damnedest."

He disappeared without saying he actually could. And if he could, why hadn't he done that to begin with? I called 911.

"Nine-one-one," a calm voice said. "What is your emergency?"

"I'm in Ocracoke, on Howard Street, in the apartment above the Moon Shell. Two people are in the shop downstairs. I think they're drunk and—I can hear them fiddling with—oh geez, they're trying to get in thedoorathebottomofthestairs."

"Ma'am? Will repeat that last part more slowly?"

I did with a few hiccupping breaths.

"I'm sending someone now. Are you sure there are two people?"

"I hear two voices. Maybe men. I can't hear what they're saying." I pulled my shorts and a shirt on over my pajamas.

"That's fine. Is anyone else in the apartment with you?"

Bonny rubbed against my legs. "My cat."

"So, she's safe with you. That's good. How do you know the people are drunk?"

"A good guess." I sat on the floor and put on my shoes.

"Is there another way out of the apartment?"

"No. I can't hear them at the door anymore."

"That's good. Someone will be with you very soon."

"Thank you. What—"

What on *earth?* Something or someone had fallen. Someone babbled. Indistinct shouts and commotion . . .

Armed with one of Allen's gargantuan chef knives, I crept down the stairs and did what no frightened householder or amateur sleuth should ever do—I opened the door a crack. Aw Shucks and Beak Booper in their blaze of Hawaiian shirt glory, cowered near the front door, on the floor, with their arms wrapped around their heads.

Like a scene from *The Birds,* Mrs. Bundy swooped around the shop, zeroing in on them with sharp jabs and thrusts from her beak—thanks to Emrys. He looked like a big kid terrifying smaller ones with a model airplane. He enjoyed it, too. More than he should have? I wasn't going to judge. What he really looked like was a younger brother who'd been at the mercy of older brothers. A younger brother who, after two hundred and seventy-four years, had gotten the upper hand and access to a stuffed seagull with a wicked beak.

Emrys looked around when I stepped into the shop. "A shame they can't hear me laugh," he said, "for 'The robbed that smiles steals something from the thief.'"

"You have fewer brains between you than a single barnacle, and the few you do have you're wasting," I told the bunglers on the floor. "Now you'll have to move away from the door because I see Captain Tate of the Hyde County Sheriff's Department there, and he wants to come in." I showed them the knife.

Tate eyed the knife when I opened the door for him but didn't comment. Then he eyed the cowed men on the floor.

"They were on the floor when I came downstairs," I said. "Except their arms were around their heads." I demonstrated and then decided the knife would be safer on the sales desk.

Aw Shucks and Beak Booper tugged at their shirts as if to smarten themselves up. Aw Shucks went as far as crossing his arms over his chest with a look of affront. "You can't arrest us," he said. "This is a business call."

"Clodpole," Emrys said. "What business?" He'd rehung Mrs. Bundy and held on to one wing tip to keep her still.

"What business would that be?" Tate asked.

"We're investiggers. Investigators," Beak Booper said. "Hired by—"

"Not by me," I said.

"By a distinguished gentleman who shall remain nameless." Beak Booper closed his eyes and swayed where he sat.

"What kind of investigators?" Tate asked.

"Panoramic," Aw Shucks said. "Paranormal. Our distinguished friend is not tall enough to climb through the back window himself."

"Allred," Tate and I said simultaneously.

"Have you seen him around here lately?" Tate asked.

"He came in yesterday for no apparent reason."

"Stop by the station tomorrow and give Matt a statement." Tate pointed at the drunks. "You two. On your feet."

"Not before we lodge a compliment. A complaint against the management," Aw Shucks said. "We were attacked by that seagull."

Tate looked at Mrs. Bundy and then back at the poor sap actually telling the truth. "That bird is dead."

"Still as the grave," Emrys said.

"Must be radio-controlled," Aw Shucks said mulishly. "Or electronic. One of those drones."

Tate, still admirably calm, looked at me.

I mimed drinking and shook my head sadly. "These guys came in the shop Monday. They spent their time looking at the ceiling, and this guy"—I picked up the knife and pointed it at Aw Shucks—"knocked on the apartment door."

"I did not."

"You did. We had a short conversation about it," I said. "You asked if it was true that Allen Withrow had died. And you were trying to get that door open when I called nine-one-one."

"Up," Tate said. "Time to go." He had his back to Mrs. Bundy, so he didn't see her take another swoop courtesy of Emrys.

Aw Shucks and Beak Booper scrambled to their feet and practically dragged Tate out the door.

Burt and Glady showed up before breakfast. Burt let Glady carry a bag with two of his muffins. He carried a fire-escape ladder and showed me how to use it.

"You need another way out of here," he said. "In case of fire or fiends."

"You heard about last night already?"

"Ran into Tate on my sunrise walk."

"And you happened to have a spare escape ladder lying around?"

"I did. Still do."

"He was a volunteer fireman once upon a time," Glady said. "He has a healthy fear of fire. Bought a dozen escape ladders. He'd hand them out to the kiddos on Halloween if I let him." She handed me the muffin bag. "We're going to need your storeroom this morning. The Fig Jams are meeting. If we're going to move fast, we can't sit around. You can duck your head in every once in a while, and we'll keep notes so you don't miss much."

"Oh. I feel left out."

"Not a bit of it." Burt patted my shoulder before heading for the stairs. "If anything goes south with this investigation, you'll get all the credit."

"Did that come out the way he meant it to?" I asked Glady.

"Certainly. You need to learn to take responsibility. You're the ringleader."

Emrys appeared across the table from me while I ate breakfast. I told him about the Fig Jams meeting and asked if he'd sit in and let me know what happened.

"Glady and Burt won't give you a report?"

"I'm sure they will, but sometimes people forget details."

"Or withhold them," he said. "My brothers excelled at that. 'Emrys,' they could easily have said, 'we're turning pirate, and so are you.' That would have been a good detail to share."

"Kind of a critical one."

"Indeed. So, yes, I will attend the meeting. But tell me, what do you think of last night's rapscallions? Should I worry about Doctor Allred sending more paranormal investigators?"

"I'm not sure Allred actually sent them. I'm sure Tate will be speaking to him, though."

"Captain Tate is a good man." Emrys traced curlicues on the table with a finger—an interesting habit to follow him down the many decades since his death. "When you walked in the churchyard in Edenton, did you find my wife's grave?"

"I looked and didn't find any graves with the surname Lloyd on them. That doesn't mean Angharad isn't buried there. The churchyard dates to 1722, but according to what I read, a lot of the early graves were marked with wooden or brick markers that didn't last. They know of more than seven hundred unmarked graves."

"She might have remarried and gone to live elsewhere. And had a good life. I could wish no less for her." He was quiet for a moment. "Any man would have been lucky to receive the favor of her love."

The Fig Jams arrived midway through the morning, coming in the back door. Glady and Burt came through the front. The meeting got underway shortly after, although Kathleen snuck out and came to say hi.

"Don't let them get carried away in there," I said.

"That ship's already been carried away on a wave of alarming ideas."

My heart lurched. "How dangerous?"

"Only to sensitive palates," she said. "Paula and Burt are one-upping each other with wild ideas for fig recipes. I'd better get back in there before the real discussion starts."

"What's on the agenda?"

"Not sure," Kathleen said. "It's probably safe enough, though. Glady called the meeting."

That didn't make me any less antsy. Neither did seeing Fake Lenrose walk into the shop. She arrived not long after Kathleen rejoined the meeting. I smiled and reminded myself not to call her Fake Lenrose. "Good to see you again," I said and looked toward the door, expecting to see Shelly for the fourth day in a row.

"Oh, don't worry about him. He doesn't know I'm here. I want to buy a present for him. Something expensive and pretty."

Pretty was subjective—expensive more specific. "A pretty shell?"

"Prettier." Her face clouded. She tapped her fingertips against her breastbone and then smiled again. "A necklace. That's what I was thinking. Because he lost one."

"That's very thoughtful. Let me show you what we have."

While she oohed and aahed and rejected seagull and sand-dollar pendants, I wondered about the ethics of selling something to someone who might not be a fraud and did indeed have dementia. And how had she gotten to the shop?

"This one." She pointed at a sterling silver shell pendant. The shell, a spiral whelk, had a design of twisting vines as though it was carved. "How lucky am I? It's perfect."

"Well, if you decide it isn't, we take returns. How do you like driving that great car?"

"Shelly doesn't let me drive it. I borrowed someone's golf cart. He told me all about your inheritance and how you've moved here. Congratulations."

"Thanks. It's a big change."

"A no-brainer, though, right? Ocracoke? A lucrative business? Follow the money, honey."

Not actually my motto or my kind of conversation. "It's hard leaving good friends and deep roots behind."

"Aw. Yeah. That's where we're so lucky. Shelly and I have always been best friends."

"My husband and I were, too."

"Until you dumped him for Ocracoke?"

I'd heard that dementia could strip away a person's filters and thought this must be an example. Whether it was or not, I didn't answer her question. She didn't seem to notice. She took her bag and stopped at the glass display case on her way to the door. She didn't say anything about the missing blue velvet, but the nautilus poem on the bottom shelf caught her eye. She crouched down and stared at it so long she might have been memorizing it.

As I wondered if I should offer to help her back to her feet, I noticed the door to the storeroom stood open a couple of inches. Kathleen hadn't quite closed it, and the open gap was right next to the display case. Not so good if Lenrose, fake or not, overheard that meeting. I slid from behind the sales desk to pull it shut.

Too late. Lenrose, her face curdled with rage, sprang up and slammed the door open. Like a riptide, her fury pulled me after her.

"What kind of game are you playing in here?" she demanded, slamming her hands on the table. "How dare you spread lies about Shelly! He never threatens or menaces *anyone*." She whirled around to where I gaped at her. "Did you tell them he threatened you?" She didn't wait for an answer before whirling back to her stunned audience. "There's a reason our figgy friendship is online only, and it should have stayed that way. You've invaded my privacy. *Shelly's* privacy."

"Lenrose," Roberta said, "We—"

"You followed me here! You're stalkers! I'm quitting the group. In fact, because I started it, I can end it. Which I did this morning. Shut it down. All the posts, all the recipes. Gone. Scrubbed. And I'll scrub the memory of all of you out of my life. And if I am losing my memory, then good. I'll forget all about you. Shelly and I thought about leaving Ocracoke early because of you but we decided not to. *We* were here first. We will stay and enjoy our vacation. Alone. If you know what's good for you!" She ran out of the shop, slamming the door behind her.

Chapter 30

I'd been behind Lenrose, in the lee of her storm, and was first to recover. Everyone else, including Emrys, looked as though they'd been face-slapped. "I am so sorry she barged in here like that."

"*Au contraire*," Paula said slowly as something like wonder dawned on her face. "That was exactly what we needed. Did you see her hands when she slammed them on the table? Proof positive that she isn't Lenrose. Remember that picture she posted with just her hand holding a jar of fig preserves? That hand had arthritic fingers. The hands on the table did not."

"And the left hand on the table had a wedding ring," Roberta said. "I notice things like that. It was . . . sumptuous."

"No way Lenrose could wear a ring like that with her knuckles," Paula said. "Remember how she said it made Shelly mad that she couldn't wear her ring anymore?"

"I don't remember that exactly," Roberta said, "but my advice is to never trust a man who'd get mad about a thing like that."

"Here, here," Kathleen said.

"So, you remember the arthritis, the ring, and the rotter, too, Kathleen?" Burt asked.

"That's when Kathleen was in the hospital with pneumonia and then in rehab to get her mobility back," Paula said.

"My social secretary," Kathleen said to Burt. "So, I guess the answer is no, I don't. But did you notice that she called him Shelly? Lenrose only called him Victor in her posts."

"This is all valuable information," Glady said. "Do you have that picture of Lenrose holding the preserves?"

"I'm looking right now to see if she really deleted the group—" Roberta smacked her phone on the table. "Gone."

"I've got something you need to see," I said. "Hang on." I checked the shop. No customers. As soon as I turned back to the room, the front door opened. I was half afraid to turn around in case it was Shelly.

"I'll go," Glady said. "You show them and show me later."

"Thanks, Glady." I took out my phone, pulled up the pictures Tate sent the night before showing the yellow shirt, orange capris, tennis shoes, and the necklace, and handed it to Kathleen. "The first picture shows the clothes the body wore. The second is her necklace."

They passed the phone around, shaking their heads. Burt looked and shrugged.

"No." Paula handed the phone back to me. "Lenrose would never wear those things."

"Why not?" Burt asked. "It looks like something seventy-five percent of the female tourists wear."

"Again, the shoes," Roberta said. "Lenrose did not do white tennies."

"And the palette," said Kathleen. "Lenrose liked what she called fig colors. Natural colors. She said it amazed her how many women's clothing manufacturers thought older women only wanted to wear pastels, pants with elastic waists, and everything with random embroidery."

"She said all this in your fig forum?" I asked.

"She had definite opinions," Roberta said.

"You know what all this means, don't you?" Kathleen asked. "It means the killer switched her clothes so she wouldn't be easily identified."

"Or it isn't Lenrose," I pointed out.

"Well, that sure wasn't Lenrose who came in here gnashing her teeth and screaming at us," Paula said.

"Speaking of teeth." I asked them if their Lenrose wore dentures. They looked at each other and back at me.

"No idea," Kathleen said, answering for all of them.

I told them about the woman's lack of original teeth and the missing set of dentures.

"So, no identification through dental records," Burt said. "Although someone made the dentures, and there should be a record of that—oh, but no dentures. Her feet, though. They might identify her if they show evidence of her foot problems. That's the kind of information Tate will get from the autopsy and something he can work on far better than we can."

"Burt," Roberta said, "maybe you can set our minds at ease about a strange character who's been haunting our yard. Haunting the fig tree, really."

At the word *haunting*, I looked at Emrys. He listened intently from the stack of chairs.

"I saw him heading for the inlet," Paula said.

"What does he look like?" I asked.

Kathleen described a squat older man. "Wearing a straw hat that made him look like . . . I don't know what."

"A mushroom?" I asked.

"Yes! I thought of 'gnome,' but he didn't look charming enough to be a gnome."

"'Troll' could work," I said. "That's Irving Allred, the local doctor. He believes he sees tokens of death before people die."

"Not in our yard," Paula said. "I hope."

"What do you suppose the old fool's up to?" Burt asked. "You can't go looking for tokens of death after the fact."

"Revisiting the scene of the crime?" Roberta asked.

"I like the way you think," Burt said. "Glady and I have wondered when he'd go off the deep end and start providing the bodies to go with his phony-baloney tokens."

"Burt." Glady appeared in the doorway. "You know I don't like hearing my name linked with the words *phony baloney*. Come on out here and watch the store. I have new and vital information."

"I'll go," I said.

"Nope. You're a vital cog. Hop to it, Burt." She waited while he hauled himself to his feet and watched until he'd ambled into the shop. While she did, I had suspicious thoughts about being a cog. She closed the door behind Burt. "Right. I've just put Maureen's recon intel of last night to good use. The Shell Inn is always looking for part-time housekeeping help. I've just had a phone interview. I start tomorrow."

"That's not why I told you where the Sullivans are staying," I said. "I told you so none of you would do anything harebrained to find out."

"Nicely proactive," Paula said. "Doing and not just talking. I think we've just taken our investigation to a new level."

"Shelly and Fake Lenrose are staying in a suite," Glady said.

"For all the notice they're taking of your less harebrained approach," Emrys said, "you might as well be a ghost." He leapt from the stack of chairs. "*En garde*, blackguards!" he cried and mimed a sword, thrusting and parrying around the table.

"Do killers stay in suites?" Kathleen asked.

"Cold-blooded killers lacking remorse do," Glady said. "Villains like that are a dime a dozen in books. And before you"—she pointed at me—"say, 'That's books, not real life,' may I remind you that people learn all kinds of things from all kinds of books. That goes for movies and TV, too."

"How did you find out they're staying in a suite?" Roberta asked.

"Invasion of privacy. I know *which* suite, too, and I'm going to search it. What do you think?"

I said, "Baloney," a word lost in the clamor for details from the others.

Glady held up a hand for silence. "Here's how it'll go down.

Burt will watch the inn and let me and Maureen know when Shelly and Lenrose leave. He'll tail them in case they make a quick return. He's had experience tailing, so no worries there. Maureen will come to the inn pretending she needs to track me down with an important message. Then she'll stay and give me a hand with the search while also making sure I don't cross any lines."

"Sound planning," Emrys said.

I rubbed the back of my neck.

"What do we do?" Roberta asked. "You can't leave us out."

"Fig Ladies, you'll be ready to create a distraction if Maureen and I need it to make our escape."

The Fig Ladies immediately started discussing distraction possibilities.

"Did you get all that, Burt?" Glady called and then whispered to us, "Ear pressed to the door. He's always been a snoop."

Burt opened the door a crack and spoke through it. "I've got to make this fast. We have customers. In the suite, make note of any reading material. Newspapers in particular. Especially if they aren't local. Check trash in the trash baskets. Look for receipts so we know where they've been shopping or eating. Take pictures. Better yet, if the receipts are in the trash, take the receipts."

"Even better than better yet," Glady said, "why don't I just bag up the trash and bring it home?"

"There you go," Burt said. "Mama would be proud."

Yanira and Coquina came in after lunch—Yanira to shadow me, Coquina to play with Bonny. "And what else?" Yanira asked her daughter.

"Dust and straighten," Coquina said. "And I brought a book to read."

"Good girl. Ask Miss Maureen where she keeps dustcloths."

I gave them both a tour of the shop and storeroom and then

turned Coquina loose to dust. She took the job seriously without a twirl in sight. She was an adorable sight, though. Today's tutu was lavender, and with the starfish headband, she looked like a housecleaning fairy.

Yanira familiarized herself with the contents of drawers and cupboards. She was a natural with customers and had no trouble with the cash register.

And then Shelly came in again. No easy smile this time. I tried one of my own, steeling myself for his reaction to whatever Lenrose had told him about what happened. He came straight to the sales desk, looked at me, and did something I hadn't expected. He bowed his head.

"I'm here to apologize." He looked at me then. "What happened this morning—Lenrose told me. She had a good cry over it. I can only think that her personality is changing with the progression of her dementia."

Coquina popped up from dusting on the other side of the center display table. "I'm sorry about your wife's dementia, Shelly."

"Niña," Yanira warned.

"I'm offering my condolences," Coquina whispered back earnestly.

"They're much appreciated," Shelly told her.

"Shelly, do you have dementia, too?"

"*Niña*. Apologize."

"I'm sorry, Shelly."

"Apology accepted." He started to turn away, when Coquina spoke again.

"Shelly? I just wanted to know if that's why you don't remember me or that I gave you your nickname."

"You're mistaken, young lady. My grandchildren gave me my nickname."

Coquina watched Shelly go out the door and then she twirled once, slowly, thoughtfully. "It's sad about his dementia because he doesn't even remember that he told Allen he doesn't have children and that's why he doesn't like children and if he doesn't have children, how can he have grandchildren? I don't think he's living up to the North Carolina state motto, do you?"

"I don't know the motto yet," I said.

"I'll tell you it," Coquina said. "It's *esse quam videri.* That means 'to be rather than to seem.' Shelly might have it backwards."

"Go read your book now," Yanira said.

"In the office?" Coquina's inner light rekindled.

"Sure," I said. "You might find Bonny taking a nap in there."

"I'll go read to her."

"Bonny might have issues with impulsive children, too," Yanira said. When Coquina was out of earshot, she apologized. "If having her with me won't work out, she can stay with her cousins."

"Let's see how it goes. There won't be many customers like Shelly." I knocked twice on the desk. "Everyone else will find her enchanting."

"Is this your book, Maureen?" Coquina came to the office door holding Emrys's open journal.

"Ghosts," Emrys blustered, standing behind Coquina, "have issues with impulsive children, too."

"*Corina* Ochoa," Yanira said, stressing Coquina's given name. Coquina froze at attention. "You were not invited to look at that. You did not ask. What do you say to Miss Maureen?"

"Are you writing poetry, Maureen?" She flipped a page. "And a pirate story?"

"Think of it this way," I said while I did the dishes that evening. "She didn't get it dirty. She treated it carefully, didn't have sticky fingers, and she apologized profusely."

Emrys, slouching against the refrigerator, said, "I shall carry it in my pocket from now on."

"Good idea. I'm sorry it happened, too."

"By my count, you've now said that three times. Thank you." He bowed. "And thank you again for the book. And the pen. Three for three. Do modern husbands write poetry for their wives?"

"Probably not much. Jeff didn't. He sang off-key to me. Songs from musicals. And he loved quoting lines from movies. Did you write poetry for Angharad?"

"And will now again."

"You must have loved her very much to write poetry for her."

"I would have laid down a pathway of stardust, were it possible, so that I could get to her or she to me."

"That's . . ."

"Poetic?"

Or flowery to the point of being purple, I thought. "I'm sure Angharad loved your poetry."

"I'm sure she still does. Somewhere."

"Was Coquina right, that you're writing a pirate story, too?"

"Perhaps not for her tender eyes. I'm writing my death scene. Capturing the essence of that dastardly barnacle of a Spaniard who shot and killed me."

"I never would have met you if that dastardly barnacle hadn't shot you."

"Or, to be fair, if I could swim. When I'm finished, perhaps I can help you write your accidental pirate story. Give you pointers for verisimilitude. Nautical vocabulary such as *mopstick, toadback,* and the like."

"Great words. What do they mean?"

"Handrail. An important safety feature for any sailing vessel, piratical or otherwise."

"I'll make a note of that. Thank you."

"And do you know how pirates know they are pirates?"

"Guilty consciences?"

"There are often complicated reasons, often of a philosophical nature, for a guilty conscience. This is somewhat philosophical, as well, but far simpler. They think, therefore they arrrrrr."

"*Will* you be my coauthor? I'm serious."

"First, show me a picture of a meerkat."

"How about a video?" I dried my hands and opened the laptop at the kitchen table. As Glady would say, meerkat videos were a dime a dozen. I opened one and scooted over so Emrys could watch as the animals stood upright, climbed up to sit on a videographer's head, and sought out the shade of another videographer. "They live in Africa."

"This is excellent," Emrys said. "Quite uncanny, too. With their thin faces and pointed noses they look exactly as I remember my brothers. I shall be delighted to partner with you on this project." He leaned closer to the screen. "Hello, John. Hello, Owen. Imagine my surprise in seeing you again."

"Do you think your brothers are ghosts somewhere?" I asked.

"Most people aren't. A question for you: Why would Shelly lie about having grandchildren?"

"Lenrose might have grandchildren from a previous marriage."

"Then either we're wrong about this Lenrose being a counterfeit, or Shelly will have a whale of time explaining the counterfeit to those grandchildren."

Before going to bed, I went downstairs to double-check locks on doors and windows. As I passed the office door, a shadow inside wavered into view: Emrys in his power position behind the desk, fingers tented, elbows not quite on the chair arms. His eyes were closed; he didn't seem to know I was there. He sat so still that he might have been asleep, but he pushed his lips in and out. On the desk in front of him were the Nero Wolfe books I'd borrowed for him. This pose and the lips—that was how Archie Goodwin often found Wolfe when he was ruminating on a case. Like Archie, I didn't interrupt. I wished I could take a picture or video of him, though, so he could see how much the pose made him look like Nero Wolfe's much younger, thinner, piratical brother. The boys would love it, too.

A text arrived from Kathleen as I turned out the bedside light.

Looking forward to your adventure tomorrow? she wrote.
Not as much as Glady.
I couldn't go to sleep without saying it, she wrote.
Saying what?
What can possibly go wrong?

Chapter 31

My plan to sleep in and have a leisurely, late breakfast Sunday morning went out the window. Nerves over meeting Glady in the Sullivans' suite woke me off and on all night. At six o'clock, I gave up and got up. Bonny, after a reproachful look for the restless sleep she'd suffered, promptly stretched out on the bed to show me how to do sleeping right. The leisurely breakfast fell through when Glady texted.

Be ready at 10:00. Will pick you up so you can't chicken out.

I sent back a thumbs-up and muttered, "Shell, shell, shell."

"Bad news?" Emrys asked.

"Bad idea. Glady will do this on her own if I don't go. But that could be worse. What if she's caught?" I clutched the hair on top of my head and groaned.

"Is that helpful?" he asked.

"Not in the least."

"Then let me give you wise advice from a wise friend." He put his hands on my shoulders. I didn't feel them but appreciated the gesture. Weird, though. "Prepare for the best, be aware of the worst, and if the worst happens, say with conviction and optimism, 'On to Plan B.'"

"Oh, for . . . I see why you didn't think much of that when I first tried it on you."

"And yet it saved your life."

I stared at my feet. "You're right. It did. You did."

"Now you might need to save Glady's."

Emrys was exaggerating, of course. There was no way Glady's life would be in danger if she snooped in the Sullivans' suite. Except she might be. They really might be killers. *Shell*.

"Did you bring something to read while you wait?" Glady glanced at me, making Dorothy Parker veer as she did.

"I was preoccupied."

"Then we're peas in a pod. I'm so excited about my first B and E, I can hardly stand it." She beeped the golf cart's horn for no good reason. Pre–B and E joie de vivre, I assumed.

"We aren't really breaking in, though, if you're supposed to be there cleaning," I said.

"Not my floor, but definitely my circus." She beeped the horn again. "When we get there, stay in the cart until I text you." She pulled into the small lot directly in front of the inn.

"They let employees take prime parking spots?" I asked.

"They told me to park in back, but if I do that, and the Sullivans leave by the back door and see you, they'll get suspicious."

"What if they come out the front door and see me?"

"Scooch over to the driver's seat. You'll look like you're here to pick up another guest. All right. Last words of encouragement before I'm late for my first shift. Try not to look like you're lurking. Don't turn tail and run. Stop worrying. See you soon."

I scooched and then stewed for a bit and probably looked exactly like someone waiting impatiently. Not a bad ploy. I was just beginning to worry about that last thought and what it meant about my moral character when my phone buzzed with a text. Glady.

Showtime.

I squeezed my eyes shut. Opened them. Trotted into the Shell Inn and had no trouble at all making the woman at the desk believe I was upset and needed to get a message to Glady quickly. Before I knew it, I was knocking softly on the suite door.

Roberta opened it.

"What—"

"Quick." She motioned me in with a jerk of her head. When I didn't move, she clucked her tongue. "It's fine," she whispered. "I'm here to help."

Somewhere behind her, Glady also made clucking noises. "Eggshell," I muttered and went in.

"It makes good sense to have a Fig Lady here," Glady said. Over her own shirt, she now wore a seafoam green smock with the Shell Inn logo. "One of them might notice or recognize something you and I won't. It was their idea. Roberta volunteered."

"You don't think too many searchers might spoil the plot?" I asked. "Maybe I should let you two do this."

"Many hands," Roberta said. "Light work. I'll take the bedroom."

"Speaking of hands." Glady gave me a pair of latex gloves. She and Roberta already wore them. Some sleuth. I hadn't noticed. Glady put an arm around my shoulders. "You look like you might be sick. Stop worrying. But you do the bathroom just in case. Go on. Scoot."

Scooting, scooching, whatever. I went. Found nothing interesting in the walk-in shower. Nothing incriminating among the toiletries and cosmetics sitting on the counter. The zippered case they must have traveled in sat in one corner. I gingerly opened it. Prescription bottles with the name Victor Sullivan. None with Lenrose Sullivan. If she'd taken medication, where had they put the bottles? I checked the trash can. Tissues and floss. Where else? I checked the back of the door. Two bathrobes, but nothing in the pockets.

"Pay dirt!" Roberta called. Too loud.

Glady shushed her, also too loud, and then let out a whoop.

"Found it on the shelf in the closet under the extra blankets." Roberta put a suitcase on the love seat in the living area and opened it. The clothes inside were jumbled as though packed in a hurry. Glady took pictures as Roberta sifted through the contents. "Do you see the colors of these clothes? These are the fig colors Lenrose loved. Oh my gosh." Roberta pulled a knitted scarf from among the tangle of tops, pants, underwear. "I'm not sure I can bear this. Lenrose knitted one of these for each of us for National Fig Week a couple years ago. She sent them with a copy of her fig truffle recipe."

"Are there shoes?" I asked. "Look for prescription bottles."

Roberta wrapped the scarf around her neck. As she plunged her hands back into the mess, the suite door opened.

"Oh, pardon me," said a woman in a smock matching Glady's. "I didn't know—wait, a second. I'm assigned to this floor. Who are you?" She jabbed a finger at Glady and then at Roberta and me. "And what are *they* doing in here? They aren't the Sullivans."

Glady planted her latex-covered hands on her hips. "Exactly what I was asking them. I saw them come in here, and I knew they weren't the Sullivans." She rounded on Roberta and me. "I am shocked. What are you doing with Mrs. Sullivan's suitcase? Explain yourselves."

"It's quite simple." Roberta calmly, confidently peeled her latex gloves from her hands and then brought a Shell Inn key card from her pocket. "Maureen and I offered to get the scarf Lenrose left behind. She chills so easily. I know she'll be happy to hear how careful you are about the privacy of your guests, though." She dipped into her pocket again and brought out two bills. She pressed one into the housekeeper's hand and one into Glady's.

"Now please put the suitcase back where you found it," Glady said. "We at the Shell Inn do not leave untidy rooms behind us."

Roberta no longer wore her gloves, so I put the suitcase back in the closet.

"Don't you worry, honey," Glady said, patting the housekeeper. "I'll make sure these two depart the premises without stopping in any other rooms."

Glady turned in her notice and smock on the way out of the inn with us.

The Fig Ladies suggested we rendezvous at one of the harborside outdoor eateries to debrief. Glady and Burt agreed. I did, too, although I felt like I was along for the ride and the ride was more like a whirlpool circling a drain.

"Might as well eat while we're here," Burt said.

We ordered and while we waited for the food, Roberta told Paula, Kathleen, and Burt about the other housekeeper arriving and Glady turning on us.

"You have to think fast in this business," Glady said.

"You thought fast, all right," Roberta said. "You thought of a way to save your own skin." A seagull on a pylon behind her laughed and flew off.

"You did a fine job of that, too," Glady said. "A natural at improv."

"I hope it was worth the risk," Kathleen said. "Did you find anything?"

"Roberta did." Glady told them about the suitcase and showed them the pictures she took.

"They're her colors," Paula said. "Why was the suitcase hidden?"

"And look at this." Roberta took the scarf from around her neck. "It's hers. It was in the suitcase."

"The Clue of the Scarves," Paula said. "We brought ours to Ocracoke, too. We thought if we wore them, they'd bring back good memories for Lenrose."

"Make that our next step," Burt said. "Wear the scarves and see if Fake Lenrose reacts."

"And if she doesn't," Paula said, "it'll be another nail in her coffin."

Coffin. Not a good word. "You know, there's another explanation for what we found," I said. The food arrived, and I waited until the server had gone again to continue.

"Like what?" Glady asked.

"The woman we've seen might *be* Lenrose. It's the simplest explanation."

"That doesn't take into account the unidentified woman," Paula said.

"It doesn't have to. You've said yourselves that Lenrose has changed. The suitcase might be proof of that change. The clothes are jumbled in it because she's lost the ability to pack. She included the scarf because she loves it, figs, this group, and because she thinks of figs when she thinks of Ocracoke. Instead of fussing with her about packing, Shelly let her pack her own bag. Then he packed another that he knew had everything she needed. He brought the one she packed, because there's room in the car. He unpacked the case he packed for her and hid the one she packed. Out of sight, out of mind. He'll put it back in the car when they leave. I'm not saying that's how it is, but can't you hear Shelly making those points if he's confronted? Or Captain Tate?"

"Way to bring down the debriefing, Maureen," Roberta said.

Kathleen came to my rescue. "She's being realistic. We have to look at all angles."

"Do Lenrose and Shelly have grandchildren?" I asked. "Or children?"

"I don't think that's ever come up," Roberta said. "What's that got to do with anything?"

"It's a normal thing to know," Glady said. "Children—family—they're a topic that comes up among friends."

"We're figs more than friends," Kathleen said with a laugh. "If there isn't an intersection between figs and whatever, kids and grandkids included, it might not come up. Even though our group is on social media, we aren't really social that way."

"You said you talk every day," Glady said. "Multiple times."

"Figs are the glue that bind us," Paula said, "but it's not like we're best friends."

"Or even want to be," Roberta muttered.

Paula leveled a look at her. "I'm changing the subject. Where did the carved shell come from? The one with the fun name."

"It's the same name as the shop," Roberta said. "Not that hard to remember, Ms. Data Manager." To me, she said, "She'd remember if it was called the Moon Fig."

"Moon Fig. I like that," Kathleen said.

"Would you two stop?" Paula said. "I really want to know."

I shrugged. "I don't—"

"You don't tell people," Paula said. "I get that. I do. Of course you won't tell people like shady Fake Lenrose. But come on. I'm safe." She leaned closer and motioned with her hands, inviting me to divulge the information.

"She can't," Glady said.

"I wasn't asking you," Paula said.

"Doesn't matter, missy," Glady said. "She can't because no one knows where Dottie got that shell."

"*Dottie*," Paula said. "I think you just told me something Maureen didn't want to. Dottie who?"

"Dottie-who isn't a secret at all. Pour me a refill on the tea," Glady said, "and I'll tell you all about her." She winked at me as Paula poured the tea. She took a long drink before starting her story. "Dottie Withrow was Allen Withrow's mother. You don't need to know about him." She waved Allen away. "Except." She raised a finger. Paula's eyes widened. "Allen inherited the shop and everything in it from Dottie. The abalones all the way down to the lowly ziti cowries."

The shop did not have—correction—no one in the entire world or known universe had such a thing as a ziti cowrie. They didn't exist.

"And Allen willed the whole shebang," Glady continued, "from angel wings to zither olives, including the cameo shell Dottie called the moon shell and named her store after, to Maureen's late and much missed husband or his heirs, should he predecease Allen, which he did." Glady had to swallow half her glass of tea after that bouillabaisse of fact and fiction. Zither olives were as nonexistent as ziti cowries, but now I wished the Moon Shell had some of each for sale.

"Dottie was an Ocracoke gal born and bred," Glady continued. "A great shell collector and able to indulge her passion due to Whit's position as a foreign service officer and diplomat. Whit was her husband."

"Was he an Ocracoke guy?" Roberta asked.

"No." Glady shushed Roberta and then turned back to Paula. "Dottie and Whit spent time in the Philippines, Guam, Malaysia, and Hawaii, and Dottie made contacts with other shell collectors wherever they were posted. After Whit died, she traveled on her own, collecting shells everywhere she went. It was her passion. Her obsession. Her calling. Then one night, somewhere in the Austral Islands, maybe Tungaru, she—"

"Discovered the carved shell!" Paula said.

"No." Glady drained the last of her tea and plunked the glass on the picnic table. "She had a dream about owning a shell shop here in Ocracoke and came home to make the dream reality. The end."

"No," Paula said. "You didn't tell us about the carved shell."

"Of course I did." Glady untangled herself from the picnic bench and stood up. "I told you that first thing. No one knows where Dottie got that shell. Coming, Maureen?"

On our way back to Howard Street, I told Glady the friction she'd felt among the Figs was real. "And not just because of their worries over Lenrose. Thanks for fielding Paula's question about the moon shell."

"It's an enduring Ocracoke mystery."

"Enduring makes it sound like people have known about the shell for a lot longer than Dottie owned it. Is that true?" That seemed like a straightforward yes or no question, but Glady didn't give a straightforward answer.

"Hard to say. I'll tell you why I took over answering Paula's questions, though."

Aha. By adding *though* to that question, Glady had possibly admitted she knew more about the shell than she was telling. Maybe.

"Well? Do you want to hear why or not?"

"Yes, sorry. Definitely."

"Good. Because I did it for you. So you could get a read on Paula's body language. Something I don't trust is going on behind those oh-so-innocent eyes and questions." Glady slowed the golf cart and turned unusually serious eyes on me. "What did you pick up as you watched her?"

"Um, it might have helped if I'd known I should be watching for something."

"You should always watch for something where strangers are concerned. First rule of amateur sleuthing. Bert and I did when we met you. You think back over your encounters with Paula, with all of them. Then let me know."

"Will do. Here's something I noticed about Roberta while we were in the suite."

"Good. Shoot." Glady jumped as soon as the word was out of her mouth. "First time I've said that since our petrifying plight in the sound last month." She gave a shiver. "Second rule of amateur sleuthing—if you want to know something, stick to the basics. Ask who, what, why, where, and how. No need to get fancy with tough-guy talk. What did you notice about Roberta?"

"Where did she get hold of a Shell Inn key card?"

"Huh," Glady said. "Good question."

Chapter 32

Groceries. I needed groceries. By the time I closed up shop at the end of that day, I was so hungry I didn't give a fig where Roberta got the suite key from. Bonny sent me off to the Ocracoke Variety Store with a flea in my ear to pick up the best, smelliest fish stuff available. Being named after a pirate queen sometimes went to her bossy little head. I kissed that head and hopped in the car.

At the store, I cruised the aisles for vegetables and fruit, bread, peanut butter, oats, milk, cheese, and eggs. Nearly swooned over the smells from the bakery goods. Was studying the selection of cat food, when a deep voice from farther along the aisle accosted me by name.

"You, Ms. Nash, hold it right there."

Guilt lanced through me. Busted for the suite B and E? I turned slowly and saw Deputy Matt Kincaid pointing one of his crutches at me.

"Ms. Nash?" He lowered his crutch, his voice returning to its normal pitch. "Are you all right?" He swung himself over and peered into my face. "I didn't mean . . . I'm sorry. Me and my lame jokes. I only meant to tell you that you never came in to give your statement about the break-in at your place. Hey, are you okay?"

"Not a good joke, Matt." I covered my face with my hands. Pulled myself together. Looked at him. "But I'll get over it."

"I am so sorry. Tell you what. To make up for it, I can stop by the shell shop tomorrow morning. Before you open, so I'm not in the way."

"I can come to the station. Save you the trip. It's my fault I forgot."

"Are you kidding? I've been cooped up way too long. But look how good I'm getting with the crutches." He swung the left crutch too wide and swiped three cans of dog food from the shelf. "Oh, geez."

I corralled the rolling cans and put them back on the shelf.

"Thanks, Ms. Nash. See you in the morning."

An invitation from Paula arrived by text while I was putting the groceries away. She and Roberta were going on the Ocracoke Ghost and History Tour Tuesday night and had an extra ticket. Did I want to join them? They'd bought three, but Kathleen had second thoughts about navigating paths and lanes in the dark, even in her all-terrain chair.

Sounds like fun, I sent back and wondered if Emrys might want to come along. Maybe if I led up to the idea with general life-as-a-ghost questions. "Hey, Emrys? Are you here?"

"I'm studying." He shimmered into view with his nose close to the mango I'd bought. "What is this?"

"A mango. A tropical fruit."

"Interesting. I never made it to the tropics."

"I haven't, either. Do you mind if I ask you about your shell?"

"Not at all."

"Where did Dottie get it?"

"*That* bothersome question."

"But you just said you didn't mind."

"The question is only bothersome because I don't know the

answer. I don't know where the shell or I have been for many of the years since my death. Someone must have found it and rescued it from the water. Perhaps I caught hold of it in the water, before I died, and my body and the shell washed ashore. I do have clear and fond memories of singing around the piano with Sam Jones and Ikey D."

"I wish I'd been there."

I knew he wasn't making this up because I'd seen a picture of Sam Jones and Ikey D. in Sam's parlor during a sing-along. Sam had been a well-loved character who'd started visiting the island in the thirties. According to Glady and Burt he'd made his fortune and was happy to dig into his deep pockets to help folks and the community when he saw need. Ikey D. was Sam's favorite horse. I'd stood in the tiny, two-grave cemetery where the two were buried.

"Do you think Sam Jones owned the shell before Dottie?" I asked.

"Possibly," Emrys said. "Why do you want to know?"

"Don't you?"

"My history is more ghost than I. There's nothing to be done about that. Have you noticed that we haven't argued in the past few days?"

"Makes for a change, doesn't it?"

"It's because you're a blithesome soul. I am, too, most of the time. Except when I'm preoccupied wondering what's *become* of my soul."

"Is that the loop you got caught in at the inlet?"

"In part. I have many empty hours to fill, so I wonder. Has my soul gone on somewhere else and just the shadow, the shade of my body remains? I don't feel soulless. But what is the weight of a soul? What space does it take up that would feel hollow when it's gone? I used to wonder why, if my soul is gone, I'm still here."

"You don't wonder anymore?"

"I've come to realize I need no justification for my continuing presence. Any more than a mollusk must justify its existence. But then . . ."

"Then what?"

"Then I wonder if this—" He looked down at himself and held his arms out, studying his hands. "Is this remnant of Emrys Lloyd of less importance than a mollusk's empty shell?"

I leaned my backside against the counter and regarded him. "You're so much more than an empty shell. Think about it this way. You lived at the tail end of the era known as the Golden Age of Piracy. Now, here you are in the information age where computers have the ability to store, search for, create, and disseminate information anywhere on earth and out into space. That makes you cool. It makes you timeless."

"Timeless." He lifted his hat and bowed. "Thank you."

"Did you know the shop up the street offers a ghost tour of Ocracoke?"

The hat went back on his head. "With real ghosts?"

"I'm going Tuesday night with Paula and Roberta. Why don't you come along and find out? I can put your shell in my backpack. Think about it and let me know. It might be fun."

"Or horrific. What if these ghosts are bloodthirsty pirates?"

"We'll run screaming. Emrys, after you found Lenrose, you came back here and wrote the note identifying her. How did you do that if you were in the loop?"

"The loop didn't take hold until the crows and I returned to the inlet."

For supper that evening, I had an egg sandwich, a few strawberries, and part of the mango. It was a good break from my peanut-butter- or grilled-cheese-sandwich loop. But I felt stuck in a loop of asking questions about the murder and never finding answers. Roberta used my name in front of the other housekeeper—did she do it on purpose? Was that going to come back to bite me? I'd already had one scare about that, thanks to Matt's dumb joke. Then there was Glady's question about noticing body language. I couldn't think of a thing I'd noticed. Except—had Kathleen been more subdued toward the end of lunch? Probably not. Probably wishful thinking. But why would I wish that? Because there was something I'd noticed without realizing it about Paula and Roberta? But if I didn't know what I noticed, then what good was it?

Bonny leapt onto the table and opened her mouth in a silent meow.

"You're right, Bonny. It's good for whispering caution around those two."

We touched foreheads, and she hopped down, flopped on her side, and stretched luxuriously with a huge, fang-baring yawn. Cats had wonderful body language. So, what about the body in the inlet? An autopsy was a kind of body language. It revealed that the poor woman had no identifying scars, no teeth. Did her hands speak of the arthritis Paula and Roberta saw in a picture? Did her feet groan with aches and ailments?

And that darn suite key—where did Roberta get it?

Well, why not ask her? I sent a group text to the Fig Jams.

Any more ideas about our next step? Curious, Roberta: Where did you get the Shell Inn key card?

Can't talk, Glady immediately sent back. **Burt and I bingeing episodes of *Columbo* for inspiration.**

Roberta sent an answer for the Fig Ladies. **We're working on ours. Where's YOUR idea?** She said nothing about the key card.

Chapter 33

Matt knocked on the Moon Shell's door at eight-thirty the next morning. Glady and Burt arrived five minutes later while he was looking at the moon shell and saying no way on repeat.

"The man lacks gravitas," sniffed the pirate who wrote love poetry.

"Is that polka-dotted golf cart out there your official Hyde County deputy's vehicle, Matt?" Burt asked.

"My grandmother's," Matt said. "It's easier for me to get in and out of."

"We saw you get out, and we came right over," Glady said. Sounding like an afterthought, she added, "To make sure everything's okay over here."

"Matt came to get my statement about the break-in," I said.

"I have news, too," Matt said. "Someone's come forward after reading the press release."

"Do tell," Glady said. She scurried behind the sales desk and brought the stool to sit on.

"The witness, a woman, remembers seeing a woman on the ferry from Hatteras wearing clothes like the ones in the photograph. This was before the body was found."

Burt glanced at Glady's capris. "A lot of women wear capris."

"And scoop-neck tees." Glady got up from the stool.

"But the necklace," Matt said.

"What about it?" Glady sat again.

"The witness remembers it. The way it caught the light when the woman played with it. Flipped it around back to front like a nervous habit, the witness said. The woman was friendly. Chatty."

"Did the witness see the Sullivans' car?" Burt asked.

"She doesn't remember seeing the woman after they docked. She remembers a UPS truck, vans, four-wheel-drive-type vehicles with surf rods in racks on front bumpers. Nothing unusual."

"Hair?" Glady asked.

"She wore a sun hat. The witness called it vintage. It had a built-in scarf she had tied under her chin." He mimed the scarf covering his ears and hair.

"Do you and Captain Tate think the body is this woman?" I asked.

"Hard to say for sure," Matt said.

"Wise answer," Glady said.

"Tate asked the witness if she saw the woman in town at any point after that. The witness said she couldn't be sure. In other clothes, without the hat or the necklace, the woman could have been any of two dozen other visitors."

"And there's no point in showing her a photograph of the woman," I said.

"Not after she'd been in the water," Matt agreed.

"And the crabs," I said.

Matt narrowed his eyes at me. "The crabs aren't public knowledge."

"Son," Burt said, giving Matt a clap on the back. Matt teetered and then rebalanced. "Anyone who knows the inlets could figure out about the crabs."

On that delightful note, Glady and Burt when back home.

Matt sat on the stool while he took my statement. Before leaving, he shook Mrs. Bundy by the wing tip, thanking her for her part in the break-in.

Emrys marched from the office as I sent a text to the Fig Jams with the information about the woman on the ferry. "I've been working out the details of my next step in the investigation," he said. "I plan to catch the husband and the ersatz Lenrose."

"Good." I hoped. "Remember, we need to work together. It's safer that way."

"I am working together by telling you as much of the plan as I can. I posit that the woman on the ferry was the counterfeit, that she dressed as she did to make herself memorable and unlike Lenrose. Further, when she and the husband killed Lenrose, they dressed her in the clothes the counterfeit wore on the ferry."

"You saw Lenrose in those clothes?"

"Yes. What's more, her ghost saw herself in them and was appalled."

"This is so hard. *You* know who the unidentified woman is. I absolutely believe you do. And there's no way to prove it. Or no easy way. Especially if Tate won't listen to us. *Argh*."

"My brothers and I never actually said *argh*. I believe that is a bit of fiction perpetrated by a Scotsman by the name of Stevenson."

"You don't say *boo*, either. You're busting clichés left and right. So, what's your plan?"

"I've written three notes that will give Captain Tate a reason to investigate the scoundrels." He took three small pieces of paper from his pocket and held them so I couldn't read them. "Here's the part you play. You'll arrange for Coquina to find the notes."

"In the shop? Why would they be here?"

"Or abandoned on the porch," he said. "Such details are up

to you. Use your imagination. When she finds them, tell her to deliver them to Captain Tate. She's to tell the captain she's giving them to him because Shelly doesn't like children and she doesn't want to bother him. Captain Tate will believe her because she's a child."

"No. We can't involve Coquina."

"I'm sure the urchin could handle herself," Emrys said, "but fine. On to plan B."

"Am I going to regret this?"

He smiled his most piratical smile. "As *les Dames aux Figues* would say, au contraire."

At the end of the lunch hour, I got a feeling of déjà vu. It was Monday, one week since I'd arrived. Glady had popped back over before lunch to let me know she and Burt hadn't yet come up with a next step. To make up for it, she shooed me upstairs for an hour while she watched the shop. It was a lovely, refreshing break with a green salad topped with mango and strawberries.

When I trailed back downstairs after an hour, Glady said, "Perfect timing," and then tossed information at me like confetti on her way to the door.

"Roberta came by to look for the recipe she left the other day."

"What recipe?"

"I didn't ask. I've already called Tate about the note on the desk. He'll be here directly, and he says don't touch it. Wish I could stay. Can't. Bye."

She was right. Tate arrived soon after she left. This time I just pointed to the office and waited. Emrys shimmered into view beside me at the sales desk.

"Plan B?" I whispered out of the side of my mouth.

"Plan B, and believe me, it is grade A."

I wasn't so sure when I saw Tate's face.

"Do you know anything about this?" He held up Emrys's envelope.

I shook my head. "It wasn't there when I went upstairs for lunch. It isn't from me again, is it?"

"No."

"Can you tell me what's in it?"

"No."

"Plan B initiated." Emrys rubbed his hands.

Tate poked around among the shells while I waited on a few customers. He came back to the desk when we were alone again. "Matt gave me your statement about the break-in. Thanks."

"Sorry I didn't get over there to give it Saturday morning."

"Not a problem. The two men are Clay Devereaux and Bill Beal. Devereaux is the taller of the two."

That made Beak Booper Bill Beal. I loved it.

"Allred denies everything they said. He says he thinks they might be mercenaries." Tate waited, silent and with a face that looked carefully controlled, while I digested that.

I attempted a carefully controlled answer. "I can't imagine."

"He also says they're not to be trusted."

"One might say Allred falls into that category, too."

"And—"

"There's more?"

A slight smile. "Almost always. Devereaux and Beal have retracted their story."

I turned to Emrys when Tate was gone. "What did you write in the notes?"

"Best that I don't tell you. That way you can truthfully say you know nothing when they grill you."

Chapter 34

Emrys watched me wrap the moon shell in a towel and put it in my backpack Tuesday evening. He hadn't said much since telling me he'd decided to come with me on the Ghost and History Tour. "I'm excited," I said. "How about you?"

At his stiffest and starchiest best, Emrys said, "I shall use the opportunity to verify the veracity of local legends."

Right. That's why, under his breath, he sang a rollicking "Drunken Sailor" as we walked down Howard Street to meet the tour at Village Craftsmen. There might have been a few capering dance steps, too. We'd been asked to gather fifteen minutes early for a start time of seven-thirty, and we were last to arrive. Emrys was first to spot Shelly and Fake Lenrose.

"Aha! Another reason to accompany you tonight. I'll take this opportunity to study the husband and this other Lenrose. To learn their weaknesses and firm my plan."

"I thought you already had your plan," I whispered. "Didn't you put it in motion with the notes this afternoon?"

"I did and I do. Just not all the details."

Roberta and Paula were talking to a woman with a clipboard. Our guide, presumably. I joined them, proud of myself for not muttering to Emrys about plans and their need for details.

"Here's our third," Paula said.

"That makes our eleven, and we can get started," our guide said. "Gather around, everyone."

"Twelve." Emrys went to stand next to the guide.

"Welcome to the tour, folks. How many of you have seen ghosts before?"

A twenty-ish guy in a hoodie raised his hand. Emrys raised his eyebrows.

"Two," the guy said. "On the ghost tour in Savannah."

"Lucky you," the guide said. "There's no guarantee we'll see any tonight, but I'll take you to some of the places where people have seen them and where a few other mysterious or spooky things have been reported."

Emrys left her side to stand in front of the hoodie guy. "Boo!" he said, leaning close. No reaction. After throwing in an "arrr, matey," for good measure, Emrys sauntered back to me.

"We'll be out for about an hour and a half," the guide said. "The nights are getting chilly, so if you want to get a jacket or something else warm from your car, now's the time."

"I have what I need right here," Paula said. She opened her purse, took out one of the scarves Lenrose had knitted, and wrapped it around her neck.

Roberta pulled her scarf from a pocket. She now stood next to Fake Lenrose. When she wrapped her scarf around her neck, she flipped an end over her shoulder—and it whapped Fake Lenrose in the face. "Lenrose, I am so sorry." The apology sounded genuine to my ears. Hard to say how Fake Lenrose felt about it. She murmured something and moved to the other side of Shelly.

"Did you know the Sullivans would be here?" I asked Paula quietly.

"But of course," she said. "This is our next step."

"We'll save the story of the fingerless skeleton for when we return to Howard Street," the guide said. "Let's start by going to see if Captain Joe Burrus, the lighthouse keeper, is around tonight. He retired in nineteen forty-six and died in nineteen fifty-one."

"Is the lighthouse haunted?" a woman asked.

"It's possible that almost any place on Ocracoke is haunted," said the guide. "That includes the beaches. The Outer Banks are notorious for shipwrecks, and we've had a good many victims wash ashore over the centuries. If you walk the beach at night, you might hear the giggles of a ghost girl. She's a playful little thing. She'll walk behind you and leave her footprints inside yours."

I glanced at Emrys and saw a glimmer of hope on his face that grew as we walked and listened to the guide's stories. We stopped at the cottage Captain Joe Burrus and his family had retired to. He'd been a kindly man, the guide said, and remained so as a ghost who walked the upstairs hallway, opening and closing doors.

My ears perked up when the guide told a story about a fisherman who'd been followed by a ghostly casket one pre-dawn on his way to his boat. "It was a token of death," she said. "And, sure enough, a beloved young woman died soon after of a burst appendix. She was buried in a cemetery next to the path the fisherman walked each day before sunup to reach his boat."

Our next stop was an example of an old-time Ocracoke house, according to our guide, and also where a visitor was shaken to his bones by the appearance of a disembodied head in the middle of the night. Emrys hung on her every word. The rest of her audience stood closer together. I'd ended up beside Fake Lenrose and thought I heard a soft whimper from her.

Suddenly, with a mad ruckus of caws, a flock of crows burst out of the myrtles and yaupon edging the yard. They flew over us, and even Emrys ducked.

"Token of death!" the hoodie guy yelled and then laughed hysterically. The crows swooped back over us to the trees again and never quit cawing. More people laughed; some covered their heads with their arms. The birds swooped again, and Fake Lenrose shrieked. In a panic, she bolted—running, crying, and waving her arms around her head.

"Like Tippi Hedren in *The Birds*," the hoodie guy said.

Shelly wasn't any good. He seemed rooted to the ground in shock. So, I pelted after Fake Lenrose, calling her name—and scared her half to death. She screamed at me, screamed at the crows, turned, and ran back to Shelly.

"Right now!" she screamed. "We're leaving right now!"

The guide tried to apologize to them, but they left without another word.

Roberta unwound her scarf from her neck and nudged Paula. "Look." She whirled the scarf around her head. "It's a token of death."

"They shouldn't laugh at what they don't understand," Emrys said.

"You understand tokens of death?" I whispered.

"I understand crows," he said. "The way she cried and screamed, I almost feel sorry for the ersatz Lenrose. What's more, I feel like crying, too. All those interesting ghosts I've never met. I'm not meeting them now, either. It's enough to make a dead pirate weep."

The moon had risen, and the crows were settling. "Come on," I whispered. "I know where we can find lots of ghosts on a night like this."

The group had moved on without us, and no one seemed to notice. We jogged back to the shop and got my bike. Then we rode to the first beach access point outside of town, left the bike, and trekked over the dunes. In the dry sand, near the tide line, I lay down on my stomach and patted the sand beside me. "Lie down."

"There are better places for naps," Emrys grumped. "Beds or the briny deep, if you're unfortunate enough to drown."

"Hush. Lie down and look across the sand around us." I

pulled out my phone and shined the flashlight across the sand—and there they were. "Sand crabs," I said. "Also called ghost crabs. We won't see too many because it's late in the year for them." But we did see several dozen of the pale little crabs walking sideways across the sand, their eyes on their eye stalks giving them a permanently startled look.

"As if someone just said *boo* to them," Emrys said. "I could watch them all night. Much better than a historic tour of places where ghosts used to be."

"So, you believe the stories we heard?"

"Do you believe in *me*?" he asked.

"Point taken. Do the crabs see you?"

"I choose to believe they do."

"You said Allen was one of the few people who saw you. Who else has?"

"There were a few, early on, who took one look and ran," he said. "Some screamed as well. You can imagine how that sort of reception might grieve a sensitive soul."

"Hurtful and lonely."

"There's been only one other whose name I knew. Ikey D. He enjoyed my singing, and he never screamed or ran when he saw me. A capital fellow, Ikey D."

"I wish I'd met him. When did Allen first see you?"

"After his mother passed. He'd been drinking."

"You said he'd been drinking when he showed you the Edgar Allen Poe book in the safe, too."

"He enjoyed his spirits," Emrys said, "in more ways than one."

"Do you know why Dottie never put the shell on display, or why Allen did after she died? Did he do it for you?"

"She didn't because she didn't want to share it, and she didn't want to tempt anyone to 'share it' against her wishes. As for Allen, I was never certain why he put it on display. He would become coy when I asked him. I rather thought it was his way of letting me know that he was in charge."

"Of what? You?"

"Considering his piratical ways, he would have been a better brother to my brothers than I could ever be. In addition to being a pirate, however, he was a poltroon. Do you know that word?"

"I've heard it. Isn't a poltroon similar to a pirate? A scoundrel of some sort?"

"A coward," he said with a neatly curled lip.

My phone buzzed with a text. Paula to the Fig Jams.

Operation Scarf complete. Meeting tomorrow 8 a.m. at Moon Shell.

"I'm getting cold," I said. "All right with you if we head home now?"

He agreed, but not before looking up at the night sky, clear and spangled with stars. "I wish ghosts could travel in outer space," he said. "We're supernatural, aren't we? Then why can't we do something completely supernatural like visit other galaxies? I've seen the most amazing pictures of them from the Bubble telescope."

"Hubble," I said. "If you ever figure out how to take that trip, let me know because I want to hear all about it when you get back."

We rode home through the quiet town, Emrys enthusing nonstop about the crabs. "How many of those fascinating creatures did you see?"

"Including the ghost on the bike with me," I said, "I bet I saw an even two dozen ghosts tonight." As those words left my lips, we passed a squat shadow at the roadside. I quickly glanced over my shoulder and saw the shadow step into the road to watch us pedal away.

Chapter 35

I stopped short of the bottom step on my way down from the apartment, the next morning, an insulated carafe of coffee in each hand. Kathleen, Roberta, and Paula had come in the back door and were settling at the table in the storeroom. Glady and Burt had arrived through the front door moments ago. But someone else had just clomped up the front stairs and tried the doorknob. And now cupped their hands around their eyes—oh. Rob Tate. I crossed to the door and showed him my full hands. "Be right back!" I called through the glass.

"Rob Tate?" Burt said when I plunked the carafes on the table.

"We saw him coming down the street as we were crossing," Glady said. "You're not open yet. Feel free to ignore him."

"Somehow I don't think so." I retraced my steps and opened the door. "What can I do for you?"

"Save me some time?" He nodded toward the storeroom. "I'd like to speak to your assembled guests."

"Come on in, Rob!" Burt hollered. "The coffee's hot and the muffins aren't bad-looking, either."

Tate and I followed the laughter into the room. Tate accepted coffee but not a chair.

"This won't take up much of your time." He swirled a finger, taking in the six of us. "Are you expecting anyone else?"

I shook my head and took the chair next to Kathleen. Emrys, our stealth member, had told me the night before that he wouldn't join us, that he needed to cogitate on his own plan's next step.

"Sheriff Tate?" Paula said.

"Captain," Glady interjected.

"Captain, how did you know we'd all be here this morning?" Paula side-eyed first Glady and then me.

"I saw you arrive."

"How'd you manage that, Rob?" Burt asked. "You were only just coming down the street when Glady and I saw you."

"Saw them first. Came around again. Thought I'd take the opportunity to fill you all in on matters."

"That's fine, then," Glady said. "We're glad to have you."

"Victor and Lenrose Sullivan came to see me last night. They made me aware of your activities concerning them. Now, I'm not saying that you've broken any laws, but it sounds like you're harassing them. Ladies, Burt, you need to cease and desist. You think someone is missing who is not."

"Captain?" Kathleen said. "May I tell you a little about the friend we haven't found in Ocracoke? You listened to the Sullivans. In all fairness, will you listen to us for a few minutes?"

Tate scrubbed a hand across his head. "I'll listen."

I admired him for that and hoped no one slipped and called him Potato Head. Or mentioned the suitcase hidden in the suite's closet.

Paula and Roberta told him about the photo of Lenrose's arthritic hand holding a jar of her fig jam. Kathleen told him about the wedding ring Lenrose couldn't wear and how that had upset Victor.

"That's another thing," Kathleen said. "Lenrose never called her husband anything but Victor. Here she only calls him Shelly."

"Then there's the recipes she gave each of us and the scarves she knitted for us." Roberta took an index card from her purse. "I have her recipe here. She wouldn't forget them or the scarves. They meant too much to her. But she has forgotten them."

"I heard a little about a scarf last night," Tate said.

Roberta sank a bit into her chair.

"Mister Sullivan told me about his wife's dementia," Tate said. "He also told me that you're aware of it. Forgetting scarves and recipe cards fits that profile."

"It's also a great cover story for a fraud." Roberta shot Tate a dirty look and then stared at the table.

"Lenrose made a scarf for herself, too," Paula said. "Can't you test the scarves, including hers? If any of the DNA is a match for the unidentified body, that'll prove the body is Lenrose."

"But if she doesn't remember the scarves, why would she have hers with her?" Tate asked reasonably. He pulled a chair over and sat next to Glady. Burt refilled his coffee and pushed a muffin across the table. "A match would only prove that the body came into contact with one or more of the scarves and that there's a connection between the scarves and the body, and nothing more. Given the expense of testing, it would be hard to justify in this case."

"How do you feel about that woman seen on the ferry?" Burt asked.

"It's a lead."

"Have you found a car no one claims?" Glady asked. "A bike? Another mode of transportation? If not, how did she get from the ferry to the village? Where are the rest of her belongings? Where would someone dispose of them? Was this a robbery? An assault? Did the villain drive her car off the island?"

"Questions you can be sure we're trying to answer," Tate said.

Glady smiled. "That makes her more than a lead, Rob. It makes her a *good* lead."

He ate his muffin and helped himself to another while we peppered him with questions.

"Was she seen talking to anyone on the ferry?"

"Was she targeted before she even got to the island?"

"Did she give her killer a ride from the ferry?"

"If the killer is a stranger who killed her and disappeared, how are you going to find them?"

"*Or.*" Roberta leaned on the word and leaned toward Tate. "If Shelly is the villain, maybe he didn't dispose of her belongings, and if you looked for them you might find them wherever he and the imposter are staying."

"Ladies. Burt." Tate got to his feet. "This has been enlightening."

"Take a muffin for the road, Rob." Burt pushed a napkin-wrapped muffin across the table.

"Thanks. For your information and your interest, too. I'd also appreciate your understanding when I say you cannot meddle in this. There have been significant developments in the case, and the best way you can help, the only way, is to understand this one clear directive: Stop."

His directive put a damper on the meeting. I took that as a sign that we were all law-abiding citizens at heart. After he left, we didn't discuss any next steps. We finished the muffins—none of us needed more muffins, but without steps to discuss, we had nothing else to accomplish. The meeting broke up when the last muffin made its last stand.

As I tried to fall asleep that night, some of Tate's words played over and over in my head. "You think someone is missing who isn't." Funny, not funny. Emrys hadn't shimmered into view since he'd shimmered out the night before to cogitate. He'd been gone roughly twenty-four hours. Not really like him. A loop? Possibly. But, considering the reason he'd looped the last time he'd gone missing for this long, this might not bode well.

I punched my pillow to rearrange it and finally slept. Fitfully, though, because two words kept repeating in my dreams like a knell—*bode well, bode well, bode well.*

Chapter 36

My phone buzzed with a text the next morning earlier than Bonny or I wanted to be awake. The sun was just getting up, and obviously someone who knew me was up, so I snagged the phone off the bedside table and squinted at it with sleep-deprived eyes. Kathleen.

Troll in our yard again. Like Rumpelstiltskin. Hopping around. Yelling into his phone.

I sent back, **Yelling what?**

Dead body! Police on the way.

I was in my car almost before I got dressed, driving faster than I should, arriving seconds after Tate. Before he sent me to stand on the porch with the Fig Ladies, I saw that Allred, or someone, had dug through the oyster and clam shells around the base of the fig tree and exposed a body. From the glimpse I got of the clothes, shoes, and length of the victim, I guessed a male. I couldn't see the face, thank goodness.

I ran up the stairs to the porch and found the Fig Ladies in various stages of dress—Paula in a robe and sneakers; Roberta in jeans, slippers, and a short, sleeveless nightgown; Kathleen in sweats and bare feet. They made no move to go in and finish dressing.

"This is like lightning striking twice," Roberta said. "I bet most people go through their whole lives without once calling nine-one-one to report a dead body. Now I've done it twice in as many weeks."

"You didn't think Allred shouting 'dead body' at them on his phone was enough?" I asked.

"He didn't call nine-one-one," Paula said. "He called Lenrose."

I stared at her, at the others. Felt ice water trickle down my spine. Knew I didn't need to ask but did anyway. "Why did he call her?"

Kathleen pointed. "It's Shelly."

I swiveled to stare at the tree. At Tate on his knees beside the body. At Allred, hands clasped behind his back, leaning close. Catching movement over Allred's head, I lifted my gaze. A crow sat in the tree, silent, watchful. As I watched, another crow landed on another branch.

People had started to gather, too. A couple with a dog stood on the other side of the road. A man in running clothes stopped, wiped his face with his shirt, and stayed. Glady and Burt arrived in Burt's cart, Minerva. As soon as Tate saw Burt, he enlisted him to keep gapers at a distance and any vehicles moving along the road.

Glady joined us on the porch. "We have a better view from here than anyone on the other side of Burt's invisible cordon," she said. "Better than Burt, too."

She was right. The tree wasn't more than fifteen feet from the porch, and we had just enough elevation to give us an advantage over the gapers at ground level. Our viewing platform didn't let us overhear Tate and Allred, though. When they spoke at all, they kept their voices too low for us to hear clearly.

"Do you two have ESP?" I asked Glady. "How did you hear about this?"

"You poor thing," Glady said with a pitying look. "Do you want to borrow a comb? Because it looks like your hair had a rough night and you didn't bother to brush it before you lit out of the house, or to notice that Kathleen sent that text to all three of us."

When she turned to look at Tate and Allred, I quickly ran my fingers through my hair. Kathleen mouthed, "It looks fine."

"But, Glady, do you know who the troll found?" Roberta asked.

"No." Glady scanned our faces. "I can see it isn't good. Who?"

"Shelly," Paula said.

Glady drew in a sharp breath. "This changes a lot. Does it change everything?"

"I don't know." I nodded at the three Fig Ladies. "How did Allred find the body? What was he doing here?"

Before they answered, Allred's voice rose. "Because I've been expecting another death. Tokens of death don't lie."

Tate said something sharp to Allred but didn't raise his voice.

"There's no need for me to remain silent," Allred said. "I've seen nothing here that wouldn't be obvious to a child. As obvious as a body in a shell pile. A ridiculous place to hide one. It's symbolic though. Symbolic and diabolical. And this murder isn't like the first. That's obvious, too."

Tate put his hand on Allred's shoulder, leaned down, leaned close, and spoke directly into his face. Still calm, voice still too low to hear. He kept his hand on Allred's shoulder when he straightened.

Allred's voice amplified. "His body was meant to be found."

Tate's only reaction was to look heavenward through the branches of the fig. There were now five silent crows in the tree. A sixth joined them and a seventh landed on the shell pile beside a pirate-shaped shadow. As the crow and I watched, Emrys shimmered into view sitting cross-legged.

A car careened down the street, snapping Tate to attention. He shouted for Burt to get out of the road and then courageously, or insanely, ran into the road himself, waving his arms at the maniac driver—of a green and white Kaiser Manhattan. The Manhattan veered into the yard, lurching to a stop only feet short of the fig tree. Lenrose flung the door open but didn't get out. She laid her arms on the steering wheel, lowered her head, and sobbed.

I couldn't stand it and couldn't think of her as Fake Lenrose anymore. "I'm going to her." I ran down the steps, crossed the short distance to the car. I didn't know any words that would reach her in that awful place her life had just been tipped, but I put my hand on her back so she'd know someone was there with her.

The gentle whir of Kathleen's chair came behind me. Glady, Paula, and Roberta came, too. And Emrys.

"We need to talk," he said. "The evidence points to one, two, or all three of the Fig Ladies."

If this were true, Glady had called it. Shelly's death changed everything. But what evidence had Tate found?

We weren't about to see or find out now. "Ladies," Tate said. "I need you all to go back to the porch."

"She needs someone with her," I said.

"I do." Lenrose raised a blotchy, tear-streaked face and pleaded with him. "These are my friends. They're all I have here now."

"We're here for you, Lenrose," Kathleen said.

Lenrose swiped at her nose with the back of her hand. "Wait." Her voice had sharpened and she pointed at Paula and Roberta. "I know you two." She looked at Kathleen. "And you. You're the ones who did this. You *did*." She struggled out of the car and shouted at Tate. "They did this! They followed us here to Ocracoke! They're obsessed! But I've been just as obsessed. I see it all now." She pointed at the women again. "Your fig group is like a cult. Shelly thought you were trying to get me away from him. He was right. But you!" She pointed at me.

Emrys, bless him, stepped between us.

"Shelly said you ran after me last night to help me. To comfort me. Just like you did a minute ago." With that, she threw her arms around me. I staggered back a step. She sobbed with her head on my shoulder, and I patted her awkwardly on her back.

Emrys, no longer facing Lenrose, turned around. "Are you all right?" he asked me.

I jerked my head for him to come closer and whispered, "What evidence?"

He whispered back. "Blackmail and roguery."

Chapter 37

It didn't feel right opening the shop as though nothing had happened. After Jeff died, so many people earnestly advised me that life goes on. *So* many. Each time, it felt like a triple-slap in the face—one slap for each word. Well-meaning encouragement to snap me out of my perfectly reasonable grief. I swore I'd never slap anyone else with those words. And yet. Life goes on.

Emrys, an unusual example of life going on, came back to the shop with me. We didn't talk on the way. He went straight to the office to sit in the desk chair, looking as deep in thought and unapproachable as Nero Wolfe ever could. And I opened the shop. Until Glady and Burt came across the street and told me Tate had arrested Roberta.

"He released a bare-bones statement," Burt said. "He charged her with Shelly's murder. Gave no motive, no cause of death."

"Does that mean he doesn't know how Shelly died?" I asked.

Glady gave one of her favorite answers. "Hard to say."

"I'm going back to the cottage," I said. "I'll leave a note on the door here. Kathleen and Paula must be beside themselves."

"You'll be a comfort," Glady said. "Burt and I will reevaluate."

"You don't believe she did it?" I asked.

"Not on the basis of Tate's bare ass—" Burt covered his mouth and coughed.

"We just want to dot the T's and cross the I's," Glady said. "For our own peace of mind."

Kathleen sat alone on the porch when I arrived, this time by bike. She stared at the fig tree, but if she saw anything at all, it was something farther away or deep inside. The crows were gone. "Hey," I said quietly and pulled a deck chair over to sit beside her.

"Deputies searched the cottage," she said. "They just left. Paula's packing. She says there's nothing we can do for Roberta."

"Tate said you can leave?"

"I think he'd like nothing better."

"Would you like help packing?"

"No." Kathleen finally looked at me. "She didn't do it."

"Can you prove it? Did you tell Tate?"

"Can't and tried. He's made up his mind."

"Does he think she also killed the woman in the inlet?"

"I don't know."

"But you haven't given up," I said. "I've never known you to give up. Glady and Burt and I haven't given up either. So, walk me through what you know. Like, when was she supposed to have killed him and dug a shallow grave in the shell pile?"

"Shelly in the shell pile. It'd be funny if it wasn't true," she said.

"It could be an alphabet book. Shelly in the shell pile. Tito in the sand. Uma in the fig tree. Wilbur in a band." I shook my head. "Nope. *That's* not happening." It eased some of Kathleen's tension, though.

"None of us have alibis for last night," she said. "Separate bedrooms, and we all use white-noise machines. I haven't heard anyone cough, snore, or get up to dance a cha-cha in the moonlight. Paula said the same."

"But why would any of you be crazy enough to bury him so sloppily and right here where you're staying?"

"Crazy like a fox?" Kathleen shrugged her left shoulder. "Or maybe they think, because we're leaving Saturday, Roberta had to do something fast and didn't expect that troll Allred to come along."

"Allred." I felt like spitting on the ground after saying his name to ward off whatever madness he carried. "Did you hear any good reason he was here in the first place?"

"You mean you didn't believe his spiel about omens? Do you think *he* believed it?"

"Yeah, afraid so. Are you really leaving Saturday?" I asked. "We haven't had a whole week together."

"We didn't get our whole two weeks here, either. Roberta had a last-minute conflict so she couldn't get here on the Sunday our rental started. It was hard enough finding this place, though, so we took it for the full two weeks and arranged to get here two days late."

"What kind of conflict?"

"We didn't ask. She didn't tell." Kathleen shook her head. "We really don't know much about each other, do we?"

"What *do* you know about her?"

"She seemed strong. Put together. But she fell apart when they arrested her. Just fell apart."

"People are good at protecting their tender inner selves with outer shells, like mollusks."

Kathleen blew her nose. "You must have learned that in mollusk school."

"Nope. Read it in a mystery—*A Clue in the Crumbs* by Lucy Burdette."

Glady or Burt must have been watching for me to get home. A text arrived from them as I let myself in the back door.

We need your brains over here. Look left and right before

you cross the street. Make sure you don't see lurking lawmen who'll come break up our cabal.

Glady opened the door before I knocked. "Ignore Burt's perpetual mess. We're in the kitchen."

We joined Burt at the kitchen table. He poured a mug of coffee for me and refilled Glady's. "Anything new from the remaining Fig Ladies?" he asked.

"Paula's packing. I didn't see her. Kathleen says Roberta didn't do it but has no proof."

"Well, it didn't surprise me one bit that Rob Tate arrested Roberta," Glady said. "I've been suspicious of the Fig Ladies from day one."

"Day one being as soon as she heard about the arrest," Burt said.

"No, sir." Glady smacked her coffee cup on the table. "Since the day we met them. But especially since Roberta finagled her way into searching the suite with us. Where *did* she get that key card? She could have used it to plant that suitcase."

"Then let's hope they have enough other evidence against her," I said, "because if we turn that information over to Rob Tate, we'll incriminate ourselves, too."

"Not at all," Glady said. "I covered our backsides with that cover story. I was doing my job. You were delivering a message to me. But here's another thing. Do you know how much top-of-the-line all-terrain wheelchairs like Kathleen's cost?"

"Glady found that model online," Burt said. "The answer is 'whoa, baby.'"

"And if that isn't suspicious, I don't know what is," Glady added.

"How does that have anything to do with Shelly's murder?" I asked.

"It's information," said Burt. "The currency of all investigations."

"Here's something *else*," Glady said. "Why did Kathleen change her mind about going on that tour Tuesday night? What was she up to instead? And that friction I felt? It's because one or more of them is a murderer."

"I don't believe Kathleen had anything to do with this." I said it firmly, flatly, to crush their suspicion of her. From the looks they gave each other, I didn't even dent it. I tried again. "Tate doesn't think Paula or Kathleen are involved. He didn't arrest them. He didn't tell them not to leave the island."

Glady smacked her cup on the table again. "How soon are they going?"

"Saturday."

"When did they get here?" Burt asked.

"A week ago Tuesday." I explained about their rental and the change of plans because of Roberta's conflict.

"*Did* she have a conflict?" Burt asked.

"Or was she here earlier, and did she kill Lenrose?" Glady asked.

"Tate will look into all that," I said. "But why would she kill Lenrose? Was she in cahoots with Shelly and Fake Lenrose? Then why kill Shelly? What sense does that make?"

"Murder is a senseless crime." This time Glady placed her cup on the table with prim precision. "Did it occur to you she might be a contract killer?"

"Good one, Glad," Burt said. "I like that. Another option—Lenrose is alive and a new widow, and the body in the inlet has no connection at all to Shelly's death."

I massaged my forehead. "What about Allred? He has to be a suspect. He's nutty. He could have done it to prove he sees tokens of death. What was he doing there? If he didn't bury Shelly, how was he lucky enough to find him?"

"He saw the toe of a shoe sticking out of the shell pile," Burt said. "I heard that while I kept those people back this morning."

"That doesn't prove he didn't kill him," I said. "We can't discount him."

"We haven't," Burt said. "But he *is* nutty, and nutty is best left to Rob to deal with. We also can't discount the Fig Ladies."

"We *can* discount Kathleen."

Glady leaned across the table toward Burt. "Let's not worry her about Kathleen anymore."

Burt nodded. "It's never fun when you have to suspect a friend of murder. Let's go after Paula."

"You know my initial impression of her," Glady said. "Suspicion. But I realize that isn't the concrete proof you're keen on, Maureen, so what have you got?"

"She's got something all right," Burt said. "Look at her eyes darting around like minnows."

Glady peered at my eyes. "Pretty blue minnows."

We all waited while my minnows darted around after a memory of Paula . . . doing what? Talking about . . . being responsible. Not Paula. Roberta. "When the Fig Ladies showed me where they found the body, Roberta said they found her and they felt responsible for her."

"Interesting word choice," Burt said.

"Isn't it? Then Paula said she wasn't just an unidentified female. She was somebody's daughter and might be somebody's mother or sister or wife. That the killer went to great lengths to hide her, so she deserved to have someone else go to great lengths to find that killer."

"Nice speech," Burt said. "I see why you want to believe they're innocent."

"Good. Because I do. Except . . ."

"Except what?" Glady asked.

"Then Roberta said even though they were horrified to find her, their horror might not be anything compared to the horror that poor woman experienced. Then they all looked at me and I imagined their eyes asking *do you understand?*"

"In other words, you got fanciful," Glady said. "The way you do."

"But now I wonder. What if their eyes asked *do you believe us?*"

Glady pointed her finger at me. "Because they're wily."

"Each one of the Figs is missing an element that would make her a successful villain on her own," Burt said. "That's what's been throwing us off. Mix them together, in the right batter, and they become invincible."

"That's an exaggeration," I said.

"Not by much," said Glady. "And not at all if we pin these murders on all three of them."

Emrys cut a dashing figure pacing the porch of the Moon Shell. For that moment, as I crossed the street from Glady and Burt's, he was the ship's captain, pacing his deck, awaiting word from the lookout in the crow's nest. When he saw me, he instantly became a worried parent. "When I saw your bike here, and your car, I didn't know where you were, and I feared the worst. If Captain Tate could make his first mistake by arresting Roberta, I thought sure he'd made a second and taken you away."

"Thanks for worrying. Let's go inside. We need to put our worries into the Fig Ladies." I left the CLOSED sign on the door, chucked Bonny under the chin, and the three of us went upstairs. Bonny and I took the settee. Emrys continued pacing. "Glady and Burt want to find evidence to prove all three Fig Ladies are guilty." I picked up Bonny and held her. She rubbed her chin against my shoulder. "They think Shelly or Fake Lenrose, or both of them, hired Roberta to kill Lenrose."

Emrys paced and said nothing.

"Hey, pirate. Will you please sit down? What did you mean by blackmail and roguery? How do you know that? Do you know what evidence the police have?"

He dropped into the recliner, elbows on his knees, and stared at the floor. "I don't know. And I don't believe the police know what they think they do. I think they're still missing something. They're aware of the gaping hole in the deck of their scurvy ship and conveniently sidestepping it. In short, there's a hole in their logic."

"I need you to look at me and tell me how you know that. What evidence do you have? What blackmail? What roguery? Does this have anything to do with those three notes you wrote to Tate?" Bonny squirmed out of my arms and went to sit in the window seat. She either didn't like where this conversation was going, or she hadn't liked my increasingly agitated voice in her ears.

Emrys raised his eyes to me. Strange to see a ghost's eyes looking haunted. "I honestly do not know if this development has anything to do with those notes. As for evidence, I know more about the evidence of crows. I'm not the only one who recognized the body of Lenrose. The two crows who led me to her body also did."

"How?"

"Lenrose fed them and left trinkets for them, the way Burt and Glady do for their crows. Crows talk to each other. Information spreads. We've seen how crows react when they see Shelly and his new Lenrose. I think the pair that led me to Lenrose's body witnessed her murder. I know they hold grudges."

"You might be projecting," I said. "Anthropomorphizing. Do you know that word? It means attributing human behavior to nonhumans. Seeing crows through your own human experience. Like calling a horse that's allowed in the parlor for a sing-along a capital fellow."

"I daresay I've spent a few hundred more years watching and contemplating crows than most people. Contemplating horses, too."

Hard to argue with experience. "What about Allred? Roguery fits him like a glove. What do the crows have to say about him?"

"Nothing at all. They give him the cold shoulder as though he does not exist."

"Serves him right."

The doorbell rang. Emrys disappeared, reappeared. "Glady and Burt wish to board. I believe they've brought food. Perhaps they see you through the lens of their crow experience and attribute crow behavior to you, a non-crow."

"I wouldn't put it past them." I trotted downstairs and invited them in. They shook their heads and stood in the doorway looking so intently at my face, they might have been reading the secrets of the ages in my incipient crow's-feet. "You're sure you won't come in?"

"Nah," Burt said. "We got carried away. Made too much mushroom lasagna, so we brought some for you and Bonny." He handed me a warm casserole dish.

"Thank you. It smells wonderful."

"We know you're worried about Kathleen and the others," Glady said. "We don't want you to think we're trying to railroad them."

"We don't have anything concrete to railroad anybody with," I said. "You really don't want to come in?"

"Nah," Burt said. "Our lasagna's waiting for us."

"Then can I ask a quick question about crows before you go?"

Emrys shimmered into view beside me.

"Crows?" Glady said. "Always."

"Have you ever heard that they can recognize people?"

"It's been proven," she said. "They remember human faces, especially the faces of people who've threatened them or treated them badly. And they pass that information on to other crows. You can look it up online. Look for the caveman mask experiment by somebody-or-other at someplace-or-other."

"That's oddly specific and unspecific at the same time," Burt said.

"Just look up caveman mask experiment and you'll find it," said Glady. "Your blue minnows are on the move again, Maureen. What are you thinking?"

"That crows react badly to Shelly and Fake Lenrose. That

crows were at the inlet where the Fig Ladies found the body. They looked like they were sitting vigil."

"Is that what they were doing in the fig tree this morning?" Glady asked.

"Maybe," I said.

"Not at all," Emrys said. "They were waiting to be sure Shelly was well and truly dead."

"Or maybe there for less sentimental reasons," I said.

"They're cunning and clever," Glady said. "More human than some humans I've met. Have you seen them react badly around any of the Fig Ladies?"

Emrys shook his head.

"No. Crows were upset about something the night Paula, Roberta, and I went on the ghost walk, but Fake Lenrose and Shelly were there, too. Most of the tour people reacted to the crows, but only Fake Lenrose overreacted."

Glady nodded solemnly. "Then I think all of Burt's silly suspicions of the Fig Ladies might be all wrong. We should listen to the crows."

"Your blue minnows are still at work," Burt said. "Let us know if you come up with anything."

"Count on it."

Donald O'Connor started singing during supper. The lasagna was so good, it was almost a toss-up over sticking with it and then licking the plate or answering. Almost. "Hey, Mom," O'Connor said. "Look at this, I called you back in less than a week. How's it going? Did you solve the murder?"

"Hi, sweetie. Captain Tate did. He arrested someone today."

"Good! Things will settle down and you can start getting in the groove of normal island life. How are Emrys and Bonny?"

"Both waiting impatiently for their turns to talk to you. I'll put you on speaker."

"Hi, Emrys! Hi, Bonny!"

I muffled the phone against my chest and whispered, "Don't mention Shelly's murder," and then set the phone on the table.

Emrys leaned over it. "Good day, Master Nash. Bonny listened to your greeting and found it congenial. As did I."

"So, what's new with you?" O'Connor asked.

"I am writing an account of my death."

I gave him a thumbs-up and went back to my lasagna.

"And your mother introduced me to several dozen ghosts." Emrys gave me a conspiratorial smile and said, "He'll never guess I'm talking about crabs."

"Emrys?" O'Connor said. "I'm still here. Being on the phone is like being in the same room with someone. Did Mom take you to see ghost crabs on the beach?"

"She did."

"Aren't they great? Kelly and I had pet hermit crabs when we were kids. They were crazy little guys. Like miniature bulldozers. They spent most of their time moving gravel around their habitat. We named them John Deere and Kubota. Remember them, Mom?"

"I do now. They were a lot of fun." While they continued talking, I finished my lasagna, barely tasting it. I'd forgotten about John Deere and Kubota and their obsessive reengineering. I chatted a bit with O'Connor before we hung up, and then I sat and thought about crabs and crows.

After doing the dishes, I sent a text to Glady and Burt about a possibility taking shape in my head. I packed my backpack before going to bed, still thinking. Crabs and crows. It wasn't much to go on.

Chapter 38

My bulging backpack and I met Burt and golf cart Minerva out front at dawn the next morning. Early for me, not for Burt. Emrys declined my invitation to join us. He wasn't keen on our destination.

Burt knew about the access road on the other side of the inlet that Tate had mentioned. It was little more than a two-tire path through tall grasses and low-growing, windswept trees. We drove along, listening to early-morning birdcalls, until the road petered out and became a path. We parked and walked single file. As we neared the inlet, Burt pointed out an American bittern doing its best, hunched imitation of Irv Allred.

At the inlet, I slipped off my backpack and pulled from it my old stream-wading, mussel research gear. Burt snapped pictures as I put on chest waders and wading boots, a bathing cap, mask and snorkel, and neoprene gloves. He sent a picture of me all dolled up in a text to Glady. She sent back a mermaid emoji.

"Explain what you're going to do. What this is about," he said, "and I'll take video."

"It's about crabs. They move things around. They rearrange their environment incessantly. My sons had a couple of hermit crabs for pets that spent most of their time bulldozing gravel from one end of their habitat to the other. The boys named them John Deere and Kubota. Once, they completely buried the little aquarium castle the boys had put in the tank.

"It's about dentures, too. If the police didn't find a set of dentures *on* the bed of the inlet, that might be because they were buried by industrious crabs. I'm going to search the muck below the surface of the bed with this." I held up a small rake. "The mask and snorkel are so I can get up close and personal with whatever's down there. Before I put my big feet in the water, I'll search a small area of the bottom from the bank. That's where I'll step in." I patted the chest pocket of my waders. "In here, I have a few plastic bags and an indelible marker in case I find anything of special interest. I'll note the time and date, initial the bag, and then get Burt to initial it. He'll also take a picture of the spot I found it. There's a clasp knife in my pocket, too, because you never know." Then I showed the mesh bag I'd tied to my waist. "Any trash I find will go in here. Wish me luck."

I knelt on the edge of the inlet's bank, a few yards downstream from where I'd found Emrys, and moved the rake slowly along the bottom in an area about two feet square. "All clear," I said and stepped into the inlet releasing the musty, earthy smells of rotting vegetation and tannin with each careful step.

Burt documented the search as I methodically worked my way up the inlet, moving from one side to the other and back again. The slow-moving tide was going out, so the silt and mud I disturbed was always behind me. Anything I found that I planned to remove from the inlet, I held up so Burt could take a picture. That included half a dozen old porcelain canning jar lids, three crushed beer cans, an unbroken fig shell, a plastic six-pack yolk, two plastic grocery bags, and a single flip-flop. The fig shell went in my chest pocket because it was a beauty. The rest went in the mesh bag for disposal.

I didn't rake up any dentures. But I did find something shiny—a silver shell pendant exactly like the one Fake Lenrose bought for Shelly at the Moon Shell. It went into one of the plastic bags with date, time, and our initials. Then I put the fig shell in a plastic bag, too, because it didn't belong in the inlet any more than the pendant or any of the trash.

"Message came in from Glady," Burt said as he helped me out of the water. "All quiet."

"Good. How long do fingerprints last in brackish water?"

"Librarian at your service." Burt tapped at his phone and said, "Depends. Maybe up to ten days."

"Rats." I shucked out of my gear. "How do you feel about looking through old sales and inventory records?"

"If I hadn't been a librarian, I would have been an archivist. Lead me to them."

On the way back to the Moon Shell, I told Burt what to look for in Allen's records.

"What will you be doing?" he asked.

"Shower. It might be my imagination, but I think I smell slightly fetid. Then I'll be down to help."

I left Burt in the office with Allen's laptop open to the inventory pages, the two labeled plastic bags, and instructions for where to find the bankers boxes of sales receipt books—dated, thank goodness. Then I took my fetid-self upstairs. I made the shower quick because I wanted time to make a deal with Emrys before going down to help Burt.

Emrys was pacing the living room when I emerged in clean jeans and T-shirt. He stopped short and asked, "False teeth?"

I shook my head. "But something else that might help. Possibly two things. And I'll make a deal with you. I'll tell you what they are if you tell me what you wrote in those notes for Tate. *And* whose name you signed to them. Deal?"

"Yes, and to show my good faith, I will start. The notes are unsigned. I learned my lesson on that after the first time. They appear to be blackmail notes written to Victor, and I have a rather good story ready to explain them if it's needed."

He told me the story, which I agreed was good, and I told him about the pendant and the fig shell.

When I ran back down to the office, Emrys came with me. Burt looked up from the laptop. "Allen only had two of those silver lightning whelk pendants. He sold the first one on August tenth last year. Unfortunately he sells a lot of fig shells."

"Ah, but this fig shell doesn't look like it's been in the inlet for more than a week or two, and the inlet isn't this particular mollusk's natural habitat. You find fig shells, also called paper figs, on a beach. They're delicate, too. You don't often find them intact." I picked up the bag. "This is an excellent specimen."

"Then let's look at receipts for the last three weeks," Burt said. "Let's see if one of the Sullivans bought the fig shell, too."

"I believe he did," Emrys said. "The day he came in to say that Allen was expecting him. I told you about his visit in my letter."

With that piece of information, it didn't take long to find both receipts. Emrys congratulated us.

"Go see Tate?" Burt asked.

"Tate."

Tate wasn't in, Matt told us, when we walked into the station. "Choir practice. Did you know he could sing? Sounds a little like a young Willie Nelson. Surprised the heck out of me. What can I do for you? Where are the rest of the sleuths?"

I started to protest the title. Burt cut me off.

"Maureen's modest. She doesn't like to toot our horn. The rest of the sleuths, minus the one mistakenly arrested yesterday, are otherwise occupied this morning. However, Maureen and I have things to share with you, starting with an educational video."

Burt brought the inlet video up on his phone. Before handing it to Matt, he asked, "Mind if we come around and watch it with you?"

"Come ahead." Matt held the phone and Burt and I leaned in to watch over his shoulders. "Is that you, Ms. Nash?"

"It is," Burt said. "Hush and you'll learn something."

When the video ended, Burt and I went back around the desk and sat down. Matt held the phone up. "Does this shake up the case?"

"The case is well shaken," Burt said. "We think what's in Maureen's envelope will flatten it."

I put the manila envelope on the desk. "I found two items of interest under the muck in the inlet—a pendant and a fig shell. They're in the envelope. So are receipts showing when the Sullivans bought them at the Moon Shell."

"Doggone it," Matt said. "All I got to do on this case was the paperwork." He opened the envelope and carefully slid the contents out.

"The pendant and the shell belonged to the Sullivans," Burt said. "They've been in the inlet maybe as long as two weeks. When was the body dumped there, Matt? They've probably been in the water since then."

"The woman calling herself Lenrose Sullivan bought a pendant identical to this one earlier this week," I said. "Probably to replace the one that was lost when she and the real Lenrose Sullivan's husband dumped her body in the inlet."

"Fingerprints, Matt," Burt said. "Has anyone searched that beautiful Kaiser Manhattan for evidence or fingerprints? If you want to do more than paperwork on this case, you could dust that car for fingerprints and see if they match any on this pendant. Then we'll know that Shelly or the fake Lenrose was involved in the woman's death. Probably both of them."

"But it's the fake Lenrose who killed Shelly, not Roberta," I said. "It has to be."

Matt squared his shoulders. "Captain Tate always tells me

that the way to get ahead in police work is to use your initiative. So, here's my initiative—I think someone framed Roberta. I can't prove it sitting around with my leg in a cast, and I can't search the car, or dust it for fingerprints, without a warrant. But I can, and I will, let you read the blackmail notes sent to Mister Sullivan." He took three handwritten notes from a folder and put them on the desk.

"Are these for real?" Burt asked. He read them aloud in wonder. "'Victor, take action or action will be taken.' 'Victor, I know your villainy. You know my price.' 'Victor, evil manners live in brass—and cash. Pay up.'"

"Does Tate think Roberta wrote these?" I asked.

"He does."

"Does he have any proof?" Burt asked.

"That first part of that last one, that thing about evil manners, is part of a quote from some play by Shakespeare. Roberta's a retired English professor, and she wrote a book about Shakespeare called *Men's Evil Manners Live in Brass*."

Poor Roberta, I thought. In this pickle because of a Shakespeare-loving pirate.

"Too thin," Burt said. "Are there fingerprints on the notes?"

"That'd be nice, wouldn't it?" Matt said. "But people are too smart these days."

Or too dead. "What does Tate think Roberta was blackmailing Shelly about?"

"He doesn't know, and Roberta isn't talking. Mrs. Sullivan thinks blackmail is possible but doesn't see how. She says she's the one with the money. She thinks Shelly would have told her about the notes. She's also sure he never met any of the Fig Ladies before. Tate told her that blackmailed people often don't know their blackmailers and many of them won't admit they're being blackmailed. She also claims there was nothing in Shelly's life that he could be blackmailed for."

"*Claims*," I said. "Okay, see what you think of this scenario," and I told them the backstory Emrys concocted for his three Shakespeare-induced blackmail notes. "The blackmailer was the drowned woman. She followed Shelly and Lenrose to Ocracoke. She went too far in her demands. Shelly killed her and dumped the body. Lenrose found out about what he'd done, knew the police would eventually find out, and in a fit of rage killed Shelly because he'd killed their dreams of a happy retirement. Killing him wasn't the reaction of a normal person, but as we've all heard and witnessed, Lenrose isn't in her right mind these days."

Matt and Burt nodded along to the whole story. Bravo, Emrys.

"That makes more sense than the theory that Roberta killed Shelly," Matt said. "If *she* was blackmailing him, why would she kill him? Blackmailers don't usually kill the money source. And he's tried, but Tate can't make the drowned woman fit into the Roberta theory."

Neither Burt nor I brought up the idea of Roberta-as-contract-killer.

Matt looked at us. "So, now what? What do we do now?"

Two phones buzzed with incoming texts. Burt's and mine.

"From Glady," Burt said. "You ask what we do now, Matt? We're about to find out."

Chapter 39

Burt read Glady's text aloud. "'FL on the move.'" He looked from the phone to Matt. "This is great. It's exactly what we hoped for."

"FL is Felon Lenrose," I told Matt. Best not to confuse him by calling her Fake Lenrose when he'd just bought Emrys's story. "We thought she might try to leave the island. Glady, Kathleen, and Paula have been keeping her under surveillance, each from a different vantage point."

Our phones buzzed again. "FL's in the car," Burt said. After another buzz, he added, "Heading into town." Another buzz. "Paula picked up the tail." Buzz. "FL parked in the public lot near the Visitor Center."

Matt came around the desk on his crutches to help us stare at our phones while we waited for the next update. We all twitched when the phones buzzed again.

FL on dock looking at boats.
FL stooped down. Retied shoelace.
Dropped key chain in water. On purpose!
FL walking back through town. Will follow.

"The keys to the car?" Matt asked. "Why'd she do that?"

Paula buzzed again. **Think she saw me, so I ducked in T-shirt shop.**

Matt grabbed Burt's phone and tapped in **Don't duck in there too long, or you'll lose her.**

We waited. Waited. And Paula sent: **Lost her. Sorry.**

Burt grabbed his phone back and shot a text off. **Glady, what's your locale?**

Stuck, Glady sent back. **Explaining to Shell Inn manager I'm not late for shift because I quit same day I started. Not getting through to him.**

"We've got ourselves a couple of clowns for operatives," Burt said. "Where's Kathleen?"

"She should be near the south end of Howard where it meets Irvin Garrish."

"And they're not clowns," Matt said. "They're amateurs who stumbled." He held up one of his crutches. "Everyone stumbles sometimes."

Kathleen texted: **FL coming this way.** Then: **Wait.**

My phone rang. Kathleen. I put it on speaker. "Hi. I've got you on speaker. Burt and I are with Deputy Kincaid at the station. What's happening?"

"I couldn't text fast enough," Kathleen said. "When I saw her, I reversed into a yard. She went right past. She's walking down Howard. I'm following slowly, keeping well back."

"Good. This is Matt, Kathleen."

"Hi. I'm afraid I'll lose her, too."

"Don't worry about losing her," Matt said. "Stay back and stay safe."

"Burt here, Kathleen. If she loops back to the highway, Glady can pick her up. I'll give her a heads-up." As he sent the text to Glady, he muttered, "Unless she's still arguing."

"Update," Kathleen said. "Mayday. She went around behind the Moon Shell. Doors are all locked, Maureen?"

"They are," I assured her. But knowing they were didn't keep my heart from crashing around in double-time.

"She's got your bike," Kathleen said. "She's probably seen

me, but she's riding away. I'll follow. She's going fast. I need backup!"

"Backup for what?" Rob Tate asked from behind us. "Who's on the phone, and who has Maureen's bike?"

Burt, Matt, and I made a synchronized turn to face Tate, who must have come in the back way. Matt stepped forward on his crutches and took charge.

"Sir, Ms. Nash and Mister Weaver brought forward new evidence that I believe shows Lenrose Sullivan is guilty of murdering her husband. I don't know where she's going on the bike, but I believe we need to get in your truck and catch her, if for no other reason than she stole the bike from Maureen."

Tate gave a curt nod. "Let's go."

Matt maneuvered his cast into the shotgun seat. I scrunched in beside him. Burt stayed behind and called Glady to pick up him and Paula so they could follow. I checked in with Kathleen so we'd know where to go.

"On the highway heading north," Kathleen said. "I lost sight of her after we passed the road to the airport."

"If you're still carrying boards in back, Captain," Matt said, "we can pull over and get Kathleen on board."

"Got 'em," Tate said.

"We're coming to get you," I told Kathleen. "Standby to board the captain's pickup."

Matt pointed. "There's Kathleen now."

Tate pulled over just ahead of Kathleen, who'd been gamely tootling along the side of the highway in her all-terrain chair. Tate lowered the tailgate and arranged a gangplank of two boards. "A good-looking vehicle," he said as Kathleen drove up and into the bed of the truck. "How's the battery life?"

"Long-lasting. Not long enough to get all the way to the ferry dock if that's where she's headed."

"Matt's calling the dock now, so they'll be watching for her," Tate said.

"All right if I ride in back with Kathleen?" I asked.

"Hop in and hold on," he said.

We pulled back onto the highway, but after a mile or two, all we'd seen were gulls and a few crows. Kathleen sent a text with our location to Glady, Burt, and Paula. Matt slid open the window at the back of the cab. "We'll pull through the parking area for the Ocracoke Beach up ahead. See if she's there."

"At least we know she can't get off the island," Kathleen said.

"She can if she planned it well enough," Tate said. "Or if she's desperate enough."

We turned off at the beach parking and drove slowly through the lot. No sign of Lenrose or my bike.

"She could've ditched the bike in the dunes and be on foot along the beach," Tate said. "Or she could've hitched a ride. With a change of clothes, and a wig, any description we gave to the ferry personnel will be useless."

We turned off the highway again at the Hammock Hills Nature Trail and then Ocracoke Campground with no luck at either.

"Hey, you dumb crow!" Matt waved his arm out the window at a crow sitting in the middle of the drive leading out of the campground. The crow nailed us with its gaze, as though beady eyes and willpower could stop us dead. Tate crept forward, and the crow flapped away with a guttural caw.

I turned to see its wings wide and ebony black against the sky—and caught a shimmer in the air at the back of Kathleen's chair. Emrys came into view and raised his hat to me. Well, blow me down.

"Tell the captain to sail for the Pony Pens," Emrys said. "The false Lenrose has docked there."

The Pony Pens? Why there for heaven's—oh! When the Fig Ladies ran into Shelly and Lenrose at the pens, on their first day on the island, Shelly had told them Lenrose rode horses as a child. "Lenrose used to ride horses!" I called through the back window.

"Bareback," Kathleen added. "Head for the the Pony Pens."

"Aye-aye," Tate called back.

"*If* Shelly was telling us the truth about Lenrose and horses," Kathleen said to me. "And even if he was, we don't know if he was talking about the real Lenrose or the phony."

We arrived at the Pony Pens as a line of cars coming from the ferry peeled off to stop there, too. Ocracoke's wild pony herd was the first glimpse of island life for many visitors. There wasn't room for more than a dozen cars but Tate found a space between two vans. He and Matt got out. Tate ran up the stairs to the viewing platform and scanned the fenced pasture. He turned and shook his head with a scowl of frustration.

I looked for Emrys. He was gone.

"But, Mommy," a child's whine came from the platform, "I want to go where *she* is. I want a pony, too."

Tate whipped back around. He looked where the child pointed and then took the stairs three at a time, stumbled briefly at the bottom, and ran back to the truck. "She has a halter and rope and got one of the ponies out of the pen. I wouldn't believe it if I hadn't seen it, but she's on the pony, and they're heading down below," he said, using the island term for the vast area between the village and the northern end of the island.

"Let's go." Matt swung himself back into the cab.

Tate backed out of the parking area, drove around the far end of the pasture fence, and set off cross-country. A hundred yards later, the truck bogged down in loose sand. Tate slammed his hand on the steering wheel. He and Matt got out to study the situation.

"We'll use the boards," Tate said, adding a few muttered words I hadn't heard him use before.

"Kathleen!" Matt called. "How does that chair handle sand, mud, and marsh?"

"Made for it."

"Then why don't I borrow the chair and go after her?" Matt said to Tate.

"Sorry," Kathleen said. "I'm under contract as a test driver for the manufacturer and can't let anyone else operate it. But give me that gangplank and I'll go after her until one of you can catch up."

Tate reluctantly agreed and set up the gangplank. "Follow her as best you can. Do not engage her in any fashion. And if anyone asks later," he said as he watched her back down the gangplank, "I deputized you."

"We'll tell them you deputized me, too," I said and stepped onto the lip at the back of the chair.

Tate pointed in the general direction he'd seen Fake Lenrose go, and we were off—like a spry tortoise more than a fleet hare.

The ride was smooth enough that I took a chance and sent a text to Glady, Burt, and Paula. Glady sent back: **Tallyho!**

We left the sounds of highway traffic and Tate and Matt swearing at the truck behind. Kathleen navigated us around stunted red cedars, and I thought we were traveling in more or less the right direction.

"Kathleen, do you see the cedar with the crow sitting on it? Head that way."

As we approached, the crow flew off and landed in another cedar twenty or thirty feet away.

"If anyone asks later," I said, "tell them this was all my fault, but I think we should keep following the crow. Crows know things."

"Good enough for me."

We rolled our way from cedar to cedar and reached the marshy end of an inlet. On the other side of the marshy area, another fifty or sixty feet farther, were Fake Lenrose and her captive pony.

"She must be a pony whisperer," Kathleen said. "Why doesn't it buck her off? Look how she has it walking in circles now. If she's that good at whispering, why isn't she racing away?"

"She might if she sees us. But at this point she hasn't got a hope in shell of getting away."

Kathleen drove the chair slowly forward. FL didn't see us until we splashed through the marshy area. As we bore down on her, it became obvious she *wasn't* the one in control. She certainly wasn't whispering.

"Stop it!" she shouted. "Stop going in circles."

The pony whinnied and trotted forward a few yards.

"Thank God," Fake Lenrose said. "Good girl." She clucked her tongue and touched her heels to the pony's sides. The pony started circling in the opposite direction.

"Why doesn't she get off and run for it?" Kathleen asked.

The answer came a moment later. The pony stopped. Fake Lenrose started to slide off. The pony bucked, and Fake Lenrose hung on for dear life.

"Get out of here!" Fake Lenrose yelled at us. "Stay back! I'll have her kick you to pieces!"

Kathleen stopped, and I hopped off the back of her chair. The pony whickered and trotted over to nuzzle Kathleen, then me. Not what I expected. Fake Lenrose wasn't prepared for that either. She kicked at me but missed when the pony pranced sideways and then turned to nip at her.

Tate arrived at a run, winded and muddy from splashing through the marsh. He caught hold of the halter. "Ms. Sullivan, I don't think you want to compound your problems by going anywhere on this horse. Please dismount."

"I can't."

"Now."

The pony snorted and pulled away from Tate.

"Lenrose Sullivan, I'm arresting you for the murder of your husband, Victor Sullivan. You have the—"

"If you think I killed my husband, you're in for a big surprise!" FL yelled.

"You have the right to remain silent. You have—"

"He wasn't my husband!" Fake Lenrose shrieked.

"You have the—"

"*You!*" she shrieked, pointing at Kathleen and me. "You and your interfering figgy friends spoiled our beautiful plan. And then Shelly put a stake through its heart by giving in to blackmail. So, yes! I did kill him. He was a messy liability. And I am thrilled, thrilled I tell you, to drop the demented act and be rid of the name Lenrose."

The pony reared, ran into the inlet, and bucked until FL fell off with a scream. She sat up, water and mud streaming from her, and yelled, "I am Darlene Bartlow and I'm not sorry about *anything*."

The pony whickered and trotted my way as Emrys appeared beside me. "The pony's been listening to you?" I whispered. Not that anyone could hear me over Darlene's mad laughter.

"Have you heard stories of a creature called a *ceffyl dŵr*, a water horse?" Emrys asked. "An enchanting, wicked animal that lets a rider on its back and won't let the rider dismount, ending in, shall we say, dire results? This pony enjoyed hearing the story. As it turns out, I knew her great-great-great grandfather."

"Don't tell me—Ikey D.?" I whispered.

"The same. She was happy to chat with me and help out. The pony also told me a joke handed down from Ikey D., who learned it from Sam Jones. How fast can a seahorse go?"

"How fast?"

"At a scallop."

How could I believe that load of scallops? And yet, how else could I explain this wild pony standing quietly while I rubbed her nose? Besides, who was I to question the word of a pirate ghost?

Chapter 40

Roberta was released after a full confession from Darlene Bartlow. Roberta and Paula left the island on the seven o'clock ferry Saturday morning. Kathleen and I took them to the dock. They planned to pick up their cars in Hatteras and not look back.

Before we reached the landing, I turned around in the passenger seat to look at Roberta and ask a question that still bugged me. "Where *did* you get the Shell Inn key card you had that day in the suite?"

Roberta had been staring out the window and turned to stare at me. "It was sitting on the dresser. When the other housekeeper came in I slipped it in my pocket."

"The simplest explanation is usually the right one," Paula said.

"We did ask, though," I said, "and it would've been nice if you'd told us."

"It would have been nice if you'd trusted me," Roberta said.

At the dock, I watched as the three Fig Ladies hugged. They assured each other they'd stay in touch. Kathleen and I stayed at the dock to wave goodbye as the ferry got underway. Paula waved back; Roberta didn't.

"I've been wrong often enough," Kathleen said as we watched

the ferry go, "but the Fig Ladies probably won't keep in touch. This adventure was a dose of real life we didn't expect and weren't prepared for. It was too much for those two."

"Not for you?"

"I don't want to be that close to murder again, but restoring truth and justice on an all-terrain? With you? On Ocracoke Island? With figs? Put me on speed dial."

Kathleen was ecstatic about the performance of the all-terrain. "I really put it through its paces. The manufacturer's going to love my report. The weirdest thing, though, and I know I imagined it, but when Darlene stole your bike and I started after her, I could swear I heard someone standing on the back of the chair yelling, 'Burn rubber!'"

"Crazy," I said.

She called the Shell Inn and, surprise, surprise, they had an unexpected vacancy. Not ready to leave the island yet, she booked the suite through the next Friday. "The story isn't finished," she said. "I want to be here to see how it ends."

Sunday afternoon, the body the Fig Ladies found in the inlet was officially identified as Lenrose Sullivan. Captain Tate did something that might have been out of character, but I didn't really think so. He called for a meeting of the Fig Jams at the Moon Shell Monday morning—breakfast, his treat. He came with a cinnamon apple French toast casserole warm from the oven. I supplied coffee. Kathleen brought a jar of local fig jam, and Glady and Burt arrived with muffins.

"Just in case," Glady said.

Matt came, too, still disappointed he hadn't thought of jumping on the back of the all-terrain the way I did. "We dusted Shelly's Manhattan," he said, "and found Lenrose's fingerprints in the glove compartment."

Tate stopped in the middle of dishing out casserole to give Matt a look.

"Matt," Burt said, "best not to intrude on another man's story. Especially when he's the one doling out portions."

"It's all right, Matt," Tate said. "You did good work." He handed Matt the last plate and sat down. "You all did good work. Not that I'm condoning amateur interference." He couldn't help catching the narrowed looks he received from the Fig Jams. Too bad he missed the snarl from Emrys. "But I'm grateful for your help."

"Reward us, then," Glady said. "We'll eat. You talk."

"I'll tell you as much as I can."

It was quite a lot. Lenrose's fingerprints were also found on a gutting knife Allred dropped at the ferry dock the day Lenrose and Shelly arrived on the island. Lenrose had picked it up and chased after him to return it. Allred said he'd noticed her arthritic knuckles at the time and only made the connection after Darlene Bartlow was arrested. He said he'd seen Shelly and Darlene from a distance several times after the murder.

"Of course he twisted the incident with the gutting knife," Tate said. "Now he claims he knew all along that *it* was a token of death—a knife cutting loose the mortal coils."

"Who blackmailed Shelly?" Glady asked after making a rude noise about Allred.

"Oddly enough, Lenrose," Tate said.

"That certainly is odd," I said.

"I'll tell you what Darlene spilled in her confession and see if you don't agree."

Darlene told them Shelly didn't want to face retirement with a wife disappearing into dementia. But he'd met Darlene, and when he realized how much she and Lenrose resembled each other, except for how they dressed, he hatched his plan to switch them. He'd do it while they were on a trip somewhere where people didn't know her well. A place Lenrose would enjoy and where one woman could slip into the other's life without notice. Ocracoke seemed like the perfect place. Darlene was happy to go along with the plan because lots of money was involved.

"I'm surprised the entire village didn't hear her shrieking about Shelly's stupid move to stay on the island after killing Lenrose. If they'd left, they could have moved to a new town where no one at all would know she wasn't Lenrose, and they might have gotten away with it."

"With murder," Kathleen said.

"Murder," Tate agreed. "I'm sorry for the loss of your friend. Darlene said it was a mercy killing. That Shelly knew Lenrose would have hated the steady loss of herself. That he would have hated it even more."

Burt tossed his fork on his plate. "I'm with Darlene, then. Not about murder. About Shelly's stupidity. Why didn't they take a boat out deep, weigh Lenrose down, and skedaddle?"

"Darlene said Shelly was convinced he could fix any glitch," Tate said. "She said he told her staying behind was damage control. I think they were stupid, yes, but also arrogant and greedy. Shelly didn't have much money of his own. It belonged to Lenrose. Shelly didn't know how long Lenrose would live or the path her dementia would take. How much money it would eat up. Her will leaves much or most of her money to charities. That gave Shelly a good reason to keep her alive so he had access to the money, but he preferred to do that with Lenrose two-point-oh. And, sadly for Shelly, two-point-oh preferred to live as Lenrose without him."

"Where was she going on the pony?" Kathleen asked.

"Closer to the ferry dock," Tate said. "Arrogance again. Because she trained horses once upon a time, she assumed she could hop on one of the ponies and stay on it long enough for an easy walk the rest of the way. She had a change of clothes."

"And a wig?" I asked.

Tate nodded. "She's the woman the witness saw on the ferry. We have the necklace she wore and played with."

"Why the cockamamie horseback stunt?" Burt asked.

"She didn't want to draw attention to herself by renting a golf cart. She didn't dare take the car because it's so recognizable."

"So, she stole a horse in front of how many visitors at the pen?" Burt said.

"Arrogant and desperate," Matt said.

Glady pointed her fork at Tate. "This doesn't tell us anything about blackmail."

"Still getting there." Tate took the fig shell from his pocket and gave it to me. "There aren't any useable prints on the shell. You can have it back."

"Thanks."

"The fig shell"—Tate nodded at it sitting on my palm—"or the *stupid* fig shell, as Darlene calls it, was a present from Shelly to Lenrose. He put it in her pocket when they went to dump her body in the inlet."

"That's an unexpected gesture," Burt said.

"Darlene called Shelly a sentimental fool. She took the shell out of the pocket and dropped it in the water. Shelly lost the necklace when he tried to find the shell. Something snagged the necklace, the clasp opened, and it slipped into the water, too. Darlene said he fretted over its loss like an old lady. She said she felt incredibly lucky to find a duplicate, but she never would have replaced it if he'd told her Lenrose gave him the original."

"And the *blackmail?*" Glady said.

"Roberta helped with that," Tate said. "Lenrose wrote three blackmail notes that were delivered to me. The handwriting on the recipe card Roberta tried to show me the other day matches the handwriting on the notes. Darlene believes Lenrose caught sight of her with Shelly, knew something was up, and in her demented state of mind tried to blackmail him."

"Excuse me for saying so," Kathleen said, "but that's mighty thin."

Tate shrugged. "I agree, but it doesn't matter. We have two facts. Lenrose and Shelly are dead, and Lenrose wrote the notes."

I wasn't about to raise my hand and say *au contraire, a pirate ghost wrote the notes.*

"We also don't need the notes or the suggestion of blackmail to convict Darlene." Tate looked at the empty casserole dish and stood up. "Thank you for enjoying my baking experiment. Thank you for listening and for your help. I'd like you to avoid such activities in the future. Oh, and one more detail has been cleared up. Irv Allred says he wrote that first note identifying the body."

"And signed my name?" I asked. "Why?"

"He said he didn't know you were coming back to the island."

"*That's* mighty thin," Glady said. "How does the old loon explain knowing the body was Lenrose?"

"He had a visitation from the ghost of Lenrose, and she filled him in."

Burt guffawed. "You believe that?"

"That he wrote the note? Yes," Tate said. "But I also believe he's cemented his reputation as a sham. No way did the ghost of Lenrose Sullivan rise up and identify herself to anyone, let alone Irv Allred."

Wednesday morning, I didn't open the shop. Glady, Burt, and I rode in Minerva to the Ocracoke Community Cemetery. Kathleen met us there, and we watched as Lenrose Sullivan was laid to rest. Many islanders came, too, including Allred. He sidled over to me during the short burial service. When it ended, he put a hand on my arm and looked eagerly into my face.

"Exactly how many ghosts have you seen?" he asked.

Glady batted him away like a fly, and we drove back home. Home. I liked that thought. I also liked knowing that I looked forward to going through the boxes in the attic with Emrys. He was waiting for me when I unlocked the door and let myself in.

"Pleasant funeral?" he asked.

"It was. A lot of people came—what are you looking at?" I followed his gaze. The moon shell no longer sat on the piece of watered silk, and the silk now lay in a heap at the base of the chipped cake plate. "Were you rearranging the silk?"

"Not I."

"Weird." I unlocked the case, lifted the shell, redraped the silk, and set the shell on it. I stood back to check the effect and watched as the shell rose slightly and the silk slipped from under it into a heap again. "Are you . . . ?" He wasn't. He was standing next to me and hadn't moved. What the shell?

"We have a guest," Emrys said quietly.

"What kind of guest?"

"She's somewhat shy and very much embarrassed by her . . . getup, as she calls it."

"*Lenrose?*"

"It's interesting," he said, head cocked, studying me, "that you look as though you've seen a ghost when you don't see her. She's grateful to us for solving her murder, by the way."

"Well, um, it was the right thing to do. So, you can hear each other? Can she hear me? Oh!" Then there I was, nose to nose, with a foggy sort of woman with an uncanny resemblance to Darlene. Shy wasn't really the right word for her. Belligerent worked better. I took a step back. "Lenrose? I'm happy to meet you."

"Can you imagine spending eternity in orange and yellow with unfortunate swaths of embroidery?" she asked. "And these shoes! A white sheet with holes cut for my eyes would be better."

"I don't blame you for being upset," I said. "Unfortunately, I think you'll have to get used to it."

"How rude." She gave me a look meant to flay like a razor clam and disappeared.

"Is she gone?" I hoped so.

"No. She says to tell you she's no longer speaking to you."

"Why is she here in the shop?" I asked. "Why isn't she haunting the inlet?"

"She says it's your fault. She came back with the fig shell you found."

"Lenrose, that shell helped us prove Darlene is guilty."

She popped back into view with room to breathe between us. "Being dead might actually be worth it if I can haunt Darlene for the rest of her life."

"If we can arrange for the shell to accompany Darlene to prison, we might be able to arrange that," Emrys said. "What is she allowed to take with her?"

"That doesn't sound like a healthy way to spend eternity," I said. "Lenrose, may I offer an alternative?"

"I can't imagine any alternative better than haunting that hussy to *her* grave, but go ahead."

"Glady and Burt, who live across the street, have old fig trees in their backyard. What if we bury your fig shell under one of them?"

"A fig tree?" Her face softened and she put a hand to her unfortunately embroidered chest. "Did you know that the tree of life is a fig tree? That fig trees are a sign of new beginnings? I will be honored to have my fig shell buried at the roots of an Ocracoke fig."

When I asked them, Glady and Burt said they didn't care one way or the other about having the fig shell under one of their trees. I didn't report that blasé attitude to Lenrose. She hummed a slow familiar tune as I dug a hole for the shell. I couldn't think what the tune was, but it struck me as appropriate. I laid the shell gently in the earth as she watched and hummed. She grew fainter and fainter as I filled the hole, until only her humming remained, and then that was gone, too.

I waved to Glady and Burt. They'd watched me through the kitchen window, looking more suspicious than people should who'd said they didn't care one way or another about a small burial in their yard.

Emrys appeared on the porch of the Moon Shell as I climbed the steps. "What's that tune you're humming?" he asked.

"Something Lenrose was humming. I can't think of the name."

Looking thoughtful, he hummed a few lines of the song.

"You know it?"

"Indeed I do. Ikey D. and I often listened to Sam and his friends sing it when they got maudlin around the parlor piano. And you say Lenrose was humming it?"

"Yes. Why? And why are you wringing your hands?"

"I'm sure I'm not." He put his hands behind his back. "It's probably nothing. It's just that I fervently hope Lenrose hummed it for sentimental reasons and not as, as—"

"As what?"

"Threat is probably too strong a word. Let's say prediction. The name of the song is 'I'll be Seeing You.'"

Here are three easy fig recipes from the Fig Ladies.

Dead Simple Prosciutto-Wrapped Figs from Paula Diamond Román

Makes 24 appetizers

Ingredients
12 fresh figs
24 strips of prosciutto long enough to wrap around half a fig

Directions
1. Remove the fig stems. Cut the figs in half lengthwise. Wrap each fig half in a strip of prosciutto.
2. Arrange on a plate and serve.

Fig, Ginger, Cardamom Truffles from Roberta McLaughlin

Makes 16 truffles

Ingredients
8 ounces dried figs
¼ cup crystallized ginger
1 tablespoon honey
½ teaspoon ground cardamom
2½ ounces dark chocolate (at least 60% cocoa solids, but 70–72% is even better), chopped

Directions
1. Remove the fig stems. Put the figs, ginger, honey, and cardamom in a food processor and process for about 45 seconds until the ingredients are finely chopped and begin to stick together.
2. Roll heaping teaspoons of the fig mixture into balls and set them on a plate or baking sheet lined with parchment or wax paper.
3. In a small bowl, melt the chocolate in a microwave or over a saucepan of gently simmering water.
4. Roll the fig balls in the melted chocolate until they're covered—one or two at a time. Return the coated balls to the parchment or wax paper. Chill the truffles in the refrigerator until set, about 15 minutes. Serve at room temperature.

Fig, Honey, and Lemon Galette from Kathleen Thomas

Serves 8

Ingredients
1 ready-made, rolled, refrigerated piecrust
10 ounces small fresh figs, sliced thin
1 tablespoon honey
½ teaspoon lemon juice
1 tablespoon coarse sugar

Directions
1. Preheat oven to 350°F.
2. Line a baking sheet with a square of parchment paper an inch or two larger than your piecrust, and unroll the crust on it.
3. Starting in the center of the crust, make overlapping concentric circles of the sliced figs. Leave a 1½-inch margin of bare crust around the outside of your fig rings. Fold the crust inward so that it just touches the outer fig ring.
4. Heat the honey and lemon juice for a few seconds in a microwave. Mix well. Brush the mixture over the crust and figs and then sprinkle with the sugar.
5. Bake 25–30 minutes until the crust is golden brown. Remove from the oven. Cool on a baking sheet for 10 minutes and then transfer the galette to a wire rack.
6. Delicious warm, at room temperature, or cold. Serve with vanilla ice cream or slices of your favorite cheese.